Malcolm Richards crafts st... e
edge of your seat. He is the ...d
mystery novels, including t... l-
nominated Devil's Cove tr... s.
Many of his books are set ...d
raised.

Before becoming a full-time writer, he worked for several years in the special education sector, teaching and supporting children with complex needs. After living in London for two decades, he has now settled in the Somerset countryside with his partner and their pets.

Visit the author's website: www.malcolmrichardsauthor.com

BOOKS BY MALCOLM RICHARDS

PI Blake Hollow

Circle of Bones

Down in the Blood

The Devil's Cove Trilogy

The Cove

Desperation Point

The Devil's Gate

The Emily Swanson Series

Next to Disappear

Mind for Murder

Trail of Poison

Watch You Sleep

Kill for Love

Standalone Novels

The Hiding House

Malcolm Richards

EMILY SWANSON BOOK FOUR

WATCH YOU SLEEP

StormHouse

First published in 2019 by Storm House Books.

ISBN 978-1-9162104-0-0

www.stormhousebooks.com

For Dutch.

1

EMILY SWANSON SAT behind the wheel of a silver Audi, blonde hair pulled back in a ponytail, green eyes vivid against her pale skin as she watched the terraced Edwardian house on the other side of the road. Few streets like this remained in Hackney. World War II had seen much of the east London district obliterated by bombs, with scores of ugly tenement buildings quickly built in the aftermath to house thousands of homeless citizens. These days those tenements were used as dumping grounds by borough councils, forcing struggling families to live in a pit of knife crime and impoverishment. But this street, where Emily was currently staked out among a line of parked vehicles, was a distinct reminder of a distant, gentler Hackney.

She'd been watching the house for three hours now, the engine switched off and the cold slowly seeping into her bones. Three hours in which she'd seen the winter sun melt through the early morning darkness and scores of workers and school children hurry by, faces burdened with grimaces as they made their way towards offices and classrooms.

But there was no activity from the house in question.

Shifting her gaze for a second, Emily glanced at the empty coffee cup that was stuffed into the side pocket of the driver door. She was tired and thirsty, her back ached, and her fingers were numb. Worse still, she had a pressing need to pee that was only growing worse. Adjusting her position in the seat, she let out a long sigh and returned to watching the house.

This was the hardest part of the job—the sitting and waiting, waiting and sitting, in a vain hope that something would happen. Something that would mark another job done. This was not Emily's idea of fun. Boredom was already setting in, and when boredom came, so did distraction, and distraction always led to mistakes. But Emily wasn't surprised—this was the second day she'd been stationed in the street with zero activity. If she didn't come up with incriminating evidence soon, Erica Braithwaite would want to know why.

Rubbing her frozen hands together, Emily shifted her gaze from the closed blinds of the living room, to the upstairs bedroom. The curtains were open. They had been closed a few minutes ago, she was sure of it. Which meant she was already making mistakes.

According to the case file, the sole occupant of the house was fifty-seven-year-old Brenda Carlyle. It was a big house for someone who lived alone and hadn't had a job in several years despite being below retirement age. Through her own research, Emily had discovered the house had been signed over to Brenda Carlyle as part of an alimony agreement with her recently divorced husband. Her *fifth* husband.

As Emily stifled a yawn, she wondered if each of those marriages had been their own carefully executed scam. Because Brenda Carlyle had procured a long track record of clever scams, all of which she'd managed to get away with. At first glance, her history of accidents appeared as circumstantial or just plain unlucky. But as you looked closer, it seemed strange that one person could have suffered so many injuries and ailments. Over the years, Brenda had encountered broken paving stones left in disrepair by the council, food poisoning from reputable restaurants, and lately, a series of falls caused by hazardous spillages in supermarkets and department stores.

Her latest incident had involved a nasty fall in the frozen food aisle at one of the larger supermarket chains, caused by an apparently leaky freezer. Despite the freezer being checked and found without fault, Ms Carlyle had sustained numerous injuries including a badly sprained ankle and a torn ligament in her shoulder. There had indeed been water on the floor around the freezer where the woman had slipped, but where it had come from was a mystery. An even greater question presenting itself was how Ms Carlyle had sustained three different injuries in three different supermarkets over a period of three years.

It was why Emily was here now—to find answers to those questions and to ensure Ms Carlyle had no further accidents.

Her left buttock was growing numb. She shifted in the seat again, trying to ignore the pressure building in her bladder and wishing she'd made herself go when she'd stopped to grab the coffee earlier. She watched the bedroom window. Still no movement despite the open curtains. Downstairs, the blinds remained firmly shut.

"Come on . . ." Emily hissed between clenched teeth, willing the front door of the house to open as the pressure in her bladder pressed down harder. A minute later, she'd taken to jigging her foot up and down. "Screw it."

She needed a break and the parking meter needed refilling. Grabbing her wallet, she pushed open the car door and stepped onto the road. The cold bit into her clothes as she circled the vehicle and mounted the pavement, frosty plumes billowing from her nostrils. She made her way towards the parking meter, past tall, three-storey houses and lines of barren trees, keeping her eyes straight ahead and her gait natural. She still felt conspicuous, but less so than her first stake out. Back then she'd been paranoid as hell, convinced every passer-by knew what she was up to and that every neighbour was picking up the phone to inform the police about the suspicious woman who'd been sitting in her car for four hours straight. After her second stakeout, Emily had realised that not a single person had even noticed her. After all, this was London, where ignoring others was a way of life.

She reached the parking meter. As she fished coins from her wallet and fed them into the machine with shivering fingers, she wished she'd accepted Carter's offer of a pair of his long johns, but even though they'd been in a sort of relationship for the best part of a year now, Emily was still bringing a toothbrush when she stayed the night instead of leaving one in his bathroom; borrowing his clothes would be akin to accepting his hand in marriage.

The meter spat out a new ticket. Emily plucked it between frozen finger and thumb, then made her way back to the car. A young mother was walking towards her, pushing a toddler in a buggy. Emily watched the woman cooing and laughing as her child watched the world zip by with large, wonder-filled eyes, his tiny gloved hands clutching a stuffed monkey. Emily offered the woman a polite smile, who retaliated with a suspicious glance. London, Emily thought as she stood on the pavement, watching mother and child grow smaller. She turned on her heels. And saw the front door of Brenda Carlyle's house swing open.

Resisting the sudden urge to duck down like a wanted criminal, she watched a glamorous middle-aged woman with coiffed silver hair and an expensive looking winter coat emerge from the harbour of the doorway and descend the steps to the street. *Completely unaided.*

According to the case notes provided by the insurance company, the injuries Carlyle had sustained had reportedly left her with mobility issues that required the use of a walking stick. Now, Emily watched as the woman made it to the gate in three quick strides and stepped onto the pavement. Brenda's eyes swept the street and landed on Emily, who quickly glanced away and continued back towards the Audi.

When she looked up again, Brenda had turned in the opposite direction and was now heading straight towards Mare Street, Hackney's busiest road, at a determined pace. A familiar rush of adrenaline shot through Emily's veins. This was it. Proof that Brenda Carlyle was the fraud the insurance company believed her to be.

And she was getting away.

Any minute now she would reach Mare Street and she would be lost in the heaving crowds. Quickening her step, Emily made it to the car and ducked inside. A digital SLR camera sat in an open bag on the passenger seat, ready for action. She scooped it up, slung the strap around her neck, locked the car, and started down the pavement at a feverish pace.

Brenda still had distance on her side, but Emily had youth. Racing forward, she started to close the gap. Mare Street was just up ahead. Streams of traffic blocked the road. Hordes of people hurried by. In just moments, Brenda would be another anonymous face in the crowd, and any opportunity to photograph her perfectly healthy stride would be snatched away. Emily broke into a run.

Brenda was now less than ten feet from the crowds.

Emily skidded to a halt, raised the camera, and quickly adjusted the lens. Carlyle pulled into focus, just as she reached the end of the road.

"Brenda Carlyle!" Emily shouted above the din of the crowd. Just ahead of her, the older woman froze. Then turned on her heels. Confusion swept across her face as she stared into the camera lens. Emily depressed the shutter release and the camera snapped away.

Brenda Carlyle's mouth swung open, her eyes grew wide with horror. Then narrowed with outrage.

Emily lowered the camera, and before the woman could utter a word, she turned and hurried back down the street. By the time Emily had reached the car, her heart was pounding. She'd taken a risk, but it had paid off. Brenda Carlyle's long history of scamming was about to come to an end.

Climbing inside the Audi, Emily put the camera away, slipped the car key into the ignition, and started the engine. As the heating began to kick in, she pulled away from the kerb and started the journey back to the office, feeling neither satisfaction nor joy about solving another case. What she did feel was a sudden guilty weight pressing down on her chest, and a now overwhelming desperation to pee.

2

GROSVENOR SQUARE WAS SITUATED in London's Mayfair district and housed an elegant public garden flanked by long terraced Seventeenth Century buildings with classical red brick facade, white pillars, and black iron railings. Until very recently, it had been home to the American Embassy, which alongside centuries-long political connections to the United States, had earned the Square the moniker of 'Little America'; a name reflected by the garden's numerous statues of former American presidents and monuments to the fallen victims of 9/11 and the Eagle Squadron fighter pilots of World War II.

Now, with the Embassy having relocated, along with the US Navy building and the High Commission of Canada, Grosvenor Square had lost much of its political connections and was currently undergoing a complete transformation into a square of luxury hotels and extortionately-priced apartments. Hidden among the redevelopment chaos was a building with a very different purpose.

Exiting the lift on the third floor, Emily hurried along a clean and brightly lit corridor until she reached a set of double doors, with the words *Braithwaite Investigations* stencilled across the smoked glass in black letters.

Pushing her way through, she entered a large, modern reception area with white walls and shiny floor tiles, and a colourful collection of armchairs in the waiting area. Sitting behind the reception desk, a tall, handsome man with dark, reddish-brown skin and large, friendly eyes glanced up from a computer screen.

"Good morning, Ms Swanson!" he said, flashing her a dazzling smile. "Forgot to go again, did we?"

"Not now, Jerome!"

Emily shot him a glare as she barrelled past and raced through the bathroom door. When she resurfaced a few minutes later, all was right with the world once more and she returned to the desk at a calm pace with a smile on her lips.

"Mission accomplished," she said, tapping the camera bag hanging off her shoulder.

"Next time you should take a bottle to pee in."

"I was talking about the job, idiot." Emily winked. "How are you getting on? It's been almost a week and you haven't been fired."

"Fine," Jerome said, arching an eyebrow as he watched Emily move behind the reception desk and slump in the chair next to his. "Although there's this one particular investigator who keeps overstepping boundaries. Thinks she owns the place."

"Funny. You should buy her dinner for getting you the job."

"You got me the *interview*. My charming interpersonal skills got me the job, thank you. Besides, I'm not sure the salary stretches to restaurant dining. How about some good, old fashioned home-cooked food?"

"It depends. Are you doing the cooking?"

"Hey, I can cook!"

"You make good coffee, I'll give you that."

Smiling, Jerome stared at his computer screen. "At least I *can* make coffee."

"Any messages for me?" Emily punched him lightly on the arm. As Jerome ran his fingers over the keyboard, she glanced down at the network of scars, some still thick and angry looking, that covered his hands. Guilt knifed her in the stomach.

"Don't," Jerome said, shooting her a warning look. "And no messages."

"Sorry. It's just that . . ." She took his hand in her own and rubbed a palm over the cruel-looking scars. "They're looking better, don't you think?"

"It's been well over a year, so I hope so. My left pinkie is still giving me grief, though. But that's the nerve damage. Not much the doctors can do about it." He was quiet for a moment, face pulled into a scowl. "I guess that's what happens when you're chased by bad guys over glass topped walls."

"If you hadn't risked your life like that, Valence Industries would still be poisoning millions of children around the world," Emily said. "You're a hero."

Jerome slipped his hand from her grip and returned his gaze to the computer screen. "Except no one will ever know about it because my moment of glory was stolen from me. I still can't believe that excuse for a journalist stole the evidence."

Emily felt anger burst through her calm mood and for a moment she fought to suppress it. "Helen Carlson always gets what she wants, no matter the cost to others. But either way, Valence Industries is sinking faster than the Titanic, several of its top dogs are headed to jail, and the world is a safer place for it. You helped to make that happen. Don't underestimate what you did."

Jerome's brow crumpled. "And yet here I am working yet another temp job while Helen Carlson lands her own damn investigative TV show."

"Well, the past is the past, and this is a new start for both of us. Anyway, maybe you should start applying for auditions again. It's been ages."

"Sure. Who's going to cast me with these monstrosities except for some crappy horror film?"

He held his hands up, showing off his scars. Emily turned away.

"Well, there's always the stage. And you've always *loved* the stage."

"Maybe. I suppose I could see what's around. But only when I'm ready, and not just so you can feel less guilty about it."

Emily opened her mouth to complain, then snapped it shut again.

"Besides," Jerome said. "I'm almost thirty. Old enough to make my own decisions. And that night I made the decision to go over that wall. So this—" he held up his hands again "—is on me."

Emily nodded, wishing she agreed. "Almost thirty? You're getting old."

"I'm a year older than you!"

"Anyway, I gratefully accept your offer of a home-cooked meal. If only so I finally get to see your new bachelor pad."

"I'd hardly call a room in a house-share with four people a bachelor pad. It's the size of a shoe box and I'll probably need to sell a kidney to afford the rent before the year's out. Plus, the walls are thin—I've heard things I can never un-hear."

Emily plucked a pen from Jerome's stationery pot and rolled it between finger and thumb. "You don't miss Daniel?"

"Sometimes."

"You sure you don't regret not going with him?"

"No. He has his whole family there. I'd just have him. Besides, what would I do in Italy?"

He snatched the pen from Emily's hand and replaced it in the pot.

"You know, if you don't like your place you can always move back in with me for a while," she said.

"What, give up my room to sleep on your sofa while you and Carter whisper sweet nothings? Thanks, but I'll pass."

Emily flashed him a smile as she walked away. "I'm glad you're working here, Jerome."

"Someone has to keep an eye on you," he said.

————

Emily's office had just enough space for a desk, two chairs, and a filing cabinet, which meant she was fastidious about keeping it tidy. Files and law books were ordered neatly on shelves. The desk was bare except for a computer, phone, and a stack of 'in' and 'out' trays. A single framed photograph hung on the wall— an image of wild cliffs and crashing ocean; a reminder of the place she once called home.

Hanging her jacket on the back of the door, Emily placed the camera on the desk and moved over to the single window that overlooked the placid green of Grosvenor Square garden. There were worse views to have to look at every day, even in the depths of a wintry January. She stood for a minute, staring down at the street, where people strolled by in warm coats and scarves, oblivious to the fact they were being watched.

Letting out a wistful sigh, Emily sat down at her desk,

logged onto the computer, then connected the camera. Once she'd transferred the morning's incriminating photographs, she leaned back and heaved her shoulders. She still felt no satisfaction for a job well done, and as she set to work on the follow-up report, she couldn't help wondering why.

A sharp knock on the door interrupted her thoughts. Before Emily could speak, the door swung open and Erica Braithwaite entered the room. As always, she wore a dark, tailored trouser suit with a white blouse beneath. Her black hair was cut short, accentuating her pronounced cheekbones, and although she wore a little makeup, she made no attempt to hide the fine lines of middle age at the corners of her eyes. Emily admired her for it, but it didn't stop her from feeling intimidated by the woman, even after several months in her employment.

"Good morning, Emily," Erica said, breezing into the room and sitting in the chair reserved for clients. She stared across the desk with piercing grey eyes. "You're back, so I assume you got what we needed?"

"Yes." Emily nodded, suppressing the urge to look away. "I have photographic evidence of Brenda Carlyle walking completely unaided. I had to chase her to get it, but . . ."

She pushed the camera across the desk and watched as Erica flicked through the images, one eyebrow arched in a sharp curve. When she was done, she returned the camera to the desk.

"How's the report coming along?"

"Just made a start but it shouldn't take long."

"Good. Mail it over by lunchtime if you can. Meanwhile, I'll inform the client that it's mission accomplished." Erica paused, her gaze dropping down to the camera. "I have another case you might like to take on."

Emily leaned forward, her mouth twitching as she pushed down a hopeful smile. "Oh?"

"It's another potential fraud case." Erica watched as Emily's expression quickly wilted. "Well, don't look too excited about it."

"Sorry. I'm always grateful for every case you send my way. Only . . ."

"Only you want to know when you'll be taking on a bigger case. Something more daring?" Erica smiled coolly.

It was true that since Emily had been hired by Braithwaite Investigations, every case she'd been given had been more or less the same—a big corporation suspecting one of its clients of fraud. Now, she felt she could solve a fraud case with her eyes closed, and she longed for something more exciting and complex. More—if she was honest—dangerous.

Erica interlinked her fingers and rested her hands across her stomach. "I'm very pleased with the progress you've been making so far, Emily. I could tell from the first day I met you that you have the makings of a fine investigator. That's why I chose you over all the other students to work for me. But becoming a fine investigator takes time, experience, and knowledge. While it's undeniable you have a natural talent, it does require honing." Leaning forward, the woman swivelled the camera around on the desk, so that the LCD viewing screen was facing Emily. Brenda Carlyle's shocked expression stared up at her, one hand raised in surprise. "One important aspect of private investigation is anonymity. While you've acquired what was needed with the Carlyle case, revealing yourself to get it was reckless, not to mention arrogant. Miss Carlyle may not seem like a threat, but who knows what kind of criminal connections she may have.

Now that she knows your face, we can only hope there'll be no retaliation."

Emily felt her skin heating up. She'd solved murders, exposed corruption, and saved several lives long before getting her private investigation licence. As much as she enjoyed working for Erica Braithwaite, and as much as she felt honoured to have been plucked from the classroom for mentoring at one of the best private investigation companies in London, she knew she was much more capable than solving petty fraud cases for a few greedy corporations.

She glanced at Erica then at the report on the computer screen.

"Point taken," she said.

But Erica wasn't finished. "I suspect this thirst for adventure stems from your achievements before we met. But refresh my memory, what happened with the case of Doctors Williams and Chelmsford?"

The question was unexpected, throwing Emily off-balance and sparking terrible images to assault her mind. She forced them out.

"They got what they deserved," she said through clenched teeth.

"They did indeed. But what happened to you?"

"Well, I suppose I almost died."

"And at Meadow Pines?"

Emily hung her head. She knew exactly where this conversation was heading and she wasn't happy about it. "Someone tried to kill me."

"And they would have succeeded from what I've read. Except Mr Miller out there—" Erica nodded towards the office door "—saved your life."

Emily looked away, saying nothing.

"And last year? All that business with Valence Industries?"

"That one I survived," Emily said, glancing back. "No near death experiences whatsoever."

"Not for you, no. But someone is always murdered during the course of your investigations, aren't they? And poor Mr Miller's hands—over a hundred stitches and permanent nerve damage."

Emily flinched. Her insides churned. She knew exactly the point Erica was trying to prove, and in that moment, she hated her for it. Mostly because what the woman was saying was true.

Erica's hardened gaze quickly softened as she let out a wistful sigh. "Look, I'm not trying to shame you or make you feel weak. In fact, quite the opposite. I'm trying to empower you. Accepting your vulnerability gives you strength because it makes you acutely aware of danger. It forces you to take steps to protect yourself—and those around you—from harm." She nodded her head towards the shelf of law books. "Continue with your studies, keep showing me the best you can do, and let me remind you of what I said on that very first day of training—much of this work isn't glamorous. It's tedious. But it *can* be rewarding. If you can accept all these things, you'll go far."

Getting to her feet, Erica moved over to the window and stared out at the Square. Emily sank a little lower in her chair.

When Erica turned back a moment later, a wry smile had spread across her lips.

"Anyway," she said, "as tiresome as another fraud case might seem, I believe you'll find this one rather more . . . complex."

Emily looked up. "Oh?"

"An old school friend of mine—Meredith Fisher—has been caught up in some rather difficult business. Her husband, John, is recovering from a stroke, so she's keen to have the problem resolved as quickly and discreetly as possible."

"What kind of difficult business?" Emily asked.

"A property dispute, if you will. Although there is more to it." Erica smiled again and headed towards the door. "Get that report to me today and I'll arrange for you to see the Fishers tomorrow. They can give you the full details then. You'll need to do some travelling—they live up in the Chiltern Hills—so keep hold of the car for now. And Emily?"

"Yes?"

"I haven't seen Meredith for a while due to John's illness— she can be very proud and very private—but I do consider her a good friend. As I'm sure you can imagine, this case is important to me and I wouldn't be handing it to you if I didn't think you were up to the job. Please don't prove me wrong."

Before Emily could reply, Erica had pulled open the door and slipped out of the office, leaving her sitting at the desk with her heart beating unsteadily in her chest. It was true that chasing after Brenda Carlyle and thrusting a camera in her face hadn't exactly been discreet, yet despite Erica's reprimand, she was entrusting Emily with a case to which she had a personal connection.

It's a test, she thought. *Erica wants to see if I can put my money where my mouth is.*

This was good. A chance to prove herself and climb out of the mire that was insurance investigation. So why was there a niggle of unease in the pit of her stomach?

3

John and Meredith Fisher lived two miles outside of Amberwell, a market town within the London commuter belt that was a curious mix of thirteenth century architecture and characterless, modern, red brick housing. Emily parked up on the gravel drive of their country cottage, complete with thatched roof and rural surroundings. Above her, the sky was huge and thick with grey clouds. To the west, a murder of crows hovered over nearby barren fields.

The drive from London had taken an hour. Since moving to the city just over two years ago, she'd only ever ventured back out of it a handful of times; some of which she'd barely survived. It was strange to think that she had grown used to city life when the endless, surging crowds had once terrified her. Stranger still was to remember her days before the city in that tiny Cornish village, where her life had been quiet and insular. Until the day it had imploded.

Emily knocked on the solid oak front door, nerves and curiosity clawing at her insides as the frosty air pinched her skin. A moment later, she heard the rattle of a chain lock being drawn back, then saw the door swing open. It was Meredith Fisher who greeted her, and she noted at once the woman's expensive but understated clothing, strong posture and confident gaze. Like Erica Braithwaite, Meredith wore no makeup, the lines and wrinkles of late middle-age on proud display. She could immediately see why the two were friends.

"You must be Emily," the woman said, her voice exuding friendliness and command. "Do come in."

The interior of the house was upmarket rustic with terracotta walls, mahogany floorboards, and tasteful art displayed in frames. Emily was shown into a drawing room furnished with plush sofas and rows of bookshelves that reached the ceiling. John Fisher was already waiting inside. He was perhaps a few years older than his wife, but where Meredith's physical presence exuded strength and confidence, John seemed to fold in on himself as he got to his feet.

"This is my husband," Meredith announced. Emily stepped forward and offered her hand, which John shook, his skin cold and clammy against her own as he smiled and said hello. "And that's Nestor."

She pointed to a sandy-coloured Border Terrier dozing on a rug in front of a crackling fire.

Emily was directed to an armchair, where she sat and waited while Meredith fussed around her husband, ignoring his pleas to be left alone as she attempted to slide a second, then a third cushion behind his back. While some stroke sufferers recovered quickly, others were left with long-lasting or irreparable damage. It was difficult to tell which camp John fell into when his wife seemed hell-bent on micro-managing his recuperation. But that was love, Emily supposed. Love and years of dedication.

A pot of coffee sat on a tray and now Meredith poured out a

cup and handed it to Emily without checking if she actually wanted any.

"How much has Erica told you about our case?"

Emily cleared her throat. Evidently the small talk was over. "A little but it would be good to hear it from you in your own words."

"I see." The elder woman was quiet for a moment, her husband also silent and staring out the window. "About eighteen months ago we moved into our former home on Raven Road. We were happy enough there, but then John was taken ill. We'd always talked about one day retiring to the countryside, and I thought the fresh air and peace and quiet would help with his recovery. So we put the house on the market, found this lovely little place just a few minutes' drive from the outskirts of town, and here we are." She paused, smiling warmly at her husband, who gently patted the back of her hand. Meredith's expression soured. "John was doing so much better—until two weeks ago, when we received a letter from the Harris family's solicitor announcing that they were suing us."

A deep line creased the centre of Meredith Fisher's brow. "We sold our house to that family in good faith. In fact, we were delighted to see children moving into our old home. We were unable to have our own, you see. I suppose for some it's not meant to be. The Harris family seemed like they'd fit into Raven Road nicely. Mr Harris was very charming. I remember his smile, bright and confident, utterly convincing. Of course, not long after we'd sold the house to them, came his arrest. We were shocked to learn of his crimes, more so to discover he'd paid us in stolen money. But what can we do? Whatever scandal has been brought to Raven Road lies squarely on Wesley Harris' shoulders, not ours."

Emily's gaze shifted from wife to husband and back again. "Why are the Harrises suing you?"

"The family say they've received a series of threatening and disturbing letters. The writer claims to be watching the house, peering in through the windows at Mrs Harris and her children. Which, of course, is terrifying when you think about it, and even more so when you learn these supposed letters have been penned by someone calling themselves The Witness."

Emily stared at the woman, open-mouthed. "The Witness?"

"That's right."

"But I don't understand. What do these letters have to do with suing you?"

Meredith glanced at John, who shrugged a shoulder, then she reached for a file sitting on the coffee table and removed a single sheet of paper. "These letters—the first one mentioned us by name. It claims that we knew all about The Witness . . . It accuses us of despicable things. Naturally, the Harris family have concluded that we deliberately deceived them. They say that had they known about the existence of The Witness, they would never have bought the house and put their children at risk. And so now we're going to court, where they'll no doubt try and win back every last penny they paid for the place."

Emily stared at the sheet of paper in Meredith's hand. "That's the letter?"

"A copy of it, yes." She held it out. "Be warned—it's a strange and disturbing read."

Taking the letter between finger and thumb, Emily carefully unfolded it, sucked in a breath, and began to read.

Harris Family,

 Why have you moved here? This house does not belong to you.

For years, I have watched and waited, observing every inch of every room, waiting for His dark arrival. I see the fresh blood you have brought. I follow them from room to room through the windows of the house. Did you bring them for Him? He will be most pleased. The Fishers gave Him fresh blood. They did it willingly and at His bidding. Now it will be your turn.

Have your lambs been down to the basement? Do they know what hides inside the walls?

They will soon. You will lead them there. Then He will show them the way.

Who am I?

I am The Witness. I am watching you all.

Goose pimples pushed through the surface of Emily's skin. She stared at the letter as if it were a snake coiled on her lap. *What the hell?* She'd been anticipating threatening words, but this—there was something insidious lurking between the lines, something unnatural, that pricked deep down to the core of her being. Instinctively, she glanced towards the open living room door and saw shadows lurking in the hallway beyond.

"I warned you," Meredith said, flashing a knowing smile.

Emily took a moment to compose herself. "This was the first time you'd ever heard of this...this Witness?"

"Of course it is." Meredith's smile had frozen into an icy grimace. "Do you honestly think you'd be sitting here now if it wasn't?"

Beside her, John cleared his throat. "Be nice, Meredith. It's a difficult question but one that should be asked."

He nodded at Emily, who smiled at him gratefully before turning back to Meredith.

"Do you believe the letter is genuine?"

"As in do I believe someone picked up a pen and committed that nonsense to paper? Yes, I do," Meredith said. "But do I think it's some depraved lunatic that we knew about and deliberately concealed? Absolutely not. The Witness is no more real than vampires or werewolves or any other figure of childish nonsense. The Witness is an invention, a clear attempt by the Harris family to squeeze us for every last penny we have. Wesley Harris is facing a prison sentence for fraud and money laundering for goodness sake! If he's not behind it, then his wife is— one last desperate attempt to make some money before she loses everything to the courts."

Emily gazed at the letter, poring over its strange words. "What do you think, Mr Fisher?"

John was quiet, his gaze fixed on the flames of the fire.

"I agree with my wife," he said at last. "Desperate times call for desperate measures. It would seem the Harris family have grown desperate indeed."

"The problem is," Meredith said, leaning forward, "the local newspapers have got hold of the story, no doubt thanks to the Harrises. You can imagine how much the press have relished the details, and who can blame them? It's all so dramatic and bizarre! But one can only imagine what will happen once we go to court. We'll be vilified, our names dragged through the mud—especially if we lose." Anger flashed on the woman's face and she closed her eyes for a second. When she opened them again, they glinted with determination. "We need your help, Emily. The stress of the past few weeks is affecting John's health. Mine too, if I'm honest. I'm afraid that if this story makes the national headlines, that . . ." Her voice trailed off as she stared at her husband, her hardened shell momentarily fracturing.

Emily glanced down at the letter, then back up at the Fishers. She'd been expecting another fraud case, but this…she didn't even know what this was.

"What is it you want me to do?" she asked.

"We want you to expose the Harris family." Meredith's steely gaze had returned. "We want you to prove that they're lying, and that this so-called 'Witness' is nothing more than yet another fraudulent attempt to extort money."

"I see."

"Is that something you're able to help us with?"

Emily swallowed. A knot of anxiety twisted her stomach as she briefly recalled Erica Braithwaite's admonishing words. She drew in a calming breath and steadily let it out. *You can do this. It's what you've been waiting for.*

"I'll do my best to find out what I can," she said. "Perhaps if I begin by talking to the Harris family, then—"

Meredith shook her head. "No. I'm afraid that won't be possible."

"Oh?"

"If the Harris family discovers we've hired Braithwaite Investigations to look into them, the first thing they'll do is use it against us by going to the press, and then it really will hit the nationals."

"But they're suing you. You have a right to prove your innocence by any means necessary—within the law, of course. And if that means questioning them—"

"No. We want this cleaned up quickly and discreetly. I understand that makes your job more difficult, but Erica has assured me you're highly skilled and more than capable of helping us achieve our aim. She's usually never wrong . . ."

The room pressed down on Emily as she stared at John Fisher's pale form. The illness he'd endured had taken its toll on both him and his wife, and all this trouble with the Harris family would only succeed in making everything worse.

Slowly, Emily nodded. "As I said, I'll do my best. I'm sure we'll get to the bottom of this soon."

"Very good." Satisfied for now, Meredith leaned back and gently squeezed John's hand. Emily smiled, but the ball of anxiety in her stomach was growing at an unnerving rate.

4

As EMILY DROVE AWAY from the Fishers' residence, she thought about the letter written by The Witness. Meredith Fisher was right—it truly was a strange and disturbing read. And yet even though it was more than likely another garden-variety fraud case with an admittedly elaborate edge, Emily found herself vibrating with excitement and curiosity. Who was The Witness? She couldn't wait to find out. Which was why, instead of turning off at the junction that would take her back to London, she drove straight on.

Five minutes later, she found herself on the outskirts of Amberwell and navigating a rabbit warren of suburban streets, until she found what she was looking for.

Raven Road was wide and long with trees lining the pavements, their bare branches like twisted claws. Large detached homes sat in clean drives with lawns that were neatly manicured despite the ravages of winter. Emily wedged the Audi between two vehicles, parking beneath a tall, barren oak. Switching off the engine, she glanced in the rear-view mirror and then through each of the windows. The street was empty of people, the only movement a few dead leaves batted about by winter winds. The sky above was steel-grey, a sure sign that rain was on its way.

With the car engine switched off, the temperature was already dropping. Peering through the driver window, her eyes found the house across the road. Number fifty-seven. Like most of the other homes on the street, it was a large, detached house with red brick walls and topped by a slate roof. There were four windows at the top, four at the bottom, and the blinds were closed in each. In front of the house was a wide lawn with a Rowan tree at its centre and a knee-high hedgerow that bordered the street, while two taller hedgerows fenced off the property from its next-door neighbours. It was an impressive looking home, Emily thought; a good size for a family and situated on a street that felt safe and ordinary.

Now that she'd seen the house with her own eyes, the letters from The Witness seemed ever more chilling and outlandish. *Why here?* she wondered. *Why target such a normal, suburban home?*

Of course, the 'why' depended on the true identity of The Witness. Meredith Fisher believed the letter was part of a hoax, a devious act perpetrated by the Harris family to dig them out of financial crisis. With Wesley Harris currently on remand while awaiting trial for his crimes, Emily could almost believe it. But staring at 57 Raven Road, drinking in its pristine appearance and calming stillness, it was hard to believe any kind of malice could stem from its inerrant walls.

Facts. They were the only thing that would prove The Witness was either an insidious figure that meant the Harris family harm or a make-believe construct borne out of desperation.

Pulling the case file from her bag, Emily quickly reviewed

its contents. The Harris family consisted of Jessica, 36, her husband, Wesley, 38, and their two children, Ethan, 17, and Georgia, 8. Flipping past the family details, Emily scanned through the rest of the contents until she found copies of deeds and contracts relating to the sale of the house. The Harris family had purchased the property from the Fishers for a sum of nine hundred thousand pounds. Wesley Harris had paid for it in cash, which Emily presumed was the reason alarm bells had started ringing, leading to his subsequent arrest.

As she waded through the notes, Emily wondered what would happen to the house. In criminal cases involving embezzlement, the prosecution could apply for confiscation proceedings to be opened in a bid to recover any financial gains made by the convicted criminal—including property purchased with stolen money. If Jessica Harris and her two children were about to be made homeless, there would be a strong impetus to save themselves from destitution by any means necessary.

Picking up her camera, Emily aimed it at the house and took a picture, zoomed in, and took more. As she reviewed the images on the camera's LED screen, she frowned. Why were all the blinds closed? It was past eleven in the morning. Jessica Harris would be at her receptionist job at a local recruitment agency, Georgia Harris at school, and Ethan Harris at college.

Emily set the camera down and spent a moment stretching out her spine—all this sitting around in cars day after day was doing nothing for her back. She made a mental note to seek out a yoga class; the last thing she wanted was to end up as bent and crooked as her neighbour, Harriet Golding. As she twisted her torso to the right, she became vaguely aware of movement out the corner of her eye. She turned her head and caught her breath. The front door of 57 Raven Road was opening. Someone was stepping out.

Sucking in a sharp breath, Emily sank down in the driver's seat, suddenly aware of how exposed she'd left herself, parked on the opposite side of the road in direct view of the house. No one was supposed to be home and yet, a young girl with long, dark hair, who was no older than seven or eight, and who was dressed in a thick winter coat and a knitted bobble hat, was standing on the doorstep, staring out at the cold, empty garden.

Slouching further in the seat, Emily noticed the bright blue ball the girl was carrying in a gloved hand. She watched as the child heaved her shoulders, stomped across the drive and onto the lawn. She came to a halt, tilting her head to stare up at the empty branches of the Rowan tree.

This had to be Georgia Harris, Jessica's and Wesley's youngest child. Why wasn't she at school? Perhaps she was sick and staying home for the day. But sick children shouldn't be out in the cold, Emily thought as she tried to make herself smaller. Sick children should be tucked up in bed, with hot cocoa and medicine to make them feel better.

She watched as the girl started a game of throw and catch. With each throw, she launched the ball higher and higher into the air, catching it effortlessly each time. After a minute of playing, she stopped still and stared at the house. Without warning, she threw the ball hard at a downstairs window. Emily heard a loud thud as it bounced off the glass and hit the drive. The girl turned, chasing after the ball, then swooping down to snatch it up before it could escape beneath the gate.

A second later, the front door of number fifty-seven was opening again and a woman in her mid-thirties with a mass of dark curls was hurrying out of the house. Emily saw the woman shake an angry finger at the child and grab her roughly by the arm. Saw her turn and shoot a terrified glance at the street.

"Shit . . ."

Feeling the woman's gaze on her, Emily sat up and reached for the key in the ignition. Starting the engine, she fumbled with the clutch, then rolled the car forwards. As she drove away, she glanced at the rear-view mirror and saw Jessica Harris dragging her daughter back inside the house.

5

THE SLAM of the door battered the house, making framed family photographs tremble against the walls. Standing in the darkened hallway, Jessica Harris winced at the noise, then felt a stab of guilt in her chest as her young daughter did the same. Neither of them spoke, the monotonous tick of an unseen clock the only sound to fill the gloom. Slowly, Georgia Harris balled her hands into tight fists and expelled an angry sigh.

"What the hell were you thinking?" Jessica said at last. Inside her chest, her heart was beating violently out of control. "I told you—you don't play outside. Not ever. And just because you're mad at me doesn't mean you can throw balls at the window. If it broke, someone could get in!"

Georgia's eyes glistened in the shadows. She's crying, Jessica thought, as another sharp burst of pain coursed through her chest. *I made her cry.* She reached out and fumbled along the wall until she found the light switch and flicked it on. The hallway lit up, and after blinking away the dark spots, she saw that Georgia wasn't crying at all. Her eyes were burning like two black flames.

"I'm bored!" her daughter hissed. "I want to go to school! We were doing art and I didn't finish my picture."

For a brief moment, the flames died, leaving behind two sad pools of tar.

"I know," Jessica said, desperate to wrap her arms around her daughter, yet unable to move. "And I'm sorry. But this isn't my fault. I'm just trying to keep you safe."

"Ethan goes to college. He's allowed to leave the house. It's not fair!"

"Yes but Ethan is—"

"A boy." The flames returned, burning brighter than before, this time joined by a clenching jaw and flaring nostrils.

"It's nothing to do with him being a boy. Ethan is older; he can take care of himself. You're eight years old."

"Grown-ups can get hurt too, you know," Georgia spat. "Just like Daddy hurt you."

The words smarted. Jessica raised a hand to her cheek, touching the coolness of the skin. "This isn't the same."

"I want to go to school!" Georgia shouted, angry eyes incinerating her mother. "I want to see my friends! You're making me lonely!"

Before Jessica could say she was sorry, that everything would be fixed soon and they'd all be safe, Georgia turned on her heels and stomped towards the stairs. When she was halfway up, she froze, then turned around. Now she really was crying.

"I hate you," she sobbed pitifully. "I want Dad."

Jessica flinched at the cruelty. Then her own fire ignited, spreading through her body in seconds.

"Well you can't have him!" she yelled. "Because he's in prison. Because he did something bad and left us all in trouble.

If you want to be angry with someone, be angry with him—because this is all his damn fault!"

She slammed her jaw shut, instantly regretting every syllable. But it was too late.

"I don't care!" Georgia screamed, acid tears splashing down her face. "He's still nicer than you!"

She cleared the rest of the stairs in a flurry of limbs and vanished into the shadows. Jessica listened numbly to her daughter's feet thundering along the landing, then flinched as Georgia's bedroom door slammed shut, sending a second wave of undulating tremors through the walls.

Her body was paralysed, her breath stuck in her throat like a dry pill. Tears were coming; she felt them filling her ducts, gathering momentum, trying to escape. But Jessica would not cry. Not for him. Not for what he had left them to deal with.

Tearing herself away from the stairs, she locked the front door and slipped the chain into place. She entered the living room, cutting through the shadows, until she reached the window. Pinching open the blinds she stared out at the front lawn and the Rowan tree with its naked branches, then at the street, which was empty save for a few parked vehicles. There had been a silver Audi pulling away just now, on the opposite side of the road. She hadn't recognised it. Maybe one of the neighbours had a visitor, she thought. Maybe one of them bought a new car.

Or maybe . . .

She pulled her hand away from the blinds and stepped back into the shadows, feeling the gloom close in on her. She wondered if this was how Wesley felt, locked up in a prison cell, awaiting trial. She hoped it was. She hoped he was in pain. She hoped that the walls were closing in on him, inch by inch, day by day, smothering him until there was no air left for him to breathe. She hoped he felt afraid. Like he was dying slowly from the inside out. Because that was how he had left his family. They were prisoners in their own home. Shunned by their neighbours. Living in fear. Slowly tearing each other apart.

Returning to the hallway, she hovered by the stairs. None of what had transpired had been her children's fault, and yet they were the ones being punished—the ones whom she was unleashing her anger upon. It wasn't fair. *She* wasn't being fair.

All Georgia wanted was a normal life, where she got to go to school and play with her friends, where parents didn't whisper and point in the playground at home time, saying, 'There goes the daughter of a convicted criminal. There goes her mother, who is probably just as guilty.'

Before they'd moved to the Chiltern Hills, they'd lived in another suburban street, in another town, where neighbours had smiled and waved, where their home had been a haven, not a prison, and they had been free to go where they pleased without people pointing and judging. And yes, sometimes it had felt dull and repetitive, and yes, sometimes Jessica had missed earlier times when they'd lived in the city and every day had been an adventure. But it had felt safe.

She could hear Georgia's muffled sobs floating down from upstairs. Feeling wretched, she backed away and stumbled into the darkness of the kitchen. Jessica flipped a switch and fluorescent lighting blinked overhead. It was a clean, modern space, fully equipped, the view of the rear garden shut out by the blinds. Crossing the room, she picked up her mobile phone from the worktop and checked the screen. Her heart raced a little faster. She quickly tapped out a message: *Did you get there? You're supposed to let me know.*

As she waited for a reply, she made herself a coffee and poured out an orange juice for Georgia, then shook out a couple of chocolate-chip cookies from a jar onto a plate: a peace offering.

She checked her phone again, tapped out another message: *Where are you? You're making me worry.*

She took the juice upstairs, knocked on Georgia's door, then winced as her daughter screamed at her to go away. Crouching, she placed the juice and the plate of cookies on the carpet, then returned downstairs to the kitchen.

She checked her phone again. Still no reply.

She tapped out another message: *I'm seriously worried now. Please let me know you're safe.*

Sitting on a stool at the breakfast bar, she drank her coffee and fought the panic that was threatening to consume her entire being.

Jessica waited another five minutes. Then she couldn't wait anymore. With trembling fingers, she sent another message: *I'm calling the police.*

Setting the phone down, she counted the seconds. *Five. Ten. Fifteen.* She gasped, suddenly aware that she'd been holding her breath. The phone vibrated loudly on the breakfast bar and she snatched it up, her fingers fumbling with the unlock sequence.

Jesus Christ! Will you stop? I'm in class. You're driving me fucking crazy!

Jessica stared at the words, feeling their rage and frustration pummel her skin. But she couldn't stop. And she didn't want to.

Not until this was all over. Not until she was certain that her children were safe.

Until then, she would continue protecting them. Even if it meant making them hate her.

6

EMILY PULLED BACK the gate of the ramshackle lift and made her way along the fourth floor corridor of the Holmeswood building; a Victorian-era construct with an interior twist of 1930s art decor that had been her home for the past two years. She was tired but her mind was cluttered, busy processing the events of the day and planning how to move forward with the Fisher case. Through the din came Erica Braithwaite's authoritative tone as Emily recalled her stern words from yesterday. They had been hard to hear and difficult to swallow, but everything that Erica had said was true. People had died, Jerome had been scarred for life, and Emily had almost been killed twice. Caution was something she definitely needed to exercise more—especially when the Fisher case involved vulnerable children.

As she approached her apartment door, any anxiety was quickly extinguished by tendrils of aromatic spices and cooking meat. Emily smiled. For once, she wasn't questioning her decision to give Carter a spare key. It had been a recent action, and one that she'd fought bitterly with her paranoia and trust issues to achieve, but Carter had so far been respectful, only using the key to let himself in when it had been prearranged. Slipping her own key into the lock, Emily stifled a yawn. All she wanted was to enjoy a quiet dinner with Carter, then put her feet up.

"Evening, dear."

The voice startled her, making her spin on her heels. An elderly woman, whose tiny frame was crooked like a question mark, stood in the doorway of the opposite apartment.

"Hello, Harriet." Emily smiled tiredly and held up a hand.

"You look like you haven't slept in days."

Good old, Harriet, Emily thought. Always full of compliments.

"Well, I've been busy."

"I see. S'pose that explains why I've barely seen you these last few weeks. Beginning to feel a lot like you've forgotten about your poor old neighbour."

Emily swayed on her feet and forced another smile to her lips. "You know that's not true. I came around last weekend, didn't I?"

"It used to be you'd pop over most afternoons for a cup of tea and a chat," Harriet grumbled as she clutched the door jamb with a pale, papery hand. "Now it's an hour here, an hour there, and that ain't much use to an old woman on her own."

"That was before I started this job. And you're not on your own, or have you forgotten about your son? Goodness knows how you could with all his junk filling up the place. It's a wonder you haven't been crushed to death by all those books."

Harriet shrugged her bony shoulders. "Andrew don't care about me. He's either in his room or out and about with the ladies these days, if you can believe it. Still, I suppose it's good he's getting out more, although I've still yet to meet one of these women. I'm starting to believe they're not the type you bring home to your mother."

Emily smiled. She thought of Andrew Golding, a fifty-year-old man who'd never moved out of home or done a day's work in his life. But everyone deserved happiness. Even Andrew Golding.

"That fella of yours cooking again, is he?" Harriet nodded at Emily's apartment door.

"Mm-hm."

"Well, I've never heard anything like it. Back in my day, the only way you could get a fella in the kitchen was when you called him to the dinner table. Then he was out again soon as he'd emptied his plate."

Emily smiled. "Next you'll be telling me I should be staying at home, doing the laundry and pushing out babies."

Harriet grumbled under her breath and turned to go inside.

"I'll come by and see you tomorrow evening," Emily called. "And if you're lucky, I'll bring you some leftovers."

"No thanks. Judging by the stench it's some foreign muck. I like British food. Good old meat and potatoes."

"Except potatoes originated from South America," Emily said, flashing a wicked grin.

The hush inside her apartment was a welcome embrace. Hanging up her coat, she walked the length of the high-ceilinged hall. As she entered the spacious living room, she heard Carter's deep voice floating out through the saloon doors that led to the kitchen on the far side. He was humming to himself, badly, and quite unaware he was no longer alone. Three large windows running from floor to ceiling looked out on the city street. Emily smiled, inhaling tantalising food smells as she padded over to the centre window and stood for a minute, watching the stream of vehicles down below, their headlights blinking like the eyes of nocturnal animals. She smiled to herself as Carter's humming grew louder. As quickly as the smile came, it vanished, replaced by a fluttering in the pit of her stomach.

Although she was slowly relaxing into the idea of sharing her life with someone, moments like these—where doubt gripped her by the throat and squeezed the air from her lungs—left her wondering if she was ready. Fortunately, Carter had a surprising stubborn streak and zen-like patience. Which was a good thing. And a bad thing.

"You know, you're lucky I'm not a serial-killer, otherwise you'd be in serious trouble right about now," Emily called out.

The humming abruptly stopped. Carter's tall and broad frame appeared behind the saloon doors, a sheepish grin beaming from beneath a shock of dark hair. His curiously-coloured eyes—one hazel-green, the other hazel-brown—fixed on Emily.

"Lucky for me, you're not," he said.

"Well, if I were, you'd have scared me off with those dulcet tones."

"I'll have you know I used to be in the school choir."

"Cat's choir more like." Emily smiled and sauntered over to the saloon doors. Standing on tiptoes she leaned over and kissed him, then peered over his shoulder. "Something smells good."

"Sri Lankan chicken curry. It's meant to have the spiciness of Indian and the creaminess of Thai." Carter stepped back to allow Emily in. "I haven't tried it before, so consider yourself my guinea pig."

Emily wandered over to a large pot bubbling on the stove. "Thanks for the warning. Harriet says your cooking smells like foreign muck."

Carter laughed. It was deep and throaty, making Emily's stomach tingle. "I have a feeling no matter what I do, Harriet Golding will always have something to say about it."

"Take it as a compliment. If she's complaining about you, it means she likes you."

Carter came up behind her, wrapping his hands around her waist and nuzzling her neck. Emily felt her body tense for a second. She shut her eyes, forcing her muscles to relax as she rested her head against his. *Try to act normal. Ask a question.*

Twisting around, she slipped her hands into the back pockets of his jeans. "Good day at the workshop?"

"If you ignore the bad parts," Carter sighed. "I mean, I love making furniture, but I don't love difficult clients. This one guy, it's like he can't make up his mind what he wants. If he doesn't decide soon, he's going to end up with a weird, table-chair-lamp thing. It's a waste of trees." Nudging Emily aside, he picked up a spoon and stirred the contents of the pot. "There's wine if you want it."

Emily eyed the bottle of red sitting on the work surface next to two glasses, one empty, the other half-full. "Maybe later."

"No pressure."

"I know. It's just weird, that's all. I've gotten used to not drinking."

"Well, it's only been a few weeks. Do whatever feels right for you."

Emily stared at the empty glass. "Three weeks anti-depressant free. Who'd have thought it?"

"Me," Carter said, flashing her a smile. "Because you've totally got this. Anyway, how about you? Good day fighting crime?"

"I guess. I solved the Carlyle case. Turns out she was a big faker after all."

"And you're disappointed because . . ."

Emily shrugged. She was disappointed, wasn't she? Not because of Brenda Carlyle. Not even because of Erica Braithwaite's reprimand. She shook her head, loosening her shoulder muscles. "I don't know. I thought being a private investigator would involve helping people who really needed it. I thought I'd be doing good."

"You are doing good," Carter said.

"Am I? I feel like most of the people I'm helping are those who're already doing fine by themselves. Namely, rich and powerful corporations. That's not what I wanted, especially after everything I went through with Valence Industries."

"Who *do* you want to help?"

Emily thought about it, her mind flooding with faces of ghosts, both past and present. Through them all came the face of a young boy. She quickly shook the image away, instead conjuring up a vision of Jessica and Georgia Harris, mother tugging on her daughter's arm, a look of terror on the woman's face. "People who really need it, I suppose."

Carter was staring at her, a slight frown crumpling his brow. He was doing it again, Emily noted with some annoyance—trying to look deep inside her, attempting to read her thoughts. She turned away from him, eyes finding the bottle of wine and the empty glass. Before Braithwaite Investigations, she had helped people who'd really needed it. Alina Engel, for instance, who had vanished without trace from this very apartment, and Anya Copeland, who had been forced into hiding so that she could protect her son's life. And of course, there was Phillip

Gerard, whom she'd tried to help but had failed—and who Carter still knew nothing about.

Who was Emily helping now? Even with the Fisher case, she was about to embark on an investigation that had the potential to bring suffering to the Harris children, and they had more than likely already suffered enough thanks to their father's crimes.

Carter's hands clasped over hers as he wrapped himself around her once more.

"Well, whether or not you think you're doing a good job, I think you're a total badass," he said, kissing her neck. Emily turned to face him and some of the tension slipped from her shoulders as he flashed her a wicked grin. "I mean, I never thought in a million years I'd be dating one of Charlie's Angels."

Emily laughed. "More like Erica's Minions. Now get slaving over that hot stove—I'm starving."

Carter kissed her again. "It'll be another twenty minutes."

"Perfect. Gives me just enough time to go over some case notes."

"You do know you're off the clock—why don't you leave it till the morning?"

"I just want to get a head start, that's all."

He was staring at her again. Emily felt her shoulder muscles tense up. She forced a smile to her lips, then pushed her way through the saloon doors and into the living room, where she sank down on the sofa. Pulling the Fishers' case file from her bag, she removed the copy of the letter that Meredith Fisher had given her and read over its chilling words.

Who am I?

I am The Witness.

I am watching you all.

The Harris family claimed they'd received further letters, Meredith had told her, although she nor her solicitor had yet to read them.

Perhaps that was how Emily would proceed—by getting hold of the rest of the letters. But how was she going to do that without making contact with Jessica Harris?

7

JESSICA LEANED against the kitchen counter, staring into the electric gloom as she waited for the kettle to boil. The blinds were still closed. She had no idea if it was light outside yet, or if the sky was a wintry blue or growing heavy with rainclouds. But it was better to shut the world out. It was safer. Even if it meant time had become liquid and unmeasurable, unless you stared at the clock. Which she did now.

7.47 a.m.

She hadn't slept well, but that was nothing new. Her mind was a constant, chaotic jumble of worries and bad memories, stuck in a never-ending loop. She wasn't the only one who hadn't slept. Georgia had woken three times in the night, bad dreams sending her running to her mother's bed. Jessica stared at her daughter, who was sitting at the table, elbows propped on the surface, one hand under her chin while the other spooned cereal into her mouth, the kitchen light illuminating the dark shadows beneath her blank eyes. An eight-year-old shouldn't look like that, Jessica thought. An eight-year-old should be buzzing with energy, her eyes sparkling with excitement for the day ahead.

Georgia looked like an old woman, someone who'd endured a lifetime of struggle and disappointment. It broke Jessica's heart. But wasn't it her fault? Partially, at least.

"Honey? What do you want to do today? We could get out the art stuff, maybe recreate that painting you were doing at . . . Or maybe we could have a Disney and popcorn day. What do you think?"

At the table, Georgia's eyes flicked towards her mother, then returned to gazing at nothing in particular as she slowly spooned more cereal into her mouth, milk running down her chin.

The kettle finished boiling. Jessica set about making coffee. She spun around again. "Or how about baking? We could make a cake. Or shortbread dipped in chocolate sauce."

Nothing. Not even the twitch of an eye to acknowledge that Georgia was listening. Jessica felt a twinge in her chest. Her gaze shifted back to the wall clock. The twinge turned into a sharp pain. Crossing the room, she opened the kitchen door and leaned out into the shadows of the hall.

"Ethan! Get up! You're going to be late!"

Returning to the counter, she finished making coffee then stood, sipping from her mug, only slightly aware that the liquid was burning her lips. She longed to sit at the table next to her daughter, to enjoy a normal family breakfast, but it was as if there were an invisible barbed wire fence surrounding it, with a sign that read: *Keep Out! Bad Mothers Will Be Prosecuted!*

The sound of feet stomping down the stairs directed her attention to the door. Ethan emerged from the shadows, thunderous eyes scowling from beneath a mess of tangled, dark hair. He froze for a second, as if he'd encountered his own invisible fence, before crossing the kitchen floor and reaching for the coffee pot.

"I can do that," Jessica said. "You sit down and grab some cereal. You've only got a few minutes."

Ethan shrugged a shoulder and stalked to the table. As he sat down, Georgia's head snapped up. Her eyes brightened, like two light bulbs switching on, and a smile rippled across her lips. It was as if her daughter had been replaced by an android, Jessica thought, activating only in the presence of her son. The pain in her chest intensified.

"Morning, Ethan." Georgia's voice was stiff and rusty.

Across the table, Ethan glowered as he poured cereal into a bowl.

Jessica fixed a coffee and brought it to the table. She didn't sit down, just stood there, her gaze hovering on her son.

"Aren't those the same clothes you wore yesterday?" she asked, staring at his black hoodie with a stain on the left sleeve. "Have you even showered?"

Ethan poured milk on his cereal and drank his coffee.

Georgia stared intently at her brother. "When you come back from college, can you help me with my drawing?"

"But I thought we were—" Jessica began. Both children ignored her.

"Maybe we can do another comic," Georgia continued, eyes bright and hopeful. "Another one with Caesar the Ninja Cat."

Ethan crammed cereal into his mouth and pulled out his phone, eyes fixed on the screen.

"Ethan, your sister is talking to you. And what did I say about no phones at the table?" The pain in Jessica's chest was starting to burn, spreading out through her veins like little trails of gunpowder, sparking and crackling. She watched as Ethan's thumb flicked across the screen, again and again. "Ethan, I'm talking to you. I know you're angry right now, but I'm still your mother. You need to show me some respect."

The tips of Ethan's fingers whitened against the phone.

"So, the comic . . ." Georgia tried again. "Maybe when you come home, we can work on it and—"

"Draw them by your fucking-self!" The words were spat from his mouth like rotten food.

"Hey!" Jessica yelled. "You don't use that language in front of your sister!"

His breakfast barely touched, Ethan stood, scraping the chair against the flagstone floor, then started towards the door.

Jessica lunged forward, blocking his path. The fire in her chest was now an inferno. "What do you think you're doing? You don't just walk away when I'm talking to you. What the hell's got into you?"

"Get out of my way." Her son's voice was low and dangerous.

"Don't talk to me like that. I'm the adult here!"

"If you say so." He stepped to the side. Jessica did the same.

"You can hate me all you want, Ethan. You can blame me for everything that's gone wrong, I don't care. All I'm asking is that you check in with me so I know something terrible hasn't happened to you. All I'm asking is that you stop disappearing."

Her hands had balled into tight, angry fists. She forced them open, flattening the palms against her sides as she stared at her son. He hadn't met her gaze for days. Even now, his head was turned away, his eyes pointed downward.

"I don't disappear," Ethan said through clenched teeth, his voice growing louder with each word. "I'm in class. I'm trying to get an education, so that I can get my grades and get the fuck away from you. It's like you want me to fail so I have to stay here and deal with your shit!"

Now he stepped to the left. Jessica moved with him, refusing to let him pass.

"I'm trying to keep you safe," she said, her fingers digging into her thighs. "I'm trying to protect you both from everything that's happening. I want you to do your best. I want you to succeed. But I need you to check in with me so I know that you're safe."

She stared at him, taking in his angry scowl, the hurt that lay in between. He was a wounded puppy surrounded by a nest of snakes. But he was the nest of snakes, too.

"Ethan," she begged. "Please, look at me."

Slowly, forcefully, Ethan raised his head and glared at her with glittering, dark eyes. Jessica gasped and flinched, the breath snatched from her lungs. *You look just like your father.* She glanced away, trying to hide her shock, but Ethan had seen and now it was as if she'd slapped him in the face. His cheeks flushed to a deep red. His eyes found the floor.

"I need to go to college," he said, his voice cracking. "You're making me late."

Shoulders sagging, Jessica nodded and turned away. *You look just like him. It's like he's staring through your eyes.* She couldn't stop thinking it, no matter how unfair it was. And she couldn't stop feeling repelled, her skin burning and itching.

"All I want is for you to text me when you get to college, or to let me know if you're going to be late home," she forced herself to say. "That's all. A few seconds of your time so I don't have to worry."

"You're crazy." The crack in Ethan's voice had become a fissure. "I didn't want to move here. I was happy where we were. I'm trying to fit in, but you're making it impossible! What you're doing to Georgia . . ." He stabbed a finger at the kitchen table.

"She needs to go to school. She won't have any friends. She won't learn anything. You're going to drive us both mad. It's not our fault what Dad did to us. It's not *my* fault. I'm not *him!*"

"This has nothing to do with your father! Someone's trying to hurt us. Someone's trying to make our lives a misery."

Ethan stepped forward until his face was inches from his mother's, forcing her to stare at him once more. *He's gotten so tall,* Jessica thought. *Only last year I could rest my chin on the top of his head.*

"The only person making our lives a misery is you," he spat.

His shoulder slammed into hers as he shoved her out of the way. Jessica spun around in time to see him vanish into the gloom of the hall.

"I'm not the one sending letters and turning everyone against us!" she screamed after him. "I'm not the one threatening to hurt you both!"

The front door slammed, sending shock waves shuddering through the walls and into Jessica's bones. Speechless, exhausted, she turned back to the kitchen, her eyes finding Georgia at the kitchen table, where she sat motionless, spoon hovering in mid-air, wide, haunted eyes staring back at her mother.

"I want to go to school," Georgia said. Then she started to cry.

8

EMILY SAT behind the wheel of the car, attempting to shut out the growing ache in her lower spine by sucking in deep breaths, holding them in for a count of seven, then slowly letting them out. It was 8.01 a.m. She'd already tried calling the local police station to see if she could speak to the investigating officer in charge of the Harris case—her way in to access the rest of The Witness' letters—but she'd been told he was unavailable and to try again later. She'd left her name and number, then made her way to Raven Road, where she'd been sitting for the past hour, watching and waiting, and feeling increasingly uncomfortable about having left Carter still asleep in her bed, knowing that he was now free to rifle through the cupboards and drawers of her apartment. Not that he would do such a thing.

Carter already knew that her deepest, darkest secrets could easily be found by searching online news archives. Emily had even encouraged him to go looking for them, but he had stubbornly refused. It would have been easier that way; to let him find out for himself about the ghosts of her past, then leave quietly through the nearest side exit, no questions asked. But

Carter was proving doggedly compassionate, loyal even, saying that he would learn of her secrets when she was ready to tell him. Emily had left him in suspense for several months now. She would have to tell him soon, she supposed—about Phillip Gerard and about all the hell that followed his death—and as she glanced out the window at 57 Raven Road, where the blinds remained stubbornly shut, she regretted not telling Carter about Phillip on the day they'd met. That way, their car crash of a relationship would never have happened. But that was the thing about car crashes and relationships—they hit you when you least expected it.

Minutes ticked by. Neighbours emerged from their homes and set off to work on foot or in vehicles. They were soon followed by clusters of parents and children ambling towards school. Emily watched them all, her head bowed, eyes shifting from side to side. It was a risk being here at such a busy time of the morning, but yesterday, Georgia Harris had been kept at home even though she didn't seem sick, and Jessica Harris hadn't gone into work. Emily needed to know if this was a regular occurrence and if the son, Ethan, was also staying at home.

Across the road, the house remained resolutely still. A car drove by. Then another. Further down the street, a young father pushed a pram along with one hand and held onto a toddler with the other. Emily glanced through the passenger window on her left. More parents were walking along with their children, deep in chatter while young friends skipped alongside. As one mother strolled by, she frowned as she noticed the silver Audi and the conspicuous blonde woman sitting behind the wheel. Emily snatched up her phone and pressed it to her ear. When she was alone again, she lowered the phone and checked the time. 8.32 a.m.

Carter would be awake now, showered and dressed after eating breakfast in her kitchen. Emily thought about calling him to see if he had left her apartment.

Perhaps she could tell him about Phillip right there and then. It was ridiculous they'd gone all this time without him finding out. Perhaps she could get Jerome to tell him. Perhaps she should just email Carter a link to one of the news stories and be done with it.

Her eyes wandered back over to number fifty-seven, where not even a branch on the Rowan tree stirred. It wasn't like she was the only person with secrets. Everyone had something they were scared to talk about for fear of judgment. Even Carter had a secret. It just so happened that Emily had stumbled upon it while checking into his otherwise uneventful past not long after they'd met. Carter's secret was called Jaimie West. She had vanished one morning, fifteen years ago, never to be seen again. He'd mentioned his sister in passing, from time to time. Occasionally, he'd had nightmares and called out her name. But he'd never told Emily about what had happened to her and she had never asked. When it came to secrets, she and Carter were well matched.

Somewhere at the periphery of her vision, a door opened. Emily turned to see a teenage boy, dressed in dark skinny jeans and a black parka jacket slam the front door behind him, the boom startling passers-by and making heads turn. Emily sank down but kept her eyes trained on the boy, who was now stalking down the drive. It had to be Ethan Harris, only son of Jessica and Wesley. She watched as he reached the gate, threw it open, and entered the street. He stood there for a long minute, his body taut, his shoulders heaving up and down, his face red and blotchy beneath a mess of dark hair. He lifted a hand and wiped at his eyes, then he was on the move, turning swiftly, storming off down the street like a fiery tornado.

Emily shifted her gaze back to the house, waiting for Jessica Harris to come chasing after him like she had done so yesterday with Georgia. But the door remained shut, the blinds closed. Ethan was moving further away with each passing second, a backpack slung over his shoulder, his stride determined and relentless. Probably going to college, Emily thought.

And the anger? That was easy.

Ethan was seventeen years old. All seventeen-year-olds were angry because no one understood them, the world was unfair, and parents only served to make their lives as miserable as possible. In Ethan's case, it wasn't so far from the truth.

Emily's fingers twitched on the steering wheel as she wondered if she should follow him. By car she would be quickly seen, probably arrested for kerb crawling. By foot she could keep a discreet distance, see where he was going, who he might meet. Even if she discovered nothing out of the ordinary, it was better than sitting here, slowly freezing to death. Besides, staking out the house was getting her nowhere. Her mind made up, Emily pocketed her phone, grabbed her camera bag, and reached for the door handle.

Two lined faces were staring at her through the passenger window. Emily stared back, mouth ajar, body frozen in a half-twist. It was an elderly couple—a short, thin woman with narrow eyes, dressed in an itchy-looking coat and a thick woollen hat, and a tall man bent over a walking stick, with a strong jaw and a hooked nose, white hair still thick and lustrous.

Emily reached over and wound down the window.

"Hello, dearie," the elderly woman said. "You must be catching your death in there."

Emily's gaze shifted uncertainly between the pair.

The man, whose eyebrows were wild and bushy, nodded towards the other side of the street. "You're watching that house. Number fifty-seven. You're watching the Harris family."

The words caught in Emily's throat. She shook her head, forced a smile. "No, I—"

"Yes, you are," the man continued. "You've been here for two hours. You were here yesterday, too."

"It's true, dearie," the woman said. "We've been watching you. You've been parked right outside our house."

Emily stared at the couple, who stared right back. Not in an aggressive or accusatory way, she noticed. If anything, they seemed curious.

She smiled again, felt her face heating up. Erica wasn't going to be happy. But then what did she expect? A stakeout on a suburban street in the middle of the day was never going to be discreet.

"You the police?" the man asked, leaning towards the window to have a good look inside. "Social worker, maybe?"

Emily seized on the idea. It was a good cover. She nodded. "We've been concerned that the children haven't been going to school."

The man arched his unkempt eyebrows. "And social workers spy on people, do they? Before they snatch the children away?"

"Oh, Raymond, don't be rude. Whatever the young lady's reasons, it's nothing to do with us, is it?" The elderly woman nudged him gently out of the way and peered inside the car. "You must excuse my husband. Whatever your reasons for watching that family, I'm not surprised. They've been nothing but trouble since the day they moved in. All that drama with the police, the husband's arrest. Then those letters. They should just pack up and leave."

Emily stared at her, momentarily forgetting about her cover. "You know about the letters?"

"Know about them?" the man called Raymond said. "Of course we know about them. We all got one. Which is why we all want that family gone."

"I don't understand. You received a letter?"

The elderly couple both nodded and Emily noticed that Raymond was blushing now.

"Why don't you come in for a cup of tea?" The woman nodded to the house behind her. "Warm yourself up a bit. We can tell you all about what that terrible family's been up to."

Emily pulled her gaze away from the couple and searched the street. Ethan Harris was just a speck in the distance now.

"Come on, then. Geraldine will put on the kettle," Raymond said.

"Oh, I will, will I? And what happened to your hands? Fall off, did they?" The woman scowled then leaned in closer. "Well, don't just sit there, dearie. We've got chocolate hobnobs."

Emily watched the couple turn and enter the front gate of their home. If only Erica could see me now, she thought. But Erica Braithwaite wasn't here, and Emily had her own methods for getting answers. Rolling up the window, she grabbed her bag, looked up to see that Ethan had already disappeared, then threw open the car door.

9

EMILY WAS SHOWN through a narrow hallway and into Raymond and Geraldine Butchers' living room, where she was greeted by cream walls, green carpet, a faded blue sofa and armchair set, and a huge flat screen television in the corner. The room was stifling hot, the air dry and musty. While Raymond disappeared into the kitchen to make tea, Geraldine directed Emily to an armchair that was covered in white cat hair. Perching on its edge, Emily spied two fat felines spread out on a rug and basking in the heat of an old electric fire.

Geraldine took a seat on the sofa and stared at Emily with curious eyes, her hands clasped together on her skirted lap.

"You don't look like a social worker," the elderly woman said, eyebrows raised.

"I wasn't aware we *had* a look." Emily smiled and shifted on the chair. Lying never sat comfortably with her, but she was here for answers and sometimes bending the truth was the only way to get them.

"Tell me about the letter," she said gently.

Geraldine's smile soured. Getting to her feet, she brushed

down her skirt and crossed the room, pausing at a side table. Opening a drawer, she fished out an envelope and let it dangle between finger and thumb, as if holding a dead mouse by the tail.

"It's best you read it to yourself. I've no wish to foul the air with such ripe language." She handed it to Emily. At the same time, Raymond shuffled into the room, a tea tray rattling in his hands. His eyes narrowed as they found the letter and he muttered something angry-sounding under his breath. Emily couldn't make out his words, but the scarlet blooming of his cheeks told her all she needed to know.

While Geraldine helped her husband with the tea, Emily carefully removed the letter from the envelope, unfolded it, and began to read. It was a short, concise letter, but by the time she'd done reading, her face was as crimson as Raymond's own.

"I see . . ." she said. She swallowed hard, tucked the offending letter back inside the envelope, and gratefully accepted a cup of tea.

"It's not the kind of letter you'd normally expect to receive in the post," Geraldine said, turning to frown at Raymond, who was now seated at the other end of the sofa and dipping a biscuit into his tea. "If you ask me, that woman needs her mouth washed out with soap and water."

"Everyone on the street received one?" Emily asked, still shocked by the salaciousness of its contents.

"Every man received one, yes. It was about two weeks ago, wasn't it?" Geraldine glanced at her husband, who grunted a confirmation. "Disgusting. Begging them to do this and do that to her, like a dog in heat!"

"Did you make a complaint?"

"To be honest, we were too shocked to do anything. But

then we learned Raymond wasn't the only one to have received such filth, and that some of the wives had decided to take the matter into their own hands."

Emily's eyes drifted to the letter sitting on the armchair. "They went to see Mrs Harris?"

"Oh, they certainly did," Geraldine said, nodding. "They hammered on the door and asked her what the bloody hell she was playing at. Of course, she denied everything. Claimed someone else had written it, that she and her family were being harassed by a stalker and that they were the victims, not everyone else. As you can imagine, it didn't go down well. Some of the women threatened her, said if she ever came near their husbands, she'd be sorry. But Mrs Harris just went on denying it and even threatened to call the police if they didn't leave. Can you imagine!"

"That family's been nothing but trouble since the day they moved here." Raymond's complexion had returned to normal. "You've got the husband getting arrested and facing jail, the police flooding the street, followed by journalists . . . pictures of our homes printed in the newspapers. We don't want that kind of thing around here. This is a quiet, peaceful street filled with families and the retired."

He let out a heavy sigh and sipped some tea.

"We saw Mr Harris arrested, you know," Geraldine said, glancing at her husband. "They frogmarched him out of that house in handcuffs while his wife and children watched. It's that little one I feel sorry for. She's a sweet thing. Innocent. Probably the only innocent one in that whole family."

Emily leaned forward. "Oh?"

"Well, how can you *not* know that your husband's been embezzling millions of pounds? They bought that house in cash, you know. And those children are always in nice clothes. The wife, too. She had to have been in on it."

Emily wondered if it was true. People didn't always know everything their spouses got up to, but the house had been paid for in cash—surely it would have set alarm bells ringing in Jessica Harris' ears.

Geraldine was still talking. "As for that son of theirs, well, you can just tell by looking at him that he's trouble. Always dressed in black. Always scowling with nothing good to say."

"A chip off the old block," Raymond said. "Like father, like son."

"You should be looking into him." Geraldine pointed a finger at Emily, who was momentarily lost in thought.

"I'm sorry?"

"The son. He's trouble with a capital 'T'. You can see it in his eyes. Besides, after what I saw, it's a wonder I didn't call social services myself."

Emily shot her a questioning look.

"I saw them, one morning in the garden, not long after their father had been carted off and the journalists had all gone home. That precious girl was in the garden, playing with a ball and looking lonely as can be, when that brother of hers came back from somewhere, all angry and bothered about something. And you know what he did? He slapped the poor girl right across the face. Knocked her down, he did, and made her cry."

"He was lucky I didn't see it," Raymond said, waving a biscuit in his hand, "or he would have had a taste of his own medicine."

Geraldine leaned back on the sofa, her face wrinkling with disgust. "He's a bad seed, that one. You can just tell."

Emily was quiet, thinking about the way the air around

Ethan had almost shimmered with anger as he'd taken off down the street. For now, she made a mental note to find out more about him, then finished her tea.

"You said Mrs Harris claimed she was being harassed?" She directed this at Geraldine, who scoffed and rolled her eyes.

"All that business in the local papers about 'The Witness', or whatever nonsense it was. Whoever heard of such a thing? No one around here believes a word of it. Why would they?"

"Sounds like something out of a horror film," Raymond agreed, nodding at the blank screen of the television. "It's just another one of their scams, isn't it? The husband's facing prison and the government's going to take away anything he bought with stolen money—including that house. The Witness, my arse. It's a desperate bid to make some money before those lowlifes are thrown out on the streets."

"It's a disgrace," Geraldine said. "The Fishers sold them that house in good faith, and now their name is being dragged through the mud. They would never have knowingly put a family in danger like that. They're good people!"

"You're friends with the Fishers?" Emily asked.

"For the short amount of time they lived here, yes. They were well liked, good, honest people. And not once did they ever mention any sinister letters or anything about someone calling themselves The Witness!"

"That's because it's a scam," Raymond said.

Emily stared from husband to wife, then down at the letter sitting on the armchair. She supposed from everything she had learned so far, the logical conclusion was that The Witness was indeed a fictitious character created by the Harris family to recoup some of the losses they were facing. But it was still a conclusion based on conjecture. Either way, she was done here.

"Do you think I could take a copy of the letter?" she asked, picking it up.

Geraldine nodded. "It can't be any good for those children to be living with a mother like that."

Fishing her phone from her pocket, Emily removed the letter from the envelope and photographed its contents. She thanked the Butchers for their time and got to her feet.

"Back to the office, is it?" Geraldine asked, standing. "Here, if you're going to file a report about what we said, you won't mention our names, will you? I don't want to be blamed for having children taken away from their families, even if they need to be."

For a moment, Emily wondered if she should tell them the truth, then quickly decided against it. "Everything you've told me today will be kept strictly confidential."

Raymond set down his cup, picked up the TV remote, and switched on the television. "Criminals, perverted letters, so-called stalkers," he said with a snort. "Next, they'll be saying that house is cursed."

"Why would they say that?" Emily asked, hooking her bag over her shoulder.

"Well, you've got that family and all their troubles, then before that poor John Fisher getting sick and he and his wife having to move out. And then before that you've got those murders."

Emily froze, staring at Raymond open-mouthed.

"Don't pay any attention to him," Geraldine laughed. "That was something we heard about when we first moved onto the street. It's an old wives tale if you ask me. Something to scare the children into behaving themselves."

"It's not, it's true," Raymond insisted. "It happened fifty years ago, something like that."

Geraldine waved a hand. "Raymond likes to make a drama out of things. Come on, I'll show you out."

At the front door, Emily thanked the woman for her time and returned to her car. After the stifling heat of the Butchers' living room, entering the vehicle was like climbing inside a chest freezer. Shivering, she slipped the key into the ignition, started the engine, and switched the heaters on to maximum power. Rubbing her hands together, she wondered what she should do with her newfound information. There were no new leads as such, but the letter sent to Raymond Butcher was of interest. It didn't make sense for Jessica to enrage her neighbours with such direct and inflammatory behaviour.

Unless it was all part of a greater plan to save her family from financial ruin.

Emily glanced across the street at 57 Raven Road. The house was silent and still, like a life-size photograph. She wondered what was happening inside.

Pulling her seatbelt across, she decided to head to the nearest cafe to use their facilities and write up some notes. And maybe, out of curiosity, she would research the history of the house to see if she could find out anything about those murders.

10

JESSICA STOOD in the shadows of the living room, fingers pinching open the window blinds. Thirty minutes had passed since Ethan had stormed out of the house in a cacophony of door slams and expletives. Now the school run was over and neighbours had returned to their houses or gone to work. And yet, Ethan had failed to let her know he was safe.

He was punishing her, she knew it. But it didn't stop her from worrying that something had happened to him. Why couldn't he respect that she was his mother? Why couldn't he understand that all she was trying to do was protect her children? Nothing more, nothing less. But it was as if Ethan believed she was trying to destroy them, that somehow it was her fault that his father was in prison.

Jessica heaved her shoulders and fought back tears. Ethan was wrong about that. But he had been right about something. Every time Jessica looked at her son lately, all she saw was his father staring back. It made her want to lash out at him, to blame him for his father's wrongdoings, just like how he was blaming her.

She watched the street, furtive eyes landing on the silver Audi parked outside Mr and Mrs Butcher's home. Wasn't it the same car that she'd spied yesterday, driving away as she'd dragged Georgia back inside? What was it doing here again? She supposed it was possible one of her neighbours had bought a new car. But she didn't think so, because most of the neighbours parked on their drives.

A visitor, then. Someone checking in on an elderly relative. Like the Butchers. They were elderly and frail, but she was sure the Butchers had no children of their own.

Perhaps the car belonged to a visiting nurse or healthcare professional. But two days in a row? Besides, Jessica had been watching the street for weeks now, noticing every single change, and she had never seen that Audi parked there before yesterday.

As she stared at it from the darkness of her house, her breaths grew thin and shallow. Who did the vehicle belong to? Why was it here, parked in the same position with a perfect view of her house, for two days in a row?

Above her, Georgia's feet stomped across the bedroom floor.

"You're being paranoid," Jessica whispered. "No one's even sitting in that car."

Maybe Ethan was right. Maybe she really was losing her mind.

Move away from the window. Go and check on your daughter.

Jessica stared at her fingers, willing them to release their grip on the blinds. They refused. Then her eyes were moving back across the road, to the Audi and to the Butchers' home.

The front door was opening and a pale, blonde-haired woman was stepping out, quickly followed by frail Mrs Butcher. She watched as the women exchanged conversation for a brief time, then the blonde woman waved goodbye and turned back to the street as Mrs Butcher went inside.

Jessica's heart raced as the woman climbed inside the Audi. She held her breath, pressing her nose against the glass to get a closer look.

"See?" she whispered. "Just a visitor."

So why wasn't relief flooding her veins? Why was the woman just sitting there, motionless behind the wheel of the car, not starting the engine, not driving away, but just sitting there, staring into space? Why was she now slowly turning her head and staring in the direction of Jessica's house?

Instinctively she jumped back, letting the blinds snap shut.

Who was this woman? What was she doing here? Why was she talking to the Butchers?

Lunging forward again, Jessica pinched open the blinds. The woman was still there, still unmoving, still staring up at the house. Nausea bubbled in Jessica's stomach. Behind her, the floorboards creaked, but she was oblivious. What did this woman want? Had Wesley sent her to spy on his family? Was she working for the police, who were convinced Jessica was as guilty as her husband, but had found no evidence to back up their suspicions?

"Mum?"

Maybe she was a damn social worker, here to take the kids away from her. Yes, that would make sense, wouldn't it? Georgia hadn't been in school for weeks now. They were beginning to suspect something was wrong.

"*Mum . . .*"

Or maybe Wesley really had sent her. In an instant, Jessica's fear was ignited by anger. Screw him, she thought. Screw him and everything he's done.

Ethan wanted to blame her for all the wrong done to the family, but everyone knew damn well who was actually responsible. As Jessica watched the woman, she wondered what she should do. The right thing would be to call the police—even if the woman was the police. But a patrol car turning up would only set curtains twitching and tongues wagging once more.

The alternative was to call Wesley, even though she hadn't spoken to him in weeks, even though he was the last person she wanted to talk to. Or perhaps she should just go out there right now, anger burning through her veins, and –

"Mum!"

Jessica spun around to see Georgia skulking in the shadows, hands on hips.

Or perhaps I should grab the kids and just run. Leave this house and all the trouble it's brought us.

"Mum, what are you doing?" Georgia shifted from one foot to the other. "You said we were going to draw. You said we could finish the picture I—"

"Just give me a minute, will you?" Jessica returned her gaze to the window. She should write down the licence plate. Give it to the police and let them know that she was onto them. Or if the woman didn't work for them, she'd be giving them a new lead to look into.

Across the road, the Audi was spewing out exhaust fumes. Now it was pulling away from the kerb. The blonde woman was going to get away.

"A pen!" Jessica cried. "Get me a damn pen!"

But the Audi was already sliding from her field of vision. Pins and needles pricked the top of Jessica's head. Nausea crested in her stomach. She turned and faced the gloom of the living room.

Georgia was gone. She could hear her daughter's footsteps hammering on the stairs, followed by the slam of a bedroom door.

You're coming apart, Jessica thought. *It doesn't matter who that woman was. Because you're going to lose your children all by yourself.*

11

THANKFUL TO BE out of the cold, Emily had been sitting in the far corner of the cafe for almost two hours now. She'd spent the time writing up notes from the morning's conversation with Mr and Mrs Butcher, and struggling to map out possible next steps in her investigation. She'd called the police station again and had succeeded in irritating the answering officer, who told her he had her name and number, and that *when* DC Ryan was available, he'd give Emily a call. At least she now knew the name of the detective.

As Emily paused to stretch her spine, she glanced around the cafe, which was small and cosy looking, furnished with dark wood, and peppered with a handful of patrons. Outside, the day was growing increasingly dark and miserable. Her gaze returned to her laptop screen and the same niggle of doubt that had been plaguing her ever since she'd left Raven Road jabbed her in the ribs. The letter Jessica Harris had allegedly written to the men of the street; after everything that had happened with her husband —the arrest, the charges, the ensuing media furore and growing animosity with her neighbours—why would she write something so inflammatory? A letter like that, so salacious in its nature, only served to incite hatred and cause further harm to her family.

It didn't make sense.

Unless it was part of a larger fabrication to make the world believe in The Witness and thereby give her further ammunition to sue the Fishers. Perhaps that was it—a last, desperate attempt by Jessica to save her children from destitution. Because if the Harrises were guilty, Jessica had to be masterminding it, didn't she? There was no way Wesley Harris could be responsible, not while he was under lock and key on remand.

But still, it seemed rather elaborate to Emily. Surely there had to be a simpler, more tangible alternative to faking a complex stalker scenario. And if Jessica really was fabricating it all, how was Emily going to prove it? In truth, she had no idea. All she had so far was a photograph of Jessica's sleazy letter, which had been typed on a computer—meaning anyone could have written it—and the Butchers' testimonial that the Harris family was bad news. Neither provided the proof Emily needed.

She sighed, sipped some coffee, then leaned back in her chair. At the counter, the server listlessly stared into space as he slowly polished the surface in rhythmic measures. At the window, two middle-aged women sat together, talking and laughing. A young man sat alone by the wall, head down, his back to Emily, his elbows resting on the table. Watching him for a second, she got to thinking about Ethan Harris. Mrs Butcher claimed to have witnessed Ethan hitting his sister. Judging from the way he'd slammed the door and stormed down the street this morning, Emily could well believe it. Adolescent siblings fought all the time, but to hit a young girl hard enough to knock her to the ground? That was a great deal more serious.

But it wasn't proof of anything.

Doubt flooded Emily's veins. How was she meant to find out the truth about the Harris family when she couldn't get close to them?

Think. There has to be another way.

She could talk to other neighbours on the street, but then she'd have to rely on their discretion. Then there was DC Ryan, who'd hopefully call her back and provide her with some new intel. Finally, there was the local press, which was always a risk, and after Emily's experience with Helen Carlson, she was highly reluctant to involve another journalist in her investigation—especially when they were already aware of The Witness.

Her shoulders sagged. Perhaps Erica had been right after all.

No. You can do this. You just need to think outside the box. What else do you know?

She scanned her notes again.

"The murders . . ."

It was probably nothing—Mr Butcher had said they'd occurred decades ago. Jumping onto Google, Emily searched for murders on Raven Road in the past fifty years. After a couple of minutes, she closed the lid of the laptop, defeated. If the murders were true, they'd taken place decades before the invention of the Internet, and she suspected the local press hadn't archived past newspapers online. It was another dead end.

What did she do now? Ignoring the mounting sense of failure, she picked up the phone and dialled a number.

"Braithwaite Investigations . . ."

"You sound so professional for someone who's only been there a couple of days."

"Emily Swanson," Jerome said. "Shouldn't you be investigating something?"

"I'm investigating the cake selection of a charming little cafe, deciding whether to have chocolate chip or banana loaf."

"So the case is going well?"

Emily let out a heavy breath. "So well that I've been sitting here for two hours, contemplating a career change."

"That bad? Surely you must have some sort of leads. Come on, you're good at this."

"Am I? Honestly, I thought I was. But I'm two days into this case and so far, nothing. No leads. Just dead ends. How am I supposed to find out anything about this family without getting close to them?"

She paused, feeling the misery welling.

"You know what you need, don't you?" Jerome said, his voice filled with mischief.

"To stop biting off more than I can chew?"

"Chocolate chip *and* banana loaf."

Emily sighed. "Maybe I should just quit."

"Maybe you should get over yourself and find another way. Or have you forgotten about all the cases you solved before you ever got your licence?"

"I suppose. But the difference now is there are all kinds of rules and regulations. The only thing I can do is sit in the damn car and watch the house."

"So go do that," Jerome said.

"Do you know how cold it is out there? Besides, they have all the blinds shut and no one ever leaves the house besides the son, and I'm not about to go following a seventeen-year-old like a creepy stalker."

"Because sitting outside their house for hours on end isn't creepy?"

"You're not helping." Emily glanced around the room, eyeing

the two women chatting at the window and the bored-looking server. "Maybe I should just go home. Try to come up with some sort of plan."

"You could always go to Erica, you know. Ask for advice."

"I may as well hand in my resignation at the same time."

"Emily Swanson," Jerome said, and she could almost hear him shaking his head. "You need to love yourself."

"Since when were you the wise one in this relationship?"

"Always was. Go home. Sleep on it. Better yet, sleep on Carter West. Nothing like a good—"

Emily hung up. Despite her growing frustration, she smiled. Perhaps Jerome was right. She'd been sitting out in the cold for two days now, freezing her bones and numbing her brain; perhaps a hot bath and a little self-care would help to clear her mind. She stared at the young man who was still hunched over his phone. But perhaps she should stop by Raven Road one last time.

———

At a little past four, darkness had already descended. Parents had collected their children from school and returned to their homes. Dinners were now being prepared, homework was being done, and noisy, psychedelic cartoon shows were being watched. As usual, the window blinds of number fifty-seven were all closed. But there were lights on now, and occasional shadows and silhouettes flickering on the slats.

Sitting in the car, Emily thought about Georgia Harris, who'd missed another day of school, of seeing her friends, of learning something new. She'd briefly thought about contacting the girl's school, but knowing how stringent school privacy policies were, she'd quickly decided against it.

Emily's usual parking space had been taken, which was probably a good thing for now. The last thing she needed was Mr and Mrs Butcher coming out with a flask of tea and announcing to the world who she was. The only parking space she'd been able to secure with a clear view of number fifty-seven was right outside the garden gate. She was taking a risk; one that could go horribly wrong.

Five minutes, she told herself. Five minutes just so she could convince herself that she'd been useful. Then she would go home, regroup her thoughts, and plan next steps. The sensible thing to do would be to talk to Erica. But then she would risk appearing incompetent.

Emily shivered as she watched the house. Five minutes. Then she would be on her way.

Four minutes. The house was unmoving as Emily began mentally composing a resignation letter. Not that she would ever resign. If Emily Swanson was anything, she was resolutely stubborn.

Three minutes. A silhouette moved across the blinds of the living room window, then was gone. The wind grew stronger, pulling at the bare branches of the Rowan tree. Perhaps she'd call Carter and invite him over for dinner. Perhaps they'd watch a movie on the sofa, something mindless that didn't require the use of her brain.

Two minutes. An elderly man strolled by with a small dog on a lead, oblivious to Emily's watchful eyes.

Or perhaps she'd spend the evening alone, have a long soak in the bath followed by an early night.

One minute. The front door of number fifty-seven swung open and a figure came racing out.

Emily jumped up in her seat. The front door was not supposed to be opening. It was supposed to remain shut, so she could sit here for five minutes, undetected while feeling less of a failure. But now the figure was hurrying down the drive and throwing open the gate. It was a woman. Jessica Harris. And now she was marching through the gate, heading straight for Emily.

Shit!

Emily's hand reached for the key still in the ignition. A loud hammering on the driver window made her cry out. She spun around to see Ethan Harris's angry face glowering at her through the glass. She swung her head back towards the passenger window. Jessica Harris had now reached the car and was peering in.

Shit! Shit!

Emily's heart slapped against her chest. What did she do? Instinct told her to turn the key and drive. But now Jessica's face was pressed against the glass and she was yelling something, and on Emily's right, Ethan was close enough to get hurt if she pulled away.

Slowly, Emily turned the key to switch on the car's electrics. She carefully reached up and switched on the interior light, then depressed the passenger window button. The glass rolled down and the cold rushed in.

Jessica Harris' pale, angry face emerged from the shadows like a ghost.

"You have exactly thirty seconds to tell me who you are and why you're watching my family before I call the police," she hissed.

Emily swallowed. She shot a glance at Ethan, who was still looming over her door, eyes burning in the darkness.

"I—"

"Twenty-five seconds," Jessica said and held up a mobile phone, brandishing it like a weapon.

"I'm sorry," Emily stumbled. "I didn't mean to—"

"Twenty seconds."

Shit! Shit! Shit!

Emily reached for her bag and pulled out her wallet. Behind her, Ethan Harris pressed his palms against the window and moved his face closer. The wallet slipped from Emily's fingers. She ducked down, snatched it up, and pulled out a card.

"Ten seconds," Jessica warned.

Emily stared at her private investigator licence. Screw it.

"My name is Emily Swanson," she said, holding up the licence. She watched as Jessica's face wrinkled with confusion, then flattened out again, her eyes growing wide and round.

"Braithwaite Investigations?"

Emily nodded. "Perhaps if I can come inside . . ."

She was fired. Fired before the investigation had even got going. And she deserved it because she was lousy and incompetent. But mostly because Erica had been right—she just wasn't ready for a case like this.

Jessica had grown silent and still, her skin almost translucent in the car light.

"Is it him?" she said, her voice flat. "Did he hire you?"

"If we could go inside and talk . . ."

"Or is it the Fishers? They've got you investigating us, haven't they? Trying to prove I'm a liar."

"Please, let's go inside," Emily urged. "I can explain."

Jessica Harris stared at her. On Emily's right, Ethan's anger had given way to curiosity. Then Jessica's shoulders sagged and the fight dimmed in her hollow, haunted eyes.

"Five minutes. That's all you're getting."

She stepped back, giving Emily room to open the door.

"Thank you. Five minutes is all I need."

Emily suspected Erica would fire her in under two.

12

EMILY WAS FROGMARCHED through a dimly lit hallway and into a spacious kitchen diner. As she entered, her eyes quickly took in the scene: modern and expensive looking mod cons, family dining table and chairs, brightly coloured children's drawings pinned to the refrigerator door, dishes piled high on the drainer, an empty brandy glass sitting alone on the counter.

Emily waited for Jessica to tell her to sit and explain herself. Instead, the woman leaned against the kitchen counter, arms folded across her stomach, and glared at her. She looked tired, Emily thought, like she hadn't slept in weeks. Her gaze flicked to the left, where Ethan hung back by the door, the shadows under his eyes accentuated by the low lights as he, too, waited for Emily to talk.

"Well . . ." she began, her gaze swinging between mother and son. "Let me begin by apologising. The last thing I wanted to do was scare you or cause you alarm."

"I don't want your apology," Jessica snapped. "I want to know who hired you to spy on me and my children."

Emily held her breath, deliberating whether she should tell

the truth. She would be breaking all kinds of confidentiality agreements but considering the situation, it was a little too late for discretion.

"Was it Wesley? Did he put you up to this? Because you can tell him from me to go to hell."

"It wasn't your husband, Mrs Harris," Emily replied. "The agency I work for was hired to investigate the validity of your claims about being harassed by the person calling themselves The Witness."

Jessica stared at her, eyes slowly narrowing. "So it *is* the Fishers. Trying to prove that my family living in terror is just made up bullshit."

"The Fishers are adamant they were unaware of The Witness and had no contact from this person prior to selling you this house. They're keen not to be dragged into court for something they know nothing about."

"So you believe them? That I'm forcing my children to live in fear, all for money?" Jessica said, jaw clenching. Behind her Ethan Harris snorted and flashed her an amused look; one that Emily thought at once odd and accusatory.

"It's not my job to believe anything, Mrs Harris. It's my job to uncover the facts."

"And what facts have you uncovered, exactly?"

"If I'm honest, nothing yet. I only began the investigation yesterday."

Jessica's mouth hung open. Then she surprised Emily by throwing her head back and laughing.

"Yesterday? And you've already been rumbled! Perhaps I should call the Fishers to congratulate them on hiring such a fine investigator!"

Blushing, Emily averted her gaze from the woman's angry

face, wanting nothing more than to leave the Harris family alone and drive back to The Holmeswood, where she would email Erica Braithwaite her letter of resignation, then bury her face in a pillow and think about an alternative career path.

"I'm sorry, Mrs Harris. I'm only doing my job."

"Well, your job sucks." As Jessica stood glaring, the lines of her face deepening with every angry breath, the woman appeared to age before Emily's eyes. "And despite what people like the Butchers across the road might say, I love my children. I would never do anything to put them in harm's way. I'm trying to protect them from all the shit that my soon-to-be ex-husband shovelled on them. All I want is for us to be left alone, so that we can get on with our lives and forget everything that bastard has put us through. But instead I have to deal with crap like this!"

Emily watched as Jessica crossed the room, pulled open a cabinet door, and reached up to the top shelf. Fishing out a plastic folder, she stood for a second, regarding it as if she were holding a dead mouse in her hand. Then she marched up to Emily and thrust the folder in her face.

"You think I have it in me to make up this kind of sick shit?"

Emily took the folder and opened it up. Her heart tripped over itself.

"Have a read of those, Miss Private Investigator. Then you tell me what kind of mother could write such terrible words about her children."

Emily's eyes moved from Jessica's face to the open folder. There were three letters in total, each one written neatly by hand.

"Go on, sit," Jessica said, as if scolding one of her children. Still hovering by the door, Ethan smirked. "Once you've read them, I'll answer any questions you have. If you can't see I'm telling the truth by then, well, you go right ahead and continue your investigation."

Slowly, Emily nodded and made her way to the table. Pulling out a chair, she sat down and one by one, slid the letters from the folder and carefully lined them up. They were photocopies, she realised; the originals no doubt held in an evidence locker at the police station.

"Go and check on your sister," Jessica told her son, who started to protest. "Please, Ethan. Just for once, do as you're told."

The boy shot Emily a warning glare before sloping out of the room. Jessica shut the door behind him.

"I'll make some coffee," she said. "Start reading."

Emily did as she was instructed. Written in the same neat handwriting, this was the first letter the Harris family had received from The Witness, just three weeks after moving into their home. Emily had already gone over her own copy of it several times, had memorised its chilling words

She closed her eyes for a second, imagining a shadowy figure bent over a table, putting pen to paper; as if doing so would reveal the writer's identity.

Pushing the letter to one side, she moved onto the next. Sucking in a nervous breath, she began to read.

Harris Family,

Now I know your names. Jessica, Ethan and Georgia. Such pretty names for pretty meat. I've been watching you through the windows, following your movements and learning your habits. You sleep at the front, Jessica. Georgia's room is next to yours and

Ethan has taken the room at the back. Every night, you stand at your daughter's window and brush her hair before she goes to bed. It's fascinating to watch, the way you gently comb out the knots. I imagine you do it with such care to protect her from pain.

If only it were possible. Pain is inescapable. No matter where you go, no matter what you do to avoid it, pain will find you and rip you open, slicing through the flesh and the guts, cutting open your liver and your heart, until you bleed out on the floor.

Poor Georgia. Has she been down to the basement yet? Has she seen what's lying in wait?

Who am I?

I am The Witness. I am watching you all.

The hairs on the back of Emily's neck stood up. She quickly read the letter again, then glanced across the kitchen at Jessica, who was busy pouring hot water into two mugs. The letter was as bizarre as the first, but now The Witness had mentioned the family by name and singled out Georgia, leaving Emily unnerved. She moved on to the final letter.

Harris Family,

Why have you shut me out? I must watch over the house like my father before me. It is my duty! As God is my Witness, I shall be yours. But if I cannot, pain will find you and your young bloods and there will be nothing you can do to prevent the cuts.

He moves behind the walls. He crawls into Georgia's room when you sleep at night. He stands over her bed, thirsty and desperate. Blood will flow in the basement, Jessica Harris. Blood will rise up from the well to drown you all.

Open the blinds before it's too late. Open the blinds. Open the blinds.

Who am I?
I am The Witness. I am watching you all.

Blood rushed in Emily's ears as she set down the letter next to the others. What the hell did it all mean? Mouth hanging open, she looked up to see Jessica walking towards the table, steaming mugs of coffee in her hands. She gave one to Emily, who took it gratefully, then slipped into the opposite chair. For a moment, her gaze dropped down to the letters and her left eye twitched. When she looked up again, her complexion had turned a sickly grey.

"They're real page-turners," she said, with no trace of a smile.

Emily stared at the letters, an anxious knot growing in her stomach. "All this talk about the basement. Have you been down there?"

"Once. I couldn't find anything. But now the door stays locked and the key stays with me." She tapped her jeans pocket. "So, what do you think?"

"About the letters? They're frightening and irrational."

"And they're only half of it."

"What do you mean?" Emily asked.

"A couple of weeks after the first letter arrived, we started getting phone calls. The caller would never say anything, not even heavy breathe, or anything like that. They were just silent. But they kept calling, over and over, day after day. I tried dialling 1471 but the number was blocked."

"You reported it to the police?"

"Of course I did. They told us they couldn't do anything without evidence, so the first thing we needed to do was report it to the telephone company. All they did was tell us to keep a record of the calls and that if they continued, they'd try to trace them. I pulled out the phone line instead. Problem solved. That's when the magazines started arriving."

Emily stared at her, one eyebrow raised.

"The pornographic kind," Jessica said, her face wrinkled in disgust. "Really nasty stuff addressed to me. Again I reported it to the police, but what could they do? Then the second letter arrived, mentioning my children by name, quickly followed by those ridiculous notes to my neighbours' husbands."

"That was when you started closing the blinds?"

Jessica nodded, staring blankly into her coffee. "If someone were watching your children, trying to turn everyone against you, wouldn't you do the same? Not that it helped. The third letter arrived a week later. Just like the others, it was delivered by hand—no stamp or address, just "To The Harris Family'. The police took an interest then, but whoever had written the letter had been clever enough to leave no tell-tale clues that would help identify them. It didn't leave them much to go on. Besides, I'm pretty sure they think I'm behind it all."

"Why would they think that?"

"Because I married a criminal, which makes me guilty by association," Jessica said. "The police couldn't help me, or wouldn't, so I took matters into my own hands. I took leave from my job, pulled Georgia out of school, and decided to sue the Fishers. If they'd been honest about The Witness, we would never have bought this damn place. And now we're stuck here, with no money and with everyone pointing the finger of blame at me.

"But I suppose that's what happens when you unwittingly marry a criminal—everyone believes you're just as guilty, no matter what you say or how much you try to defend yourself. Everyone's mind is already made up: 'Look at her expensive clothes, her flashy car and her fancy house. How could she not have known about the money? How could her husband have hidden it right under her nose without her ever finding out? She's guilty as sin and we don't need the evidence to prove it, either.'" Jessica brought her hands to her face, rubbing her tired eyes. "I suppose that's what you think, too."

Emily glanced away, finding the children's drawings on the refrigerator door. "In my job I'm required to investigate every angle."

"Even so, you must form opinions. You have to have a hunch or an idea to start you on the right path. Of course you've thought about my guilt. You wouldn't be doing your job if you hadn't."

"True. But opinions aren't the same as facts. The fact that the police aren't pressing charges against you in connection with your husband's crimes indicates that they believe you're innocent."

"Oh, they believe I'm guilty, they just can't find any evidence to incriminate me. But whether I'm guilty or not is irrelevant because people will believe what they want to believe. Newspaper headlines will help them believe it, too."

That was true, Emily thought. She'd had her own horrific experiences with the press and understood only too well how public perception could be easily manipulated to sell more newspapers. She watched as Jessica leaned back in her chair, dark shadows and lines making her look years older. Her grief and anxiety certainly seemed genuine.

"The third letter," Emily said, staring at it on the table. "It's a direct threat. Open the blinds or you'll be sorry. Surely the police have to act upon that?"

"What can they do? They're just letters. Whoever wrote

them hasn't acted upon them. To the police they're just words. To my family they're bars of a cage. How can I let my daughter go to school without knowing she'll be protected? How can I let her out of my sight for fear that this sick bastard is still watching us? I can't. I *won't*. My children are all I have left. The court is trying to claim this house as criminal property. The only thing that can delay them from seizing it right now is my name on the mortgage agreement. If I try to sell it, they'll go for the money and my family will be left on the street. But if this harassment continues, what choice do I have but to leave?"

Emily stared at the letters, chewing on her lower lip.

"I understand why the Fishers are investigating me," Jessica said. "If I was in their position, I'd do the same thing. That first letter, it named them—'the Fishers gave Him fresh blood'. If they'd been honest with us, we would never have bought this place and my children wouldn't be in danger. But here we are, and I will do what it takes to protect my children, even if it means making an enemy of everyone on this street. Even if it means suing the Fishers. Because they should have been honest. Just like my son of a bitch husband should have been honest." She stared at Emily, her eyes boring into her. "What will you do now? What will you tell the Fishers?"

Emily thought about it. If she told them anything, the assignment would be over in a second, most likely her employment under Braithwaite Investigations, too. But she was already beginning to doubt the woman's guilt. Could even the most gifted of actors feign the tired lines of exhaustion and the dullness of anguish? Possibly, but a person capable of such deception was usually a dangerous sociopath, not a mother of two trapped in a suburban nightmare by her husband's crimes. She met Jessica's gaze and shrugged.

"Honestly, I don't know."

Jessica leaned forward, her eyes suddenly sparking with life. "I have an idea. Instead of proving my guilt, why not prove that The Witness is real? Why not help me and my children by showing everyone we're not lying, that we are being harassed by someone; someone who's not in their right mind."

"I don't—"

"Think about it for a moment. By helping us to prove The Witness is real, you'll be doing your job anyway. I'll answer any of your questions. I'll give you access to whatever you need." Tears were brimming at the corners of Jessica's eyes, threatening to spill down her cheeks. "Please, I just want this to stop. I just want our lives to go back to normal."

"I don't know if I can do that," Emily said, removing her hands from the table. "Not without compromising my position."

"Your position is already compromised. All I have to do is pick up the phone and call my solicitor."

"Your solicitor will tell you the Fishers are doing nothing wrong by conducting an investigation. They might even welcome one if it proves your innocence."

The tears came now, spilling down Jessica's cheeks and splashing on the table.

"Do you have children?" she asked. Emily didn't answer. "Of course you don't. Because if you did you wouldn't hesitate to help me. You'd know how vulnerable my children are. You wouldn't hesitate for a second to protect them."

"That's not fair."

Through her tears, Jessica laughed. "You know what isn't fair? Having someone like you spying on my family when we're already at breaking point. If you don't want to help, then you should leave. Now."

Emily didn't move. She stared at the woman across the table, conflicting thoughts and feelings colliding in her mind. Instinct told her to help the Harris family, to do everything in her power to prove The Witness was real and that the family was in potential danger. Her sensibilities told her to leave now, to report back to Erica Braithwaite as a matter of urgency, then brace herself for the consequences.

Jessica looked up through her tears, anger pushing through the sorrow. "Well, what are you waiting for?"

"I'm sorry. I—" Emily got to her feet, the chair scraping noisily against the flagstone floor. "I'll . . . I'll go now."

The last thing she saw before turning and hurrying towards the hall, was the unadulterated look of defeat on Jessica Harris' face.

13

"So, what do you think?"

They were sitting in a corner booth, Emily slouching against the cushioned seat while Jerome sat opposite, elbows propped up on the table as he sipped a garishly-coloured cocktail. The bar was still surprisingly busy for a Wednesday night at 10 p.m. It was a nice bar; one Jerome had introduced Emily to a few months ago. She liked its brick walls and low lighting, hues of red and green shimmering on the chrome bar, where young bartenders served fashionable drinks to their equally fashionable patrons.

Jerome set down his drink and shook his head. "To be honest, I don't know what to think. I guess you have to ask yourself whether you believe she's telling the truth or if she's trying to suck you in. Either way, it's up to you to decide what to do about it."

Emily frowned as she circled the rim of her glass with a finger. "That's not fair. I asked you here to tell me what to do, not to tell me what I need to hear."

"You're the private investigator, not me. Besides, since when does Emily Swanson ask for advice?"

Emily pulled a face as she glanced across the room, staring at her fellow twenty-somethings scattered around the bar. For a moment, she envied their carefree lives. Except, of course, she had no idea how carefree they actually were. For all she knew their lives were just as complicated as her own.

"What does Carter think about it?" Jerome's voice pulled her back to the booth. She glanced at him, then down at her drink; a vodka tonic that she wasn't particularly enjoying.

"I haven't told Carter. He doesn't need to know right now, does he? Besides, it's not as if he tells me every detail of his working day."

"You do know how relationships work, right?"

"Yes, I don't need you to mansplain, thank you very much. Anyway, it's not that I don't want to include him, it's just that he doesn't need to hear about it."

"So you're not worried about him judging you or anything?"

Emily glared across the table. "I didn't ask you here for relationship advice, either."

"I know. You asked me here to tell you what to do, but I'm afraid you're going to be sorely disappointed. Now answer the question: Do you believe this woman is innocent or do you think she's trying to take you for a ride?"

Grabbing her drink, Emily took a hefty swig, winced at the taste, and set the glass back down. She didn't know why she was drinking. Just because she could now, she supposed.

"Jessica Harris doesn't strike me as someone who'd come up with something so weird and outlandish as The Witness. I mean, yes, she's married to a criminal, but the police have found no evidence of her involvement. And those letters were so creepy and strange, far too bizarre for someone in their right mind to dream up."

"Maybe she's not in her right mind."

"I've seen crazy. Jessica Harris isn't that. What she is, is tired and desperate. She's got her kids locked down in a fortress of darkness, the youngest one pulled out of school . . . It's all so extreme." Her eyes drifted across the room again, coming to rest on a young couple sitting at the edge of the bar, their heads tipped toward each other and their bodies dangerously close. "If I was Jessica Harris in this situation, I would take my children and run. But she can't. The courts want the house. If she tries to sell it, they'll take the money, and she and her kids will be on the street. She has no choice but to stay."

"What about family?" Jerome asked, staring into his empty glass. "Parents, siblings. Someone who could put a roof over their heads while Jessica tries to start her life over."

"If there was someone, wouldn't she have turned to them by now for the sake of her kids? I get the feeling she's on her own."

"Which would make her desperate. And wouldn't a desperate mother go to any lengths to protect her children?"

Emily stared at Jerome, her mouth open but no words coming out. Slowly, she clamped her jaw shut and slumped her shoulders. "Well, I don't know what to think."

"You'll figure it out. You always do."

"What I do know is that come the morning when Erica Braithwaite finds out I've messed up, the only job I'll be assigned is to clear out my desk."

"You don't know that. I mean, truthfully Erica Braithwaite terrifies me, but she wouldn't have given you this case if she didn't think you were up to the job."

"Except I was the one who insisted I could do it and she was the one who said I have a lot to learn. I should have listened to her. Besides, today is just more evidence that the whole private investigation thing isn't for me."

"But you wanted to help people."

"People who need help, yes. Not big corporations or the wealthy, but people who . . ."

"Deserve it?"

Picking up her glass again, Emily tipped her head back and drained the rest of its contents.

"What do you think I should do? Do you think I should come clean with Erica or help Jessica Harris prove that The Witness is real?"

Jerome stared at her, one eyebrow cocked, his gaze hard. "The Emily Swanson I used to know would never admit defeat. Oh, she was a bull in a china shop, stamping on people's feelings and smashing her way towards the truth. But she would always get there in the end."

"That Emily Swanson was medicated and out of her mind."

"Maybe. But she always figured out the right thing to do. And so will you."

"You're not helping."

Emily slumped against the seat once more, her shoulders sinking as she pictured Erica Braithwaite's disappointed face.

"Maybe you should sleep on it. See what the morning brings."

"Or maybe," Emily said, tapping her empty glass with a finger, "We should have another drink."

Jerome sat up, a smile, bright and wide, spreading across his lips. "Now you're talking my language."

14

THE HOUSE WAS QUIET. Jessica stood on the upstairs landing, yellow light casting long shadows on the walls. It was late. Georgia had gone to bed two hours ago and for now, was silent. She wondered how long it would be before her daughter's screams would send her running into her room to comfort her. The night terrors had begun shortly after Wesley's arrest, and had only grown worse with the passing of time; more so since Jessica had been keeping her home from school.

Light was seeping out from beneath Ethan's door. Pressing her ear to the wood, Jessica heard the rhythmic tapping of fingers on keys. She heaved her shoulders, then gently rapped her knuckles on the wood. The clacking continued, growing louder and more frantic in Jessica's ear. Irritated, she reached for the door handle and snapped it open.

Ethan was sitting cross-legged on his bed, dressed in boxers and an old black T-shirt, his usual mess of hair draped over his face. As Jessica entered, his eyes flicked up from the laptop screen and grew wide and startled. He immediately pulled the laptop lid closed.

"Jesus, don't you knock?" he growled, pulling headphones from his ears and dumping them on the bed.

"I did," Jessica replied as she cast an eye around the room. It was typical seventeen-year-old boy: small hills of clothing scattered across the carpet, obscure film and music posters tacked to the walls, and an underlying odour of stale sweat and hormones.

"What do you want?"

"It's late," she said softly, staring down at her feet and willing them to move forward, but it was as if invisible clamps had fastened them to the floor. "You need to get some sleep or you'll be tired tomorrow."

Ethan glared at her, the bitterness in his eyes sharp and stinging. Jessica stuck a foot out, testing the boundaries.

"Listen, I'm sorry about earlier, okay? I know I shouldn't be texting you like that. I know it must seem weird to the other kids. But I'm just trying to keep you safe, that's all."

Anger flared in Ethan's eyes like flickering candlelight, but then something shifted and the flames died. He nodded, causing hair to fall across his face, which he swept away, tucking strands behind his ear.

"I know, Mum. I get it, I really do. It's just that . . . Well, it's hard enough to fit in around here as it is. Dad made sure of that. But I'm not a kid anymore and you checking up on me every two minutes isn't helping."

Jessica slid a foot forward, then another, glancing at her son to see if he would object. When he offered no resistance, she moved further into the room and eyed the edge of the bed.

"I'm sorry," she said at last. "With everything going on right now, after everything you kids have been through, I'm just trying to protect you."

She stood there for a while, not speaking, eyes fixed on the space between them. How else could she explain it to him?

On the bed, Ethan shifted uncomfortably and stared at his laptop.

"Mum?"

"Hmm?"

"Do you think it's Dad sending the letters?"

Jessica glanced up, saw the wounded look on Ethan's face, as if the very idea was like a knife in the gut.

"Your dad loves you," she said. "He would never hurt you."

"What about you?"

"I . . . Well, he's on remand. He couldn't pull this sort of stunt from prison."

"What about that woman? The private investigator—do you think she can help?"

"The Fishers hired her to prove I'm making the whole thing up. I showed her the letters, told her about everything that's happened. She's not going to help us and it doesn't matter what she tells them because we know the truth, don't we? We know we're the victims in all of this."

Ethan stared at her then glanced away, his gaze coming to rest on his laptop.

"Don't we?" Jessica repeated.

"Sure, Mum."

There was something there. Something he wasn't saying. Jessica felt it pulsing from his body in waves. Did he think she was behind the letters? That she could be so cruel to her own children?

"Lights out," she whispered, her chest tightening as Ethan continued to avoid her gaze. "You should get some sleep or you'll be—"

A loud buzzing shattered the silence. Jessica's heart jumped into her throat. On the bed, Ethan's head snapped up. Mother and son stared at each other, wide-eyed and open-mouthed.

"What was—"

The buzzing came again, quickly followed by loud hammering.

"Stay here," Jessica said, her words short and sharp. But Ethan was already moving off the bed.

Leaving the room, Jessica crossed the landing and reached the top of the stairs. Seconds later, Ethan appeared behind her.

"I mean it," she hissed, her eyes shooting towards Georgia's bedroom door. "Stay where you are."

The buzzer filled the silence, sounding like a swarm of bees.

Reaching out a trembling hand, Jessica flipped a switch and the downstairs hall light flickered on. From where she stood, she could see the painted wood of the front door and its two small windows of frosted glass at the top, where darkness lurked on the other side.

Her breaths coming thin and fast, she descended the stairs. She reached the hall and slid to a halt.

"Hello?" she called out.

Ethan had reached the fourth step but was now hanging back, his face pale and taut.

Silence settled over the house. Jessica stepped forward and pressed her eye to the peephole. Darkness stared back at her.

"Who is it?" Ethan whispered. Ignoring him, Jessica continued to stare, her eye twitching from side to side. "Mum?"

"Go and check on your sister."

Grasping the chain lock, Jessica fastened it into place, then one after the other, drew back the door bolts, barely aware that

Ethan was no longer on the stairs and was now hurrying along the hall and into the kitchen.

Jessica pinched the door key between finger and thumb, then twisted it clockwise until she heard the lock snap open. Ethan returned, a large steak knife clutched in his fist.

"What the hell are you doing? Put that down!"

Ethan shook his head. "Open it."

Slowly, carefully, Jessica turned the catch and opened the door. The chain lock snapped tight. Cold air crawled over her skin as she stared through the gap. The garden lay in darkness. Beyond it, the road was quiet, pools of streetlight offering islands of protection.

"Can you see anyone?" Ethan called from behind.

Jessica shook her head, reached for the wall and found a panel of switches. She flicked one and immediately the porch was bathed in harsh yellow light.

Something was there. Sitting on the doorstep.

Jessica stared at it, her pulse quickening.

"Mum?"

It was a package of some kind. A shoe box wrapped in a bright red ribbon.

"Give me the knife," she said.

"What is it?"

"Now, Ethan."

She reached a hand behind her and felt the hilt of the blade slip into it. Gripping the knife, she carefully sank down and reached her free hand through the gap. A gift card was attached to the ribbon. Pinching it between finger and thumb, she flipped it over and read the message.

To Jessica. With love.

"What's going on?" Ethan called out, fear pinching his voice.

"Nothing. Just stay back."

"Shall I call the police?"

Yes, Jessica thought. Good idea. But tell them what? That someone had left a gift for her on the doorstep? She didn't even know what was inside. If it was nothing, calling them would only cement their already maligned opinion of her family. But what if it wasn't nothing? What if it was something that was meant to cause her harm?

"Mum?"

"Stay back."

Reaching out a trembling hand, Jessica pushed the box closer with the edge of the knife. Setting the blade down, she found the end of the brightly coloured ribbon and gently pulled. The bow loosened. She pulled harder. The knot disappeared and the ribbon fell away.

Picking up the knife again, she sucked in a breath, then inserted the tip of the blade beneath the lid of the box.

"Mummy? What's going on? Was someone at the door?"

Jessica glanced back over her shoulder to see Georgia standing halfway down the stairs, a bird's nest of hair sticking out at crude angles as she rubbed her tired eyes.

"Stay there!" she yelled, then glared at Ethan. "Keep her back!"

Something was rustling on the doorstep.

Blood rushing in her ears, Jessica returned her gaze to the shoe box. With the edge of the knife, she forced the lid up and over, until it slipped off and landed on the step.

A mound of colourful tissue paper sat inside the box. Nausea bubbled in Jessica's throat as she saw the paper moving up and down.

Before she could register what she was doing, she reached

out and tore the paper away. She leaned closer and saw what looked like a writhing mass of knotted hair.

Fingers trembling, Jessica pressed the tip of the knife into it. The mass burst apart, forming thousands of spiny legs and bodies. The spiders spilled over the lid of the box in black, undulating waves. Hitting the step, they launched forward, scuttling towards the open front door.

Jessica fell back, hitting her elbows on the floor and drawing in a sharp, shocked breath. Behind her in the hall, her children began to scream.

15

THE BRIGHT OFFICE lights of Braithwaite Investigations were piercing flames in Emily's eyes, the closing of the double doors thunderous crashes. She was sleep deprived, dehydrated, and the pounding in her head was growing worse by the minute.

Her ill-health was reflected in Jerome's pained expression. He nodded as she approached the reception desk, then winced.

"You look how I feel," he said, his voice filled with sand.

Emily tried to smile but all she could manage was a grimace. Spying Jerome's mug of coffee on the desk, she snatched it up and took a sip.

"Hey, get your own!"

"But you make it so well," she croaked. "Besides, the only reason I feel like death warmed up is because of the vat of cocktails you made us drink."

"You're blaming me? Since when does Emily Swanson do anything she doesn't want to?"

Much to Emily's protest, Jerome snatched his mug back, placing it out of her reach.

"Now I remember why I don't drink," she groaned. Her eyes

wandered around the empty waiting area, moving from office door to office door. "Is anyone here?"

"If you mean Erica, she's in her office," Jerome said, wincing at the sound of his own voice. "Have you decided what you're going to do?"

"I emailed first thing this morning, asking to see her."

"Oh. Then let me wish you the best of luck. It's been nice knowing you."

Emily swallowed nervously as she stared at Erica's office door.

"Are you sure this is what you want? Because you can always change your mind." Jerome gently squeezed her arm. "Just turn around and go. I'll make up some excuse, tell her you're out in the field."

Emily thought about it. It was a tempting idea, but would it change anything? She still felt the same this morning as she had last night—helping the rich and powerful stamp on the small and vulnerable was not what she had signed up for. Besides, it was only a matter of time before Jessica Harris picked up the phone and Emily's failings found their way back to Braithwaite Investigations.

Slowly, she shook her head. "No. I messed up, and by doing so I've put Erica's reputation on the line, not to mention her friendship with Meredith. I need to make things right."

Circling the desk, Emily picked up Jerome's coffee mug, drained its contents and set it back down. Then she began a slow walk towards Erica Braithwaite's office. Halfway across the room, her phone began to buzz in her bag. She pulled it out and stared at the caller ID. It was a number she didn't recognise.

At the desk, Jerome arched an eyebrow. "Saved by the bell?"

Emily pressed the phone to her ear. "Hello?"

"Miss Swanson?" The woman's voice trembled uncontrollably. "It's Jessica Harris."

Emily caught her breath and glanced towards Erica's office. "Jessica? What's wrong?"

There was a pause before the woman spoke again and Emily realised it was because she was crying.

"Something's happened. Please, I'm begging you. Won't you reconsider my offer?"

"Has there been another letter?" She looked up, catching Jerome's concerned gaze. "Are the children safe?"

"They left a box. Something terrible was inside. Please, can you come to the house?"

Emily hesitated. "I—I don't know if I can do that."

"Please, I don't know who else to turn to!"

Erica Braithwaite's office door swung open. A moment later, Erica stepped out and caught Emily's eye.

"I have to call you back," Emily said to Jessica.

"Please, wait. Don't—"

"I'll call you back. I promise."

"Everything okay?" Erica asked as Emily disconnected the call and dropped her hand to her side. She nodded, shrinking under the weight of the woman's scrutinising gaze. "You wanted to see me?"

At the reception desk, Jerome cleared his throat and fixed his eyes on the computer screen. Emily was frozen to the spot, her throat drying up as she stared at the office door.

"Emily, is everything okay?" A frown was creasing Erica's brow. "You seem troubled."

"Actually, something's come up," Emily said, glancing down at the phone in her hand, "A possible lead in the Fisher case. I should probably follow it up."

"All right. Later then, unless it's something you think I should know about now?"

Emily shot a glance towards Jerome, whose eyebrows were almost touching his hairline.

"Later is fine. Just a couple of questions that can wait." She took a step towards the exit doors. "I should probably go . . ."

Nodding, Erica turned back to her office. "Before you do, Meredith called this morning. She'd like an update." She was staring at Emily strangely now. "I told her you'd drop by the house later today. I'm assuming you'll be in the area?"

Slowly, carefully, Emily forced herself to nod. "Yes. That's fine. I'll visit her later."

Frowning, Erica shot her a confused glance then disappeared inside her office.

When they were alone, Jerome let out a shuddering breath.

"Not a word," Emily warned.

"My lips are sealed."

Circling the reception desk, she stalked towards the exit doors, then came to a stop.

"Last night, you told me I'd figure out the right thing to do," she said. "Well, this is me figuring it out."

Jerome flashed her a knowing smile. "You're welcome."

Emily pushed her way through the smoked glass doors and headed for the lift. Her head was pounding. Her heart was racing, threatening to give up on her. But she felt a sudden determination flowing through her veins. There had to be a way to help the Harris family *and* give the Fishers the peace they needed. She just needed to figure out how she was going to do it without getting caught.

16

EMILY PULLED up outside of the Harris family's house just after eleven. Jessica was waiting for her in the garden, arms hugging her ribs, eyes darting up and down the street. The two women exchanged uncomfortable looks, then Jessica nodded toward the house.

"Be careful as you come inside."

As Emily followed her along the path, she spied the black, gunky mess splattered over the doorstep. Grimacing, she stepped over it and entered the hall. It took her a second to adjust to the gloom and just like last evening, she felt a heavy weight press down on her shoulders. It was strange, she thought, how a person's negative energy could manifest in such a physical way.

Jessica was pressed up against the kitchen counter. In the electric light she looked as if she'd aged another ten years since their last meeting.

"Where are your children?" Emily asked, shrugging off her jacket and watching the way Jessica's hands trembled as she reached for the kettle.

"Georgia's upstairs in her room. Ethan wanted to stay home, but I sent him to college. It's his final year and he needs to get his grades for university."

Emily headed for the table and sat down. She waited for Jessica to explain what had happened, but the woman seemed fixed on first serving coffee. It was ingrained, Emily supposed; a long-standing habit of playing the gracious host. She waited until she'd been handed a steaming mug and Jessica returned to the counter, her hands twitching by her sides.

"So, last night . . ."

Nodding, Jessica nervously eyed the back door, as if some unnamed horror were lying in wait on the other side. "Someone rang the doorbell at around ten. By the time I answered they were gone. They left this on the doorstep."

She picked up a gift box and dumped it on the table, then slipped into the chair opposite. Emily leaned forward. The lid had been removed and a pretty red ribbon trailed from the side. A black, sticky mess smeared the side of the box—the same gunk that was splattered over the doorstep, she noted. A card was still attached to the ribbon. Producing a pencil from her jacket pocket, Emily used it to tip the card up so that she could read the message: *To Jessica. With Love.*

"What was inside?" she asked, then glanced up to see Jessica shudder.

"Spiders. Hundreds of them. They all came spilling out, all climbing over each other to get to us. I just crouched there, screaming, doing nothing. Georgia ran forward and started stamping on them. Ethan too. Until every last one was dead."

Emily stared at the box, mouth hanging open. "Do you know what kind?"

"What do you mean?"

"The spiders—were they poisonous?"

"How should I know?" Jessica glared at Emily as if she were the sender of the grisly gift. "Sorry. I'm still a little jumpy from last night."

"It's fine. But you should take the box to the police."

"Why? So they can stick it on a shelf somewhere and forget about it?" Jessica leaned forward, linking her fingers together and resting them on the table. "Who do you think's doing this?"

"Shouldn't I be asking *you* that?" The woman's eyes were desperate and pleading. Emily cleared her throat. "Well, the obvious explanation would be that whoever's behind this has an axe to grind with your husband. I've been reading up on his court case—he tricked at least fifty investors out of three million pounds. Most of them won't see that money returned. Perhaps one of them isn't happy that you're managing to hold onto the house. Perhaps they believe you were involved and you've gone unpunished."

"I told you I wasn't," Jessica snapped. "Which is why the police found no evidence that said otherwise."

Emily stared at the box, then up at Jessica. "But I'm not entirely convinced The Witness is one of your husband's victims."

"What makes you say that?"

"The letters. Whoever wrote them claims they've been watching this house for a long time—long before your family moved in. If it was one of your husband's investors, why go to the extreme of inventing something as bizarre as The Witness? Why not just send more boxes of spiders?"

Jessica flinched. "Maybe they want to scare us."

"Possibly. What about your neighbours?"

"I know we're not exactly popular on this street, but if people don't like their neighbours, don't they usually just avoid them?"

"Unless someone wants you gone for good."

"My children and I have done nothing wrong. And even if our neighbours aren't happy about the attention my husband's brought to the street, they'd have to be seriously messed up to go to such horrible lengths to get rid of us."

Emily's gaze was still fixed on the gift box. "When was the last time you spoke to your husband?"

"I'm not sure exactly. Four or five weeks ago."

"You haven't visited him?"

"Why would I do that?" Lightning strikes of anger flashed in Jessica's eyes. "He destroyed our lives. He lied to me and played me for a fool. I have no reason to visit him or to listen to anything he has to say ever again."

"What about the children? Don't they want to see their father?"

"What they want and what they need don't always match up. And right now, the last thing they need is their waste-of-space excuse of a father making everything worse."

Emily chewed her lip, watching Jessica. "Have you considered that your husband could be behind the letters? Behind everything else that's happened?"

"Wesley may be a self-obsessed prick, but he would never try to hurt his children."

"Would he try to hurt his wife? After all, the box of spiders was addressed to you. The men on this street all received salacious letters supposedly from you. Is it possible your husband is trying to get back at you for something?"

"Like what? The only thing I did wrong was to fall for his

shit." Jessica lifted her hands to her face. "Please. Won't you help us? Can't you find out who's doing this to my family?"

Glancing away, Emily thought about leaving, about all the trouble she was causing herself just by being here. But sitting at the table, drowning in the desperation flooding from Jessica's body in great waves, she felt a sudden and deep longing to put things right. Because this was what she wanted, wasn't it? To help.

"I have three conditions," she said. "One, if I agree to help you, I need you to be completely honest with me. Even when I ask difficult questions."

Jessica's fingers parted then slipped from her face.

"Two, you need to agree to give me access to any information I ask for, no matter how personal or unconnected it may seem to my investigation. Three, and most importantly, if I agree to help you, I'll be compromising my position and risking my job. That means no one can know about my involvement. You do not mention me to your solicitor, to your husband, or to anyone else for that matter. The second I hear someone knows, I'm out. Do you agree?"

Jessica stared at her, a frown rippling across her brow. "If it means risking your job, why would you help me?"

"Do you agree?" Emily repeated.

Slowly, Jessica nodded. Her shoulders sagged with relief. "Of course. Thank you. Where do we start?"

"Well . . ." Emily began, then cut herself off as she looked up to see Georgia Harris hovering in the doorway, a curtain of lank hair pulled across her features. Shock fired through Emily's veins. Had the child been standing there the whole time, listening in to every word? If so, how could an eight-year-old be trusted to keep

Emily's involvement a secret? Then Georgia lifted her head and her hair parted to reveal eyes, hopeful and desperate, glinting in the dull electric light.

Emily turned back to Jessica. "We start with you reporting that box to the police so they can test for prints."

17

EMILY'S MIND raced as she drove away from Raven Road. She knew what she had just agreed to do was categorically wrong—not only was she breaking her agreement with the Fishers, she was also betraying Erica's trust—yet she could not deny she felt a warm glow of satisfaction. She would need to be careful, but as long as she was discreet, she'd not only be able to solve the case and prove that she was a worthy investigator, she'd also achieve what she'd set out to do in the first place—which was to help those who really needed it. She knew there was still a chance that Jessica Harris was lying to her, but what better way to find out than from on the inside? Besides, Emily had a plan; one that could quickly prove the woman's innocence or guilt. Before she could put it into action, there was something else she needed to do.

As Emily parked on the drive and made her way towards the cottage, the front door swung open and Meredith Fisher appeared dressed in a scarlet ankle-length winter coat and a pair of leather black gloves. The Fisher's Border Terrier stood at her heels, eyeing Emily curiously and wagging its tail.

"Would you mind if we went for a short walk? Nestor here needs his exercise," Meredith said. "John usually takes him—he needs his exercise, too—but he had a bad night and needs to rest."

Ignoring the flutter of nerves in her stomach, Emily smiled. "A walk would be nice."

Buttoning her coat, she walked alongside Meredith, skirting around the side of the house. Nestor pulled excitedly on his lead as they silently crossed the frosty rear garden and passed through a wrought iron gate that led to a grassy lane with tall hedgerows flanking its sides. The air was bitter cold, the sky icy blue above their heads. Despite the freezing temperature, it was nice to be out in the countryside, Emily thought.

"So what do you have for me?" Meredith asked as the lane opened onto a grassy field with a copse of trees at the far end. She bent down and unclipped the lead from Nestor's collar, then smiled as the dog shot forward, bounding excitedly through the grass.

"Well, it's early days," Emily began. "What I can tell you is that the Harris family seem to be on lockdown."

Meredith frowned. "What do you mean?"

"I've been watching the house for the past couple of days. All the blinds are closed. The only person I've seen go in or out is Ethan Harris, the teenage son, who I assume is going to college. The daughter, Georgia, on the other hand, hasn't been going to school at all."

Nestor was already a smudge in the distance, but now he slid to a halt, investigating something hidden in the grass. Emily fixed her gaze on him, hoping the sudden guilt she was feeling was not seeping into her voice. They walked on a little, Emily stealing glances at the elder woman.

"Nothing else?" Meredith asked.

"As I said, it's early days. But I'll also be investigating other angles, other suspects. It's part of the process. We investigate, eliminate, see what we're left with."

"And what are these angles? Who are these other suspects?"

"Well, there are the clients that Wesley Harris stole from. It's possible any one of them could be behind the letters; not as a means to extort money from you, but as a means of revenge against Mr Harris."

"That doesn't make sense. Why would they involve me and John? We had nothing to do with the man's crimes."

"As I said, it's just an angle."

Meredith nodded, watching the dog in the distance. "What else?"

"Well, the fact that Jessica has shut herself and her children away seems strange to me."

"Perhaps it's part of the act to make her claims more credible."

"It seems quite extreme, though. Would a mother keep her daughter locked away for weeks, risking her education and emotional wellbeing, just for money?"

"I suppose it would depend on what kind of mother she is. And how do you know it's been weeks?"

Emily bit down on her lip, suddenly aware she was saying too much and thinking aloud in front of the wrong person.

Meredith stared at her coolly, frosted breath billowing from her nostrils. "You talk about them as if you know them. Calling them by their first names . . ."

"Just trying to put myself in their place to get a better understanding of what's going on."

The women walked on. Meredith produced a rubber ball

from her coat pocket and Nestor came racing back, tongue lolling from the side of his mouth. Throwing back her arm, she pitched the ball across the field. Emily watched it sail through the air, saw the dog shooting after it like a bullet.

"What else?"

"Well, there are the neighbours to look into, which might take a bit of time."

Meredith laughed. "The neighbours? Really?"

"Every angle needs to be investigated."

"My dear girl, I lived on that street for eighteen months, which, granted, isn't a long time, but it's long enough to know that while some of the neighbours could be irritating, I can assure you that not one of them is malicious enough to do something as vile as this. They're just families, older people. Peaceful folk." She paused, the humour gone. "The angle you should be looking at is the one you were hired to investigate. A criminal bought our house and now he and his wife are trying to take us for every penny we have."

They'd reach the centre of the field. Emily was silent, face heating up despite the cold. Nestor bounded back, tail wagging, red ball clamped between his jaws. Ignoring the animal, Meredith turned to stare at her.

"I'm sorry to ask, but you are keeping a low profile, aren't you? Like we discussed? All I want is for this whole frustrating mess to be over and done with as quickly and as *quietly* as possible."

Emily's heart tripped over itself as she held the woman's questioning gaze. "Of course."

"I'm afraid that if you go snooping around the neighbours and asking questions, it will only be a matter of time before the Harrises find out, and I can guarantee that the first thing they'll do is go straight to the newspapers, who will make a meal out of us." She glanced away and expelled a trembling breath. "John . . . it'll be no good for him. No good at all."

Guilt pressed down on Emily's shoulders as she watched the woman's fortress-like veneer start to crumble. She felt a sudden need to confess, to admit that she had indeed made contact with the Harris family, that it seemed the quickest and most direct way to find out the truth. And actually, that Jessica Harris seemed desperate and alone, and not the type of person who would run to the newspapers or dream up something as awful as The Witness. If anything, she seemed like the type of person who wanted to be left alone, so that she and her children could get on with their lives without living under the shadow of their criminal husband and father.

Mud sticks, Emily thought, not for the first time in her life.

"Don't worry, Mrs Fisher," she said, placing a hand on her shoulder. "I wouldn't be doing my job if I wasn't exercising discretion."

Meredith grew tall and straight again. She stared at Emily for a long time. At last, she nodded. "Let's go back. The temperature's dropping by the second."

Pursing her lips, she let out a short, sharp whistle and Nestor came racing towards them. By the time they'd reached the house, it was so cold that Emily's feet felt like heavy, lifeless rocks.

"Well, thank you for coming to see me," Meredith said quietly, her gaze meandering. "Perhaps I should just leave you alone to get on with things. After all, the sooner this awful business is out of the way, the sooner we can put it behind us and get on with our lives."

Emily nodded, glancing over the woman's shoulder to see

John Fisher standing at a downstairs window. He smiled and raised a hand. Emily waved back.

"For goodness' sake!" Meredith huffed. "That man will be the death of me—he's supposed to be resting!"

"I should go." Emily turned to leave, then stopped as a thought struck her. "Mrs Fisher—"

"Call me Meredith."

"Do you happen to know anything about the history of the house on Raven Road?"

"The history? Not really. I mean, all old houses have histories, but I've never heard anything out of the ordinary about number fifty-seven. Why do you ask?"

"It's just that, well, I did happen to speak to one of the neighbours—just in passing, without saying who I was or what I was doing—and they told me something curious."

"Yes?"

"They told me some murders took place at the house."

"Murders?" Meredith exclaimed, eyebrows reaching for the sky.

"Yes, about fifty years ago now. You never heard about them?"

"Who told you that?"

"An elderly couple from across the street. I think they were called the Butchers?"

Meredith's frown was quickly swept away by a knowing smile. "In that case, I wouldn't believe a word of it. That dear couple are very sweet, but they do love to tell a tall tale. Raymond, in particular."

With that, the woman clucked her tongue at Nestor, and together, they disappeared inside the house, leaving Emily standing on the gravel drive. She stood for a moment, watching as Meredith appeared in the window and scolded John like a naughty child. She smiled to herself, but only for a second. The Fishers had been through so much already. They'd asked for Emily's help and yet here she was, lying through her teeth and going against the couple's wishes.

But as guilty as she felt, lying was a necessary evil because one way or another, Emily was going to give the Fishers the peace they so desperately deserved.

18

THEY SAT in the cluttered and cramped kitchen, oily, food-stained walls closing in on them. Jerome leaned over the stove, stirring a pot with one hand and holding a wine glass with the other. Emily sat at the small, square table, knees pressed together as she clutched a glass of orange juice between her fingers.

"I don't know how you can even look at that wine after last night," she said, wrinkling her mouth in disgust.

"Years of practice," Jerome called over his shoulder.

Emily glanced around the kitchen, at the refrigerator plastered in various magnets and the sink piled high with dishes. "How on earth do five of you cook in this kitchen?"

"We don't. Two of the guys work in catering, so they mostly eat at work, and the other two are hardly ever here."

"So you're responsible for this mess?"

"I like to think of it as a creative kitchen. What do you think of the rest of the place? I know it's not The Holmeswood, and let's be honest, it's kind of a shit hole. But it's cheap at least—by London standards."

"Are we even in London? It took me ages to get here."

"It's Walthamstow, not the North Pole. Anyway, you're being a snob. We don't all have fancy jobs, you know."

"You're right. I'm sorry. But I wouldn't call my job fancy—I basically sit around in a car for a living. And the only reason I've been able to afford The Holmeswood is because I sold my house in Cornwall. That money's gone now."

"What does that mean? You have to move out?"

"I don't know. Maybe. I don't want to think about it right now."

"You could always move in with lover boy. You know he'd say yes in a shot."

"No," Emily said, too quickly. "I mean, we've been together for a year. It's too soon for that kind of thing."

"In that case, welcome to the reality of London living." Jerome flourished a hand around the kitchen, and the light glanced off the network of thick scars. "I'd love to have my own place, but that would mean having a well-paid job—and an actual career."

"You do have a career," Emily said quietly.

"Did. I *did* have a career." He returned to the table with two steaming bowls and set them down. "Dinner is served."

Emily stared at the food in front of her. "Pasta?"

"I told you—the salary Braithwaite is paying me is like being a student again, only with more bills and actual work to do." He attacked his meal with vigour. "Anyway, I take it you decided not to confess all to our esteemed yet terrifying leader?"

"Not yet." Emily shot him a glance. "I may have gone to see Jessica Harris again, and I may have agreed to help her."

"There she is! The Emily Swanson I used to know. Welcome back."

"Not funny."

"It's a little funny. Are you sure you know what you're doing?"

"Not really. I mean, sort of. But having Jessica on my side means I have a better chance of finding out if she's The Witness."

"I thought you didn't think it was her."

"I don't. But I could be wrong."

"Hang on. Did I just hear Emily Swanson admit that sometimes she makes mistakes?"

"No, you didn't. And why do you always have to refer to me by my full name every time you want to prove a point?"

Jerome shrugged. "I didn't even realise I did that."

"Well, you do and it's annoying. Anyway, if I can get Jessica to trust me, I can kill two birds with one stone. I can prove she's not The Witness and at the same time, I can convince her to drop the lawsuit against the Fishers. Everybody wins."

"Except you're forgetting one small thing," Jerome said, picking up his wine glass.

Emily frowned. "What?"

"If Jessica Harris isn't The Witness, someone else is."

"Actually, I haven't forgotten that at all. In fact, I have an idea of how to catch whoever it is red-handed." She paused, staring at him. "But I need your help."

Jerome's amused expression suddenly faded and his eyes dropped down to his scarred hands.

"No. Nothing like that," Emily said quickly. "I'm never putting you in that kind of danger again."

"What, then?"

"It's a different kind of danger. A sort of 'if Erica finds out we're both in trouble' kind of danger."

"That sounds worse." Jerome picked up his glass and took a large gulp. "Well, go on then—tell me."

"I need some security equipment. Cameras, mostly. Normally, I'd sign it out, but I don't want Erica asking questions."

"So you want me to risk my low-paid, temporary job to help you sneak them out?"

"Basically, yes."

Emily waited for the rebuke to come. Instead, Jerome shrugged. "Fine. Erica's got an appointment tomorrow morning at nine. Swing by and pick up what you need then."

"That's it? No lecture?"

"You're not the only one who's changed, Emily Swanson. Besides, I need to start looking for another job sooner or later."

"You mean auditions?"

"No. I told you—that part of my life is over."

"Jerome . . ." Emily set down her cutlery and let out a sigh.

"Don't make this about your guilt. Sometimes people don't get what they want, that's all. It's no big deal."

"Except it *is* a big deal. It was your dream. It was all you ever wanted to do."

"Exactly. Past tense." Avoiding her gaze, he stood and grabbed the wine bottle from the counter. Returning to the table, he filled his glass to the top.

Silence fell. As Emily picked at her food, she stole little glances at Jerome, wishing she could turn back time. Wishing that she had never put him in the path of danger. And yet, here she was, asking for his help again, as if she hadn't learned a damn thing.

19

THE NEXT MORNING, Emily was back at Raven Road, the icy wind slapping at her skin as she balanced on a step ladder on the front porch, screwdriver in hand, working on the installation of a small security camera. When she'd arrived at Braithwaite Investigations just after nine, Jerome had been waiting with a silver case hidden at his feet, all ready for her to take. She'd thanked him and he hadn't quite met her gaze, making her feel even worse for having asked for his help yet again.

Now, with the camera fixed to the wall, she angled the lens until it pointed directly over the doorstep. Climbing down from the ladder, she rubbed her hands together and blew hot air over them. Her fingers were already stinging and red, as if she'd dipped them into hot bathwater, and on the back of her hands the thin scars that were barely noticeable on a normal day were now bone white and glowing. Digging into her pockets, she slipped on a pair of gloves. Above the street, the sky was clear and eggshell-blue. Up until a week ago, winter had been damp and mild, but now the country had transformed into a giant ice box, with snow most definitely on its way.

Removing another security camera from the silver case, Emily glanced around the garden until her eyes came to rest on the Rowan tree. Five minutes later, she had the camera attached to its lower branch and pointed at the street. Making her way down the stepladder, she brushed flakes of dried bark from her winter coat. Her body shivered beneath her clothes, but she still had one more camera to place before returning indoors to defrost.

Something stirred at the corner of her eye. Emily turned to see Geraldine Butcher standing on the other side of the hedge, large eyes peering out from beneath a colourful headscarf.

"Hello, dearie. Just on my way home from shopping and saw you up the tree," she said, staring up at the camera. "Is that part of a social worker's job? Putting in cameras?"

Emily followed her gaze, forcing a smile to her lips, realising her cover was well and truly blown. "Oh, they have us doing all sorts of things these days."

The elderly woman was still gazing up at the tree. "Well don't be out here for too long. You'll catch your death."

Waving a hand, she crossed the street, heading for home. Emily's shoulders sank. It probably wasn't the best idea to be giving the street's residents more to whisper about, but if one of the neighbours was The Witness, perhaps her presence would act as a deterrent.

She watched Geraldine disappear through her front door. A few seconds later, she saw the tall, crooked form of Raymond Butcher appear at the living room window. Even from this distance, Emily could tell he was watching her. She held up a hand and waved. Raymond waved back, continuing to stare. If Emily needed help to spread the word about the cameras' presence, she had a feeling she'd just got it.

Her feet heavy and numb, she picked up the metal case from the doorstep and followed a narrow path along the side of the house. The rear garden was a good size, consisting of a rectangular patio, where moss and weeds grew up from the cracks, and a large, untidy lawn bordered by tall hedgerows that offered privacy from the adjacent households. A few of Georgia's toys littered the ground: a shiny red bicycle lying on its side, a rainbow-coloured football sitting in the centre of the lawn. Large ceramic pots lined the back of the house, the plants they'd once contained killed off by winter.

Removing another camera from the case, Emily attached it to a metal stake and stepped onto the lawn. Selecting a cluster of shrubs, she pushed the stake in the ground until the camera rested a few inches above the hard soil, before pointing the lens at the back door. She frowned, then smiled in the direction of the kitchen window, where a pair of young eyes watched her through a gap in the blinds. A second later, the blinds snapped shut.

Emily heaved her trembling shoulders. *A girl that age should be going to school and playing with her friends, living a normal life.* She knew only too well what happened to a child when they were isolated from the world. She absentmindedly scratched the back of her gloved hand, feeling the thin scars sting with lonely memories as her teeth began to chatter in her skull.

Activating the camera, she got to her feet and crossed the lawn, heading straight for the back door to let herself into the kitchen. The lights were on but the room was now empty. She stood for a moment, stamping her feet on the mat and rubbing her hands, but it was as if the cold had seeped into her bones and frozen the marrow.

From somewhere inside the house, she heard movement.

Heading to the kitchen door, she peered out into the hall. Jessica's voice floated down from upstairs and was quickly followed by sulky, indignant murmurs. Silence resumed. Her heart racing, Emily closed the kitchen door, then set the silver case on the kitchen table and flipped the lid. Removing a tiny camera the size of her thumb, she quickly looked around, scanning cupboards and shelves and pots of kitchen utensils. Spying a shelf of plastic potted plants, she reached up and inserted the camera between the leaves.

The silence was disturbed by a piercing shriek. Emily spun on her heels. She let out a breath as she realised it was the telephone. Turning back to the plant, she angled the camera so it was pointing at the kitchen, then switched it on. The phone was still ringing. Above her head, footsteps rolled across the ceiling like distant thunder. A second later, the phone cut off and she heard Jessica's voice.

Leaving the kitchen, Emily made her way along the hall and came to a halt at the foot of the stairs, where she cocked her head and listened in on Jessica's conversation. Her voice was strained, the words coming out in short bursts.

"Yes, I know that, but . . . No, she's still not well . . . I already told you why . . . I'm sorry but her safety is more important than your damn attendance levels!"

As Jessica continued to talk, Emily glanced along the hall, noting the door, halfway down on the right.

Have your lambs been down to the basement? Do they know what hides inside the walls?

Shivering, she tip-toed into the living room. Like the rest of the house, it was shrouded in darkness, and Emily took a moment to find the light switch. It was a large space with two sofas, shelves filled with books, a huge television, and family photos hanging on the walls. Just a normal family living room, Emily thought, except now she was noticing the missing pictures and the dark rectangles left behind on the walls where sunlight hadn't bleached the paintwork. Every trace of Wesley Harris had been erased.

Her gaze moved to the window blinds, which were pulled down like security shutters. Emily frowned, tiny childhood memories sneaking in through the cracks. Forcing them back out, she focused on a large, marble mantelpiece, where an array of ceramic jars stood in a row. Tiny camera in hand, she moved towards them. Then froze.

Footsteps were raining down on the stairs. Spinning on her heels, she slipped the camera inside her pocket, just as Jessica entered the room. At first, she didn't notice Emily. But Emily noticed the deep frown that was slashed across her brow and recognised the desperate expression of someone who was close to giving up. Then Jessica's head snapped up and their eyes met, and a curtain immediately fell across her face.

"Oh," she gasped, a hand reaching to her collar bone. "I didn't see you there."

Emily smiled. "Everything okay?"

Jessica nodded unconvincingly. "That was Georgia's school. They're demanding I send her back."

"Do they know what's going on?"

"With her father, yes."

"What about the letters?"

"I told them Georgia was sick, but they know. How could they not when it's been all over the local newspapers? And God knows there are enough gossips around to help spread the word."

"Maybe she'd be better off at school," Emily offered.

"Someone's threatening my family. How am I supposed to trust they'll keep my daughter safe?"

"They must have security. These days, most schools have locked gates and electronic doors."

Jessica stared at her, then glanced away, her eyes finding the wall of family portraits and the gaps in between. "Are you done putting up the cameras?"

Emily followed her gaze. "Let's go into the kitchen. I'll show you the set up. Do you have a laptop?"

"It's upstairs. I'll go get it. Why don't you fill the kettle and I'll make some coffee? You must be frozen."

"Like an icicle."

Emily smiled as she watched Jessica exit the room. As soon as she heard footsteps on the stairs, she hurried towards the row of vases on the mantelpiece, changed her mind, and darted towards one of the alcoves of shelves. Removing the camera from her pocket, she activated it and reached up on tiptoes to slot it between two books on the highest shelf.

———

Minutes later, Emily was seated at the kitchen table, a tablet device in her hands, while Jessica sat beside her in front of a laptop. She'd already downed half a mug of coffee and now heat radiated through her body, blooming out from her chest in blissful petals.

"I've installed three external cameras," she explained, nodding at Jessica's laptop screen, where the display showed three grainy black and white images of the front porch, the street, and the back of the house. "What you're seeing now is a live feed with a delay of a few seconds."

"And it's recording this?" Jessica asked, eyes bright with curiosity.

"No. The cameras have built-in motion detectors, which means they'll only start recording when they pick up movement and stop once everything is still again. That way, you save on battery power and it means we won't have to spend hours trawling through footage to see if something—or someone —shows up."

Beside her, Jessica let out a trembling breath.

"You can access the live feeds at any time from this dashboard, as well as any recorded footage. I'll keep an eye too, and I'll review the recorded footage each morning. If someone is harassing your family, if they try to deliver another letter or anything else, the cameras will catch them in the act."

Jessica was staring at her, eyes flitting left to right. "You said 'if' someone is harassing us. You still don't believe me?"

Emily stared back, unblinking. "It was a figure of speech. If I didn't believe someone was sending those letters, I wouldn't be here."

The two women continued to stare at each other, until Jessica's shoulders softened and her gaze returned to the laptop screen.

"Well, I'm glad you are here. And the cameras already make me feel safer."

"All the same, I wouldn't suggest sitting here watching them, twenty-four seven. Not unless you're determined to drive yourself crazy."

Emily tapped the tablet screen, selecting the Rowan tree camera feed and zooming in. The street was still, with not even a car driving past. Leaning back to stretch her shoulders, she stared at the kitchen door.

"Can I see the basement?"

Startled, Jessica stared at her. "Why?"

"Because it's mentioned in all the letters. I'd like to take a look around."

The fear on the woman's face was palpable. "I—I suppose that would be okay."

Emily followed her out of the kitchen and into the hall, where Jessica stood, hovering outside the basement door, her face pale even in the yellow electric light. Slipping her hand inside her jeans pocket, she produced the key and slid it into the lock. The door opened with a slow creak and a cold draft rushed out.

Both women shivered as they stared into darkness.

Blood will flow in the basement. Blood will rise up from the well to drown you all.

Jessica reached out and flicked a switch. The darkness vanished, revealing a set of wooden steps leading down towards a rectangle of concrete floor.

Her skin crawling, Emily went first, conscious of the tightness in her chest as she descended the stairs. Reaching the bottom, she glanced over her shoulder to see that Jessica was still up in the hall, her silhouette haunting the doorway.

"It's okay," Emily said. "I'll just take a quick look."

It was cold down here, the air damp and acrid. Wrapping her arms around her ribcage, she stepped from the harbour of the stairs, moving further into the basement.

The room was wide with a high ceiling, and it was lined with shelves of junk and forgotten-about items. Emily glanced around at the boxes of memorabilia, spying old toys and piles of clothes, and a collection of trophies that was collecting dust. The letters had made the basement sound terrifying, but she saw no torture tables, no manacles, no arterial slashes of blood on the walls, and certainly no well. It was just an ordinary basement in an ordinary family home on an ordinary street. Emily heaved her shoulders with relief, although she couldn't deny she also felt a twinge of disappointment.

"Everything all right down there?" Jessica called.

Emily walked along, rapping her knuckles against the walls. If there was something nasty lurking behind them, it was clearly shy.

"Emily?"

She returned upstairs to the hall, where Jessica quickly locked the door and pocketed the key.

"Nothing?"

Emily shook her head. Returning to the kitchen, she checked the camera feeds on the laptop. Jessica joined her, pressing her face close to the screen.

"I'd like to make a suggestion," Emily said, watching the empty gardens and the quiet street. "One that you might not be comfortable with, but one that might hurry things along."

"Go on."

"I think you should open all the blinds."

Jessica's mouth fell open. "I'm not giving that psychopath an open view of my family."

"I know I'm asking a lot and I completely understand that you're afraid, but The Witness was urging you to open the blinds. He made threats. He said something terrible would happen if you didn't. The spiders were very likely just the beginning. But if you do as The Witness says, if you open the blinds, perhaps it will stop him from escalating. Perhaps it will keep your family safe for now, maybe even lure him out into the open and in front of the cameras."

"But he'll be watching us!" Jessica cried. "He'll be watching my children!"

"Which means we'll have a better chance of catching him without putting you and your children at greater risk."

Jessica shook her head as she stared at the closed kitchen blinds. "I don't want to look up and see him staring through the window."

"You won't. He's cleverer than that. But if you keep the blinds shut, we have no idea what he'll try next."

Emily stared at the camera feeds. A shadow moved at the corner of her eye. Georgia hovered in the kitchen doorway, pale skin sickly looking in the artificial light.

"Anyway," Emily said, watching the girl cautiously enter the room and approach the kitchen table, "it would be good to let a little light in here."

Georgia moved between the women and stared at the camera.

"Is that our street?" she asked, jabbing the screen with a finger.

"It is," Emily smiled. "We're making sure you're safe and sound."

The girl's gaze shifted back and forth as she viewed each feed. "Can *I* have a camera?"

"Well, they're kind of expensive and they're not really toys. Maybe you can help by keeping an eye on these feeds. And by not touching the cameras . . ."

Jessica wrapped an arm around Georgia and drew her near, kissing the top of her head and inhaling the scent of her hair.

"We're just trying to keep you safe, sweet thing. You and your brother." She glanced at Emily. "You'll be watching?"

"Watching is what I do best."

Releasing her daughter, Jessica slowly got to her feet and moved over to the kitchen sink.

"Well, I hope your best is good enough," she said. With a trembling hand, she reached across the counter, hesitated, then pulled the cord of the window blinds. The kitchen filled with startling winter light and all three of them raised their hands to protect their eyes.

When her vision had finally adjusted to the brightness, Emily stared at Georgia and her heart spasmed inside her chest. Jessica saw it too, and she clutched her hands together as she blinked away shocked tears.

In natural daylight, Georgia Harris looked like a ghost—pale and gaunt, skin the colour of dishwater, shadows circling her eyes like two black holes.

But she was smiling. Which was something, Emily supposed. And a sign that she had made the right decision after all.

"I know you feel unsafe right now," she said to Jessica, as her phone began to buzz inside her jeans pocket. "But we're already one step closer to finding out who's behind this."

Removing the phone, she pressed it to her ear.

"Good morning, this is Detective Constable Ryan returning your call," a deep, confident voice said. "You wanted to speak to me about the Harris family?"

She froze, shooting a glance at Jessica, who was studying her closely, mouth hanging slightly open.

"Yes, that's right. Thanks for getting back to me. I was wondering if I could come down and speak with you. It wouldn't take long."

"I'll be here for the next hour or so, if—"

"That's great. I'm on my way."

She hung up. Now both Georgia and Jessica were staring at her.

"Everything okay?" Jessica asked.

Emily nodded as her eyes flicked towards the shelf of artificial plants and the first of her hidden cameras, then moved down to the counter where the gift box still sat, dried spider guts smeared across its front. "I thought you were taking that to the police."

Jessica followed her gaze. "I will. It's just that . . . Well, I—"

Crossing the room, Emily slipped on her gloves and carefully picked up the box. "I'll drop it off on my way back to the office. But you have to leave the house at some point. It's not good for you to be inside all the time. For either of you."

Jessica stared at the box uncertainly. She opened her mouth, then closed it again.

"I'll be back tomorrow," Emily said. She nodded at the camera feeds on the laptop screen. "And I'll be watching."

20

THE LOCAL POLICE station was appropriately sized for a small town, with only a handful of patrol cars parked in bays. With the gift box now inside a plastic bag, Emily pushed through the double doors of the two-storey building and made her way to the reception desk, where the middle-aged station duty officer, whose sedentary lifestyle had taken a toll on his waistline, sat behind Perspex glass, typing on the keyboard of a computer. No one else was around.

Coming to a halt, Emily cleared her throat. The duty officer glanced up, barely acknowledging her, then continued typing for a few more seconds.

"Excuse me, I—"

The man held up a silencing finger. Emily watched him through narrowed eyes. Finally, he looked up.

"Yes, can I help you?"

"Emily Swanson, here to see DC Ryan."

The officer shot her an unimpressed glare. "No journalists."

"I'm not a journalist, I'm a private investigator. DC Ryan is expecting me."

Producing her licence, she pressed it against the Perspex screen. The man leaned closer. "That thing real?"

"Of course it's real. I'll be happy to wait while you verify it for yourself."

It wasn't the first time someone had questioned her private investigator licence. Sometimes she wondered if it was because she didn't look like the stereotypical PI, but she suspected it was more to do with the fact that private investigators weren't a common phenomenon in Britain. There were agencies, of course, but they were few and far between, and rarely dealt with the types of cases seen in film and television.

Shrugging a shoulder, the officer picked up the reception phone and nodded to the row of plastic seats behind her. "You can wait over there. I'll see if he's available."

Emily thanked him through clenched teeth, then sat down on one of the uncomfortable-looking chairs, setting the gift box next to her. While she waited, she glanced at the various posters on the walls, mostly crime prevention paraphernalia, and a brightly-coloured petition to prevent further budget cuts to the police force. The way that police numbers were being slashed in this country, it was only a matter of time before the crime rate exploded.

Heaving her shoulders, she returned her gaze to the front desk. She was wondering if she was wasting her time when a door in the far wall swung open and a man dressed in a charcoal suit moved towards her. He was in his early thirties, with tight, curly hair and a pleasant smile.

"Good afternoon," he said. "I'm DC Ryan."

Emily got to her feet and shook his hand, then fumbled for her licence again. "Emily Swanson. Braithwaite Investigations."

"A private investigator?" DC Ryan raised an eyebrow as he

stared at her ID, but unlike the officer on the front desk, he seemed more surprised than amused. "We don't get many of those around here. How can I help?"

Relaxing a little, Emily slipped the licence back inside her wallet. "I'd like to talk to you about a current harassment case. The Harris family of Raven Road? You're the investigating officer?"

"That's right. And what's your involvement?"

Emily quickly explained about the Fisher family and about the lawsuit they were facing. DC Ryan nodded, giving her his full attention. When she'd finished, he turned to speak to the office at the front desk. "Andy, can you sign Miss Swanson in, please? And two coffees would be great."

The duty officer looked up, a flash of irritation in his eyes.

"One more thing," Emily said, picking up the plastic bag and handing it to the detective.

"What is it?" he asked, peering cautiously inside.

"A gift. Not one you want to open without gloves."

———

Now signed in and cradling a plastic cup of coffee, Emily sat at a table in a small interview room with DC Ryan. A memory flashed briefly in her mind—of being questioned in a similar room after Philip Gerard's death—and she quickly shooed it away. She'd now brought the detective up to date with her involvement with the Harris family and he'd sealed the gift box inside an evidence bag and had it taken away for testing.

"Sounds like you've made more headway with this case than we have," DC Ryan said.

"Well, I don't have a hundred other cases breathing down my neck or budget cuts to worry about."

"Don't get me started. So, apart from making me look inferior, is there anything else you can help me with today?" The detective constable flashed her a smile.

"Actually, I came here to ask for your help," Emily said, blushing.

"With what? You seem to be doing just fine by yourself."

"I need information. Anything you're allowed to tell me about the case. I've seen photocopies of the letters that Jessica Harris received, and I know about some of the harassment she claims to have experienced, but beyond that . . ."

"I'm not sure I can enlighten you further. Forensics tested the letters for fingerprints and DNA, but whoever wrote them was careful. Everything came back clean, so I wouldn't get your hopes up about that box." DC Ryan sipped his coffee and grimaced. "We also had the handwriting analysed, even took samples from the Harris family—but nothing matched."

"So you think the Harrises are telling the truth?"

"Most of them," DC Ryan replied. "Those letters didn't write themselves. At first, I thought it was one of the clients Wesley Harris stole from, out for revenge. But it doesn't make sense that one of his clients would involve the Fishers—all that does is complicate things. No, my money is on Harris."

"But why? What reason would he have to terrorise his family? And how could he mastermind it while he's on remand?"

"Maybe it's not about terrorising his family. Maybe it's about securing them a future seeing as how he's screwed up everything else. And you'd be surprised what criminals behind bars can do when they have connections. Harris may have lived the high life, but he would have used some pretty shady characters to launder his clients' stolen money."

"You've been looking into that?" Emily asked.

DC Ryan leaned back in his chair and smiled. "Not me. That's one for the big boys—Fraud Squad."

"But what about The Witness?"

"If Harris is behind it, he'll be rumbled soon enough."

"If he isn't?"

"You mean what if there really is some nut job out there, intent on doing the Harris family harm?"

Emily nodded.

"Unlikely. Look at the threats they've received so far. A couple of creepy letters, a few pornos through the door, and now a box of house spiders. It's playground stuff. Harmless. I'm telling you, it's Harris. He's a dick but he's not going to hurt his own family. Excuse my language . . ."

Emily shifted on her chair as DC Ryan gazed at the door. Despite his cockiness, she found herself liking him—but he undoubtedly had more pressing cases that he needed to return to. Once Emily had finished with him.

"What about Jessica Harris? Do you think she could be involved?"

"There are those who believe she's cold and manipulative," he said, his knee jiggling up and down now, "that she knew all about her husband's criminal activities but chose to live the high life instead of turning him in. I'm not so sure."

"Why?"

"I was there on the scene; the day Wesley Harris was arrested. It was her eyes, I suppose. People can fake tears and gasps of horror, but it's much harder to fake genuine shock. That day, Jessica Harris looked like a rabbit in the headlights. The few times I've seen her since, she seemed genuinely afraid, convinced that someone's trying to hurt her family."

Emily nodded. She'd thought the same.

"But maybe I'm completely wrong. Maybe I'm a snowflake and she's a better actress than I give her credit for."

"Well," Emily said, "whoever The Witness may be, it's only a matter of time before we find out. I have cameras set up all around the house."

"If only the police force had the time and resources for something like that, you wouldn't have to do our job for us. Speaking of which . . ." Ryan smiled as he eyed the door once more.

"Of course. I should let you get back."

As they made their way along the corridor towards reception, Emily wondered if the detective—and the Fishers—were right. Was Wesley Harris really The Witness?

DC Ryan stopped by the door and went to open it. Emily wrapped her fingers around the handle.

"One more question before I go," she said. "Say I wanted to arrange a visit to a prisoner on remand—how would I go about doing that?"

The detective constable stared at her, a smile spreading across his lips. "You're not convinced it's him, are you?"

Emily shrugged. "I'm exploring my options."

21

Harriet Golding's apartment was more cramped than ever. As usual, books and journals covered every available service, but they seemed to tower higher than before. The air was thick and pungent, as if the windows hadn't been opened in days.

"I'm worried about you," Emily said, studying the woman's bony form. "You've lost more weight."

Harriet waved a spindly hand in her direction, skin papery with age and marked by liver spots. Sitting in the armchair, a blanket draped across her lap, she looked small and childlike.

"Nonsense," she wheezed. "It's a bit of a chest infection, that's all. Give me a few days and I'll be right as rain." She erupted with coughs and splutters. Emily passed her a tissue. Harriet waved her away and produced a cotton handkerchief from the sleeve of her cardigan. "Stop fussing. Anyone would think I was already in my grave!"

"Someone's got to fuss over you. This place is a mess. Where's that son of yours, anyway? He should be taking better care of you."

Emily cast another glance around the room, then picked up

her teacup. Tucking her handkerchief back inside her sleeve, Harriet patted her bun of silver hair, checking for loose strands.

"Andrew?" she said, as if she had other sons she'd never mentioned before. "He's out. Got a meeting."

"What kind of a meeting?"

"Something to do with history, he said. You know what he's like. He'd be happy sitting around with all those other lazy good for nothings, talking about books till the end of time. Still, I can't blame him, I suppose. He can't work with that back of his. It's just a shame the only women who'll go near him aren't the marrying type." Harriet adjusted her blanket and shut her eyes for a moment. "He's just a bit different, that's all. At least he's got the love of his mum, eh?"

"Still, it's not right that he's leaving you in this mess. What if you trip and fall over these books?"

"It's not the books I worry about. It's this." The elderly woman stabbed a finger at her temple. "The minute my mind goes, I don't want no part of this world anymore, thank you very much. Just put a pillow over my face and be done with it."

"Don't say things like that! Besides, you're as sharp as a needle, so you don't need to worry about losing your marbles just yet." Emily reached over and patted her neighbour on the knee. "And the only reason I'm worrying is because I care about you. Evidently more than your son."

"Oh, rubbish! My boy loves me to the moon and back. But he's a grown man, and you know what men are like."

"Only too well."

Both women smiled. They were quiet for a minute, sipping their tea, and Emily found herself thinking back to Georgia's ghostly face that afternoon, white as bone in the winter sunlight. She hoped that now the blinds were open that some colour would return to the girl's face. No matter the reasons behind what was happening to the Harris family, it was criminal that an innocent child was suffering the greatest impact.

Emily was still unsure what to make of Jessica Harris, though. She wanted to believe her, she really did—yet she couldn't ignore the feeling that something was there, concealed beneath the woman's outward anguish; something that she didn't want to share. It was why Emily had installed the hidden cameras. She had conflicting feelings about doing so—and not only because she was breaking protocol—but the truth was she'd been tasked with proving Jessica's innocence. Or guilt. Right now, Emily's instincts told her it was the former. She just hoped her instincts were right.

"I've lost you," Harriet said. "Honestly, I never see you, and when I do, you're a million miles away."

Emily smiled. "Sorry. It's this new case I'm working on."

"Keeping you up, is it?"

"You could say that."

"Well, I hope it isn't dangerous, especially after everything you've been through. All the jobs in the world you could do, and you choose private investigator! If you ask me, you should have stuck with teaching. That's a much better job for a woman."

Emily rolled her eyes. "And I suppose private investigation is men's work, is it? You do know that it hasn't been the 1950s for quite some time? We get to choose our own jobs now. Some of us even choose not to get married or have families."

"What I meant is all that investigation business is police work. You should leave the detecting to them. Honestly, I don't know what that man of yours must think about you gallivanting all over the place!"

"If you must know, Carter is very supportive."

"That's not what I hear." The elderly woman pursed her lips, then dunked a chocolate chip cookie into her tea.

Emily stiffened "How would you know what Carter thinks about my career?"

"Oh, you know, women's intuition or whatever you call it. Besides, I happened to hear your door opening yesterday morning and popped my head out to say hello. But instead of you it was your fella."

"You just *happened to hear*?"

"Yes. It's not like I stand at the door every minute with my eye to the peephole, is it? Anyway, me and him had a nice little chat. If you ask me, he's rather concerned about your line of work."

A flash of heat ignited Emily's stomach and quickly grew in momentum, sparking and crackling its way up to her chest. "Is that so? What exactly did he say?"

Harriet waved a dismissive hand. "Oh, nothing to worry your head about. He's a good-looking fella, isn't he? A bit wet behind the ears but nice enough."

Emily set down her teacup and clenched her jaw. "Harriet, what did he say?"

"Just that he's worried about you. I expect he doesn't want you to get hurt. It's very gentlemanly, I reckon. Better than not caring if you live or die."

Emily could feel the irritation bubbling in her gut. Who did Carter West think he was? What she chose to do with her life was her own damn business. If he didn't like it, well, he knew what to do. She glared at her empty teacup. She would have it out with him when he came around later. Set him straight. Or perhaps she would say nothing at all. People were entitled to their opinions, she supposed. In any case, Harriet's proclivity for exaggerating the truth was well documented, and if past experience had taught Emily anything, it was that if Carter West had something to say, he would say it to her face. He was that kind of person—honest and upfront.

Except for when he's gossiping with my neighbour behind my back.

No. She would leave it alone for now. If she could help it.

Harriet was staring at her, one eyebrow raised, an amused smile etched on her lips. "It's funny. A year ago, you were Miss Independent, never getting married, never having children, determined to sit on a shelf for the rest of your life. And now look at you, all hot and bothered because a nice-looking fella's taken a fancy to you. You're a funny fish, Emily."

Emily narrowed her eyes as she got to her feet. "Well, this funny fish needs to go. I have work to do, bills to pay, people to help—regardless of what others have to say about it."

Harriet sucked in a faltering breath, then let out a guttural, phlegm-filled cough. Any irritation Emily felt quickly disintegrated.

"I should call the doctor."

"Don't you dare. I'm fine." The woman sucked in another breath as she scrabbled for her handkerchief.

"Well I'll check in on you tomorrow," Emily said, reluctant to leave. "And the next time I see Andrew, I *will* be having a word about keeping this place tidy."

"Leave the boy alone, he'll do it in his own time."

"Boy? He's fifty years old!"

Harriet wiped spittle from her mouth with the handkerchief. "The problem with you Emily Swanson, is you spend too much time worrying about other people and not enough worrying about yourself."

"Since when was worrying about the people you care about a bad thing?"

"Except if it's your fella worrying about you, eh?" Harriet rasped.

Emily frowned. "See you later."

22

EVENING FELL OVER THE CITY, painting the skyscrapers in grey-green light—the closest London ever came to darkness. Inside her apartment, Emily sat at the dining table, case notes and files spread across the surface. Her eyes were glued to the tablet screen, which showed the grainy black-and-white images of the camera feeds. She studied each one deliberately, looking for signs of activity. Raven Road was quiet and still, pools of streetlight making islands in the dark. Curtained windows were illuminated in neighbours' homes. A car drove past, cutting through the shadows. Stillness resumed.

The camera above the front door displayed a darkened doorstep, the motion-triggered porch light currently dormant, while the camera hidden in the rear garden showed the back of the house, windswept shadows dancing over the brickwork. But there was nothing to report.

Emily's fingers twitched as they hovered above the tablet screen. She tapped an icon and was presented with two more live camera feeds. The living room was cast in night-vision black and white, with glimmers of streetlight splashed along the walls. Good, Emily thought. At least Jessica had kept the blinds open.

The second feed showed the kitchen, the fisheye lens elongating the view to encapsulate the entire room. The Harris family members were all present and accounted for. The children were seated at the table, Ethan with his phone out, tapping away at the screen, while Georgia scribbled on what looked like a sketchpad. Behind them, Jessica Harris was busy preparing dinner.

Emily watched her closely, noticing the way she turned every twenty seconds or so to peer out the kitchen window, then at her children. Georgia could also be seen turning to look at the windows. Only her body language was different to her mother's. Where Jessica was tense and nervy, her head twitching on her shoulders, Georgia's movements were loose and relaxed, her gaze lingering comfortably on the dark world outside.

Emily turned her attention to Ethan, who neither looked up nor acknowledged the open blinds. Which was strange, considering the house had been locked away in shadows for weeks.

As she continued to watch the family, she felt a strange, voyeuristic thrill. She was a secret, hidden away on a kitchen shelf; a pair of omniscient eyes, watching from the dark. Not unlike The Witness, she realised.

The thrill quickly left her, leaving behind a guilty weight on her chest. Yet she continued to watch the grainy black and white images. It was a necessary evil, she told herself, to discern whether Jessica Harris was telling the truth. Besides, the hidden cameras provided an extra level of security—even if the Harris family was oblivious to their presence. On the downside, the micro cameras were too small to carry motion detectors. Instead, their live feeds were being recorded continuously, which meant hours of footage for Emily to trawl through. But it was a small price to pay if it gave her what she needed.

Emily leaned back and continued to watch the screen, guilt and curiosity battling it out in her mind.

A loud buzzing shattered the quiet. Emily's spine twitched and her conversation with Harriet returned to taunt her. Getting up, she walked into the hallway and pressed the intercom call button.

"You know, you can let yourself in," she said, all too aware of the brittleness of her voice. "That's why I gave you a key."

Carter's voice crackled through the speaker. "I'm too British for that. I have to knock first."

She pressed the buzzer, unlocking the electronic entrance door on the ground floor, then returned to the living room without saying another word. When Carter entered a few minutes later, Emily felt the muscles in her shoulders knitting together in a tight ball. Normally she would jump up to greet him with a kiss, but now she only offered him a brief smile before returning her attention to the tablet screen.

Moments later, she felt his lips, warm and ticklish, on the back of her neck. The tension in her shoulders grew tighter.

"What's this?" he asked, peering over her shoulder to stare at the camera feeds. "Covert surveillance?"

"Something like that." Emily tapped the screen and the camera feeds disappeared. She forced another smile to her lips. "Good day?"

"Actually it was," Carter said, brushing hair from his forehead. "That annoying client I told you about finally decided what he wanted. A day or two and I'll be rid of him forever."

Emily's gaze wandered back to the blank screen of the tablet. "That's a relief."

"How about you? Good day? Or is that classified?"

Emily flashed him a look. Pulling away, she stood and headed for the kitchen. "Dinner's going to be late. I went to see Harriet when I got home. She's not well."

Carter followed behind and came to a stop, the saloon doors bumping up against his back. "What's wrong with her?"

"Sounds like a chest infection. I told her she should see a doctor, but she wasn't having any of it. And of course, Andrew's nowhere to be seen. Again. He needs to take better care of his mother." Emily pulled open cupboard doors and stared apathetically inside. "I don't know what to cook. Pasta or rice?"

Carter shifted his weight from one foot to the other. "Is everything okay?"

"Why wouldn't it be?"

"I don't know. You seem—"

"What?"

"Bothered by something."

"I do?"

"Yes. Is it the new case?"

Emily shot him a glare. "Why would you think that?"

"I don't. I'm just taking a guess."

Crossing her arms over her chest, Emily leaned against the counter. She felt Carter's eyes on her, searching out answers, and she thought about telling him to mind his own business. Instead, she shrugged a shoulder. "It's not dangerous, if that's what you're worried about. I'm just helping out a family, that's all."

"Okay . . ."

"I'm not chasing murderers or tracking down hardened criminals. It's just surveillance. Sitting and watching a camera.

So you don't have to lose any sleep, worrying about me getting killed."

A smile spread across Carter's lips and quickly turned into a full-blown grin. Emily clenched her jaw. Was he laughing at her? Did he think she was being ridiculous?

"What now?" she growled.

"Why don't you tell me what's on your mind?"

The muscles in Emily's shoulders were starting to hurt, and now an invisible hand was pressing down on her chest, squeezing her heart. All these questions that she didn't want to answer, all these layers Carter was trying to peel back, knowing full well there was something dark and nasty waiting inside.

She turned away and glowered at the floor. "Look, all I'm saying is that if you want to know things about me just look online like I told you to do when we first met. It's all there in gory detail to read at your leisure. You don't need to be snooping around, whispering with my neighbours, and you certainly don't need to be side-stepping around me like I'm made of glass. I'm —" The words caught in her throat. She dropped her arms to her sides, then wrapped them around her ribcage. "I'm fine, actually, thank you very much. I've been through enough crap to know I can take care of myself."

Carter was beside her in a second, his hands reaching out, then drawing back. He was quiet for a moment. They both were. Then he took her hand in his and Emily felt his skin, warm and comforting against her own.

"I know there are things that you're scared of me finding out," he said softly. "And I know you think me worrying about you is a judgement on your character. But actually, I worry because I care about you. That isn't a crime. And yes, I do worry about your job because there is an element of danger. But at the same time, I know you can take care of yourself."

Emily glanced up at him, but only for a second.

"You should go online," she said. "Read the stories. Find out what you're really dealing with."

Carter shook his head. "Whatever it is, we'll deal with it together. But only when you're ready to tell me. Because that's how it should be—when you're ready and not before." Now his fingers were travelling along her forearm, reaching up to stroke her face. Emily met his gaze again and this time she held it. "We've all got secrets, Em. Fortunately for the rest of us, they're not hung out like dirty laundry on the Internet. I don't know how that feels, but I do know how it feels to carry an emptiness inside. I do know how it feels to carry a burden."

The muscles in Emily's neck loosened a little. Angry flames died down to little petals.

"Your sister," she said. "You never talk about her."

Carter nodded, his eyes suddenly drowning in sadness. "Like you, I will at the right time."

He leaned forward and kissed her. Emily didn't resist. Instead, she melted into him, wrapping her arms around his waist.

"I wish I could tell you," she said. "But I just can't get the words to come out. What if I tell you and that's the end of it? Of us? Better for you to find out alone and walk away than for me to have to see that look in your eye. I've seen it before, Carter. I don't want to see it again, especially not from you."

"You won't."

"You can't know that."

"And you can't know that I won't stay. Besides, unless you're a mass murderer, how bad can it be?"

Emily was silent as Phillip Gerard's young face emerged from the recesses of her mind. She had made her peace with him. She'd forgiven herself and said goodbye. But whether he knew it or not, Carter was bringing the boy back from the dead.

It's not Carter, Phillip whispered. *It's you. You'll never let me go. Unless you tell him.*

Emily stared into Carter's searching eyes. She opened her mouth, tried to force the words out. But she only managed silence.

23

MONDAY MORNING CAME AROUND QUICKLY, the weekend passing without further events. It was 7:10 a.m. Jessica stood by the kitchen counter, one arm wrapped around her rib cage, the other clutching a steaming mug of coffee as she gazed through the open blinds. She still wasn't used to the light, and even though the winter sun had only just begun its ascent, the brighter it got, the more exposed she felt. But her children—the light had transformed them.

For the first time in weeks, Georgia hadn't seemed to mind being kept indoors and had spent much of the weekend playing happily or staring through the windows at the outside world with fixated curiosity, despite Jessica's warnings to come away. Ethan had also spent much of Saturday at home without protest, only slipping out yesterday for a few hours, but for once texting Jessica that he was safe and sound without needing to be reminded. He hadn't told her where he'd gone though, or who he'd been with. When she'd pressed him, he'd growled that he'd been with friends, and Jessica had left it at that; it had been such a long time since she and Ethan had been able to have even the briefest of conversations without it turning into a fight.

Now Jessica shifted her gaze from the view of the backyard, where early morning frost glinted on the lawn, to her children sitting at the breakfast table, spooning cereal into their mouths and exchanging small talk—it was truly a miracle. This is how it's meant to be, Jessica thought. A normal Monday morning, brother and sister getting on, smiles all around the table. And yet there was something still crawling just beneath her skin, taunting her, reminding her that nothing about their lives was normal.

Her eyes wandered over to the open laptop on the sideboard, to the grainy live camera feeds filling the screen. She had spent much of the weekend glued to the feeds, watching and scanning, desperate but terrified to catch someone watching the house. But the camera feeds had revealed nothing out of the ordinary.

A scrape of a chair on the tiled floor pulled Jessica from her thoughts, and she turned to see Ethan taking his cereal bowl to the dishwasher. As he passed by, he shot a curious glance at the laptop screen.

"Do you have lunch money?" Jessica asked, watching her son. He was getting so tall, she thought. His face changing, maturing. Looking just like his father. *No, don't think that!*

Ethan nodded, actually making eye contact for a second before his mop of hair fell across his eyes. "And yes—I'll text you as soon as I get to college."

"Thanks." She had a sudden urge to go to her son, to wrap him in her arms and cradle him like the child he once was. Then his gaze returned to the camera feeds and a vertical crease appeared at the centre of his forehead, identical to the crease that always appeared when his father did the same. Jessica caught her breath and turned away. "Hopefully this will all be over soon and we can get back to normal."

Mother and son both stared at the screen in silence.

"Does that mean I can go to school now?" Georgia called from the table, the hope in her eyes as bright as daylight.

"Soon," Jessica said, eyes still fixed on the feeds. "Once this is all over."

Georgia let out a heavy sigh, shoulders slumping. "Please, Mum. I'm so bored!"

"I'll ask the school to send more work."

"But they told you I have to go back."

Jessica turned, mouth agape. "Have you been listening to private phone calls?"

"They're not private if they're about me."

"She's got a point," Ethan said.

Jessica turned away from the laptop and moved over to the sink, avoiding her children's stares.

"Maybe you should think about it," Ethan continued. "I mean, now we have a private investigator on the case, maybe it would be fine for Georgia to go to school."

Her shoulder muscles were tightening, her heart beating a little faster as her children's eyes burned into her back like red hot irons.

"You're going to be late," Jessica said. She turned to see her son's eyes slowly narrow.

"Fine. Whatever."

At the table, Georgia sank into her chair, shadows darkening her eyes. Ethan was by the door now, throwing it open and stepping into the hall.

It's me, isn't it? I'm the cause of their unhappiness.

"Ethan?" Jessica called.

"What?"

"I'll think about it, okay? We'll give it another couple of days and I'll think about it. Georgia, is that all right?"

At the table, Georgia shrugged her shoulders. "You said that before."

"It's true," Ethan said.

Jessica stared at her daughter, then at her son, the muscles in her neck growing unbearably tight. "I—"

The cheerful tone of the doorbell sliced through the air. Mother and children both tensed, eyes widening, jaws clenching. They stared at each other, then at the camera feeds.

Georgia jumped up from the table. "Who is it?"

Ethan and Jessica followed, crowding around the laptop. There were people standing on the doorstep—a man and a woman, both middle-aged and conservatively dressed, both with serious expressions. They watched as the woman eyed the security camera above her head then pointed it out to the man.

"Are they police?" Ethan breathed.

Jessica shook her head. "They don't look like police."

The woman reached out and pressed the doorbell again, the sound cracking open the silence.

"What about journalists? They could be local press."

"I'll answer it," Georgia called out, hurrying across the kitchen floor.

"Stay where you are!"

The girl froze, staring at her mother with hurt, wide eyes.

"I mean it," Jessica said, then spun back to the cameras. Who were these people? They looked official; business-like and deadly serious. Perhaps this was something to do with her husband. Someone from the courts maybe, here to rob them of the last of their money.

Growing impatient, the man on the doorstep rapped his knuckles on the door.

Jessica flashed a look at Ethan. "Wait here and keep an eye on your sister. Do not let her out of your sight."

Then she was crossing the room, concentrating on keeping her breath calm, her heart rate in check. She walked along the hall, eyeing the locked basement door, brushing creases out of her clothes, sweeping lank hair behind her ears. Reaching the front door, she drew back the two deadbolts, turned the key, and slipped on the chain lock. Letting out a trembling breath, she let the outside world in.

"Yes? Can I help you?"

The man and woman smiled politely. The woman produced an ID card and held it up.

"Mrs Jessica Harris? I'm Rita Whitlock from Children's Services. This is my colleague, Geoff Newman. We'd like to talk to you about your daughter, Georgia, if we may. The school has been very concerned about her continued absence. Can we come in?"

Jessica glared at the woman, then at the man, who so far hadn't said a word.

"My daughter's not been well," she said, eyes flitting between the two, at the street beyond.

"Yes, the school mentioned that. But there's been no doctor's certificate? Perhaps if we could come in and have a chat about things? Perhaps see Georgia for ourselves . . ."

"We can talk fine just here." Blood rushed in Jessica's ears. Were they here to take Georgia away from her? They didn't take your children away from you just for missing a few days—weeks —from school, did they? But what if your husband was a convicted criminal? *No, don't be ridiculous. Get a grip on yourself.*

The man leaned forward slightly, a condescending smile on his lips. "All the same, Mrs Harris, we do have some concerns for your daughter's welfare, and it would be better for everyone if we could come inside to talk. It's just a chat, just to see what's going on and how we can help."

"Mum?" Jessica shot a look over her shoulder to see Ethan standing halfway along the hall, eyes darting past her. "What's going on?"

"Go back to the kitchen. Everything is fine."

Ethan stood still, eyes flitting between her face and the gap in the door.

"Mrs Harris," Rita Whitlock said, her smile sympathetic. "It really would be best if we could come inside to talk. I understand things have been difficult lately. We're here to help, that's all. Nothing more."

The nausea in Jessica's stomach was bubbling up to her chest. She thought about slamming the door, sliding the bolts back into place.

"*Mum,*" Ethan said again, this time more forcefully.

Jessica stared from man to woman, then let out a trembling sigh. "Just give me a second."

She shut the door, slipped off the chain lock, turned to Ethan and saw the worry in his eyes.

"Everything is going to be fine," she said. "They're just here to talk, that's all. You should get going or you'll be late for college."

"I can stay."

"No. There's no point getting you into trouble as well. We'll be fine, I promise."

Ethan stared at her.

"I promise," she repeated. This time, she almost believed it herself.

Turning away from him, Jessica squeezed her eyes shut and sucked in a calming breath. She opened the door.

"Please, come in," she said to the people from Children's Services. "Georgia is in the kitchen. I'll make some tea."

24

THE ROADS WERE JAMMED with traffic, the air noxious and gritty. Horns honked, engines growled, faces sneered through windscreens. All was as usual on a Monday morning in the city. Emily sat behind the steering wheel, fingers drumming, lower lip pinched between her teeth as she waited for the traffic lights to change. Travelling through rush-hour was not her idea of a good time, but today it was necessary.

The weekend had passed uneventfully. She'd spent most of it in her apartment, obsessively watching the Harris family through the hidden camera feeds. She'd had moments of guilt, knowing that the family was completely unaware they were being watched—by her, at least—but the more she watched, the harder it was to look away. Something had happened to make all the deception worthwhile—the Harris family appeared to be getting along, which made Emily feel less guilty about lying to both Meredith Fisher and Erica Braithwaite. Besides, she was helping people, trying to make things right for both parties, and sometimes doing the right thing required doing the wrong thing first.

The traffic lights changed from red to amber, and the air turned ugly as impatient drivers honked their horns once more. Emily drove the car onward through the city, past towering buildings and pavements filled with thousands of pedestrians, all dressed in winter greys and blues, all sharing the steely London grimace that she had grown quite accustomed to. Occasionally, her eyes flicked to the dashboard clock. Her appointment wasn't until eleven, but with the way the traffic was moving this morning, she was relieved she'd left earlier than planned.

As she continued to drive, her mind wandered back to the weekend. She'd declined to stay over at Carter's house on Saturday night, instead opting to meet him on Sunday for a walk around Hampstead Heath, where an icy breeze had chased them through green open spaces and small wooded areas, before they'd abandoned their stroll for a late lunch and an open fire at a nearby pub. Conversation had been stilted at first, neither of them mentioning the near-fight they'd had on Friday evening. After two glasses of red wine, it was as if the disagreement had never happened, and Emily had found herself quite relaxed and reflecting that it was nice to have someone to share weekends with. If only she didn't have to drag her past behind her like a body wrapped in carpet.

An hour later, she had finally broken free from the city centre and was now heading south towards the outskirts. The roads were still busy, but the traffic was flowing with greater ease. She thought about her destination and her body immediately tensed. She'd been lucky to get an appointment at such short notice, but she'd already prepared a list of questions, which she now went over in her mind, checking that she hadn't forgotten anything important to the case.

Her phone began to ring in the cup holder. Reaching above

her head, she pressed a button on a small device attached to the sun shield, which connected the phone line to the car speakers.

"Hello, this is Emily Swanson."

Jessica Harris's voice came through the speakers, taut and panicked. "I've just had Children's Services on my doorstep, demanding to come inside my house. The school reported me! They're concerned about Georgia's welfare. They say she's missed too much school with no valid reason. As if being stalked by a psychopath isn't a valid reason!"

Emily frowned and turned the wheel, manoeuvring the car on to a wider road, where industrial buildings grew up on both sides.

"Well, I suppose it was only a matter of time," she said. "And it's a sign of a good school if they're that concerned."

"You think Children's Services turning up is a *good* thing?" Jessica's voice was sharp and waspish. "Well, I can tell whose side you're on."

"It's standard practice. Georgia's school has a duty of care to every single student. Would you rather they ignore that one of their children has been missing for weeks?"

"Of course not. But they know what's going on, what we're going through."

Emily heaved her shoulders, pressed her foot down on the accelerator a little harder. "What did Children's Services say?"

"They said she needs to go back to school. *Today.* Or things will get more serious."

The road turned and Emily turned the car with it, straight into halted traffic and yet another red light.

"Perhaps Georgia should go back to school. I know you're worried and that's completely understandable, but maybe it would be good for her—to be with her friends, to get back into a normal routine. The same goes for you—wouldn't you be better off returning to work instead of driving yourself mad at home?"

"How safe is she going to be? We still don't know who's behind all this. What if they're still watching us? What if they find a way to get into the school?"

"Most schools in this country have good security measures. Locked gates during lesson times. Key fobs. Staff IDs. Electronic doors. And I'm sure that under the circumstances Georgia's teachers will double down on making sure she's safe. They're not your enemy, Jessica. They want what's best for your daughter, just like you do."

The lights changed. The traffic got going again. Jessica was quiet, the phone line crackling.

"Are you still there?" Emily asked.

"You sound just like Children's Services." Defeat weighed down Jessica's voice.

"That's because I want what's best for Georgia, too. And in a past life, believe it or not, I used to be a teacher."

"Really? How the hell does a schoolteacher end up becoming a private investigator?"

Emily's voice caught in her throat. She turned the vehicle onto a quieter road. "It's a story for another time. Look, you can drive Georgia to school, the teachers can meet you and take her in—and then return her to you in the playground at home time. She'll be perfectly safe. What's more, she'll thank you for it."

"And if I don't?" Jessica's voice trembled through the speakers. "If I decide it's not safe for her?"

"Then you can expect Children's Services to investigate further, which will only complicate things, and it certainly won't help your case against the Fishers."

Silence. A large building was coming into view. Emily stared at it, anxiety making her stomach squirm.

"Georgia will be fine," she said.

"Can you promise that?"

"I—" An image flashed in Emily's mind: a tiny, broken figure lying face down in the playground, a dark pool of blood widening in a growing circle. "She'll be fine. Completely safe."

More silence on the line. The building was growing larger, looming in the near distance.

"Okay," Jessica said at last. "We'll try today. But if there's the smallest sign of anything wrong, I'm pulling her out again, Children's Services be damned."

"Okay. That's good. You're doing the right thing."

"I hope so," Jessica replied. "How about you? Have you discovered anything yet?"

"The cameras were quiet all weekend, but I'm looking into a few leads."

"Oh? To do with investigating The Witness or to do with investigating me?"

The building was filling the windscreen now. Emily stared up at its imposing towers and high walls topped with barbed wire. She slowed the car as she approached a security barrier and tall gates beyond.

"Emily? Are you there?"

"Just some leads," she said, half-listening. "Nothing I can talk about right now."

"You know you can ask me anything you want to. I told you I'd cooperate without you having to dig things up."

She was coming up to the barrier fast, where uniformed guards stood on duty. "I have to go."

"But—"

"Good luck with the school. It's all going to be fine."

Emily said goodbye and hung up. She slowed the car to a halt. One of the guards approached and signalled for her to roll down the window.

Smiling nervously, Emily removed her investigator's licence from her wallet and held it up.

"Emily Swanson, Braithwaite Investigations," she said. "I'm here for visiting hours?"

The security guard stared at her credentials, a bemused smile twitching on his lips. Returning to the security booth, he took his time to check the records, then pressed a button. Slowly the barrier lifted and he waved Emily through. She drove on, heading for the visitor car park and the mountainous slab of concrete, bars and wires that was Stollingbrook Prison.

25

STANDING ON THE DOORSTEP, her breaths coming fast and shallow, Jessica scanned the street. It was quiet, no signs of movement except for a stray piece of litter being pushed along the pavement by a breeze. Swallowing nervously, she glanced back over her shoulder into the hall, where Georgia stood, blue winter coat over her grey school uniform and thick winter tights. She was silent, staring at her mother in equal measures of excitement and nerves.

"Ready?" Jessica asked, instantly hearing the fear in her own voice. She pushed it down, forced a smile to her lips, but it was too late. A dark frown surfaced on Georgia's brow as she watched her mother, her eyes growing wide and round.

"If we leave now, you'll make it in time for lunch." Jessica wiggled her fingers, surprised by Georgia's reaction. For days all she'd wanted was to return to school, but now she was reluctant. Frightened, even, staring past her mother at the open doorway and the street beyond, as if a monster were lurking behind the hedgerows.

"We go together," Jessica told her. "I'll hold your hand all the way to the car. And when we get to school, I'll take you to Mrs Wernick myself."

Georgia hesitated. Slowly, she walked forward. Jessica clamped her fingers around her daughter's hand, then loosened her grip when she saw her wince in pain.

"Everything's going to be fine," she said, forcing another smile. She glanced up at the camera pointed down at her head. A small red light winked at her reassuringly. Still holding onto Georgia's hand, she locked the door, pulled on the handle twice.

"Ready?"

Georgia's eyes were fixed on the street. She nodded.

They made their way down the drive, their eyes shifting left and right, hands clamped together. They reached the gate and slid to a halt. It had been weeks since Jessica had left the house, even ordering the food shopping online and having it delivered to the house. Now, by opening the gate she felt like she was letting in danger. But it had to be done. Children's Services were insisting Georgia had to go to school, that if she didn't, a formal investigation would be initiated and things would escalate. Jessica had suggested home-schooling as an alternative, but the horrified expression on Georgia's face had told her all she needed to know.

She stared at the gate, then at the security camera sitting in the Rowan tree. Emily Swanson had told her the school would be safe. That letting Georgia return to the normal world would be good for her. As Jessica swung open the gate, she hoped that Emily was right.

The car was just up ahead, a battered old red Ford Escort that she'd purchased with her own dwindling funds after the courts had confiscated the Mercedes. The Ford was all that she'd been able to afford and she'd deliberately kept it parked on the road instead of the drive, so the neighbours couldn't further relish in her family's downfall. As they approached the vehicle, Jessica stared at the car's chipped and dented paintwork. It seemed appropriate somehow—a reminder of all that they had once had, now stolen from them just like her husband had stolen from others.

"Okay?" she asked her daughter, whose grip on her hand was growing tighter by the second. Georgia said nothing, kept her eyes fixed on the car.

Now they were by the passenger door. Jessica shot a glance both ways down the street. Two elderly women were walking away on the other side of the road. A cat tiptoed its way along a garden wall, fur bristling in the breeze.

Jessica fumbled with the car keys, pressed the unlock button with a trembling thumb, and wrenched open the back passenger door. Hustling Georgia inside, she pulled the seatbelt across her thin body and locked it into place.

"There you go. See? We're safe and sound."

As Jessica shut the door, movement blurred at the corner of the eye. She snapped her head up and whirled around.

A woman in her early thirties was approaching with a gurgling toddler in a pushchair. She smiled as she strolled by. Jessica tried to return the smile but all she managed was a grimace.

"Get a grip," she whispered to herself, as she stepped off the kerb and onto the road. Wrenching open the driver's door, she checked the street one last time and climbed inside.

Trembling fingers inserted the key into the ignition, then she adjusted the rear-view mirror.

"Everything all right?" she asked her daughter's reflection.

Georgia nodded.

"Good. Then let's get you to school."

———

Located at the end of a residential street, Oak Tree Primary School was just a five-minute drive from Raven Road—walking distance, even, for families who weren't living in fear. Lunchtime had already begun, and the playground was filled with scores of young children, dressed in winter coats and bobble hats, all running and screaming at the top of their lungs.

Jessica found a parking space on the already cramped road and pulled in. Now that they were here, Georgia's nervousness had quickly dissipated. She stared keenly through the passenger window, eyes bright with excitement. This was good, Jessica thought. If only she could feel the same.

Checking the rear-view mirror, then the wing mirrors, she scoured the empty street for signs of danger. Next, she focused her attention on the tall chain-link fence that surrounded the school. At over three metres tall, it would be difficult to climb, but perhaps not impossible to someone who was strong, agile, and determined.

Her eyes shifted to the towering school gate, its black, wrought iron bars topped with sharp spears. As Emily had predicted, the gate was locked.

Good, she thought. Guilt pinched at her chest as she tried not to think about the weeks that she'd kept Georgia locked up in the darkness of their home.

She twisted around to see her daughter had already unfastened her seatbelt. "Are you ready?"

Georgia nodded emphatically and reached for the door handle.

They got out of the vehicle and crossed the road. As they approached the gate, the din of the playground became a deafening waterfall of noise. Jessica winced, tightening her grip on her daughter's hand. She examined the solid electronic lock securing the gate, then glanced up at the security camera watching them from above.

She pressed the intercom button. As she waited for a response, she saw two women approaching the school on her left. She vaguely recognised them from the playground at home time—parents of children in Georgia's year group. They noticed her as they drew nearer, then slowed down and whispered to each other. Jessica turned away, felt her face heating up despite the cold. The sudden urge to run was overwhelming. How easy it would be to turn around and drive back to the safety of the house, where no one stared and no one pointed. But the intercom was buzzing. The gate was unlocking and swinging open. The two parents brushed past Jessica and into the playground, shooting accusatory looks over their shoulders. She stood frozen to the spot.

"Come on, Mum." Georgia's voice rose above the noise, desperate and hopeful.

She pulled on Jessica's hand, but Jessica resisted. Georgia stared up at her mother, confusion and disappointment dulling her eyes. Slowly, Jessica forced one foot forward, then another, until she had cleared the gate. She watched as it swung shut behind her and the electric lock snapped into place. The sound made her feel safe. Secure.

"Georgia! You're back!" Two little girls came running towards them. Georgia tore away from her mother's grip and the three children collided, arms wrapping around each other as they jumped up and down. Jessica's heart melted. And then it shattered.

What had she done to her daughter? To her family? She'd been trying to protect them, but now she felt as though all she'd achieved was to drive them further into anguish. Jessica watched her daughter and her friends laughing together, and for the first time in months, she smiled a genuine smile. Perhaps Emily was right after all. Perhaps everything was going to be fine.

A large, middle-aged woman with dark hair in a ponytail and a determined stride was wading through the sea of school children and heading straight for Georgia. Jessica tensed, her heart crashing in her chest as the woman came closer. Then she relaxed, expelling a sigh of relief. It was just Ms Craven, the teaching assistant from Georgia's class. She came to a halt beside Georgia and her friends, smiling warmly as she spoke to them before looking up in Jessica's direction.

"Hello, Jessica," Ms Craven said. "How lovely to see you. Mrs Wernick's at a lunchtime staff meeting, but she's asked me to bring Georgia straight inside. Has she eaten?"

Jessica avoided the teaching assistant's gaze, instead focusing on her daughter. "Not yet."

Ms Craven wrapped a protective arm around Georgia. "Well, don't worry. I'll make sure she goes straight into the dining hall. If you could check in with Mrs Wernick at home time, that would be great."

The woman smiled again, but Jessica couldn't bring herself to look at her or any other adult in the playground.

"You'll be all right?" she said to Georgia, whose excitement had faded, replaced by worried glances. The girl nodded. Then Ms Craven was whisking her away, with her two friends bobbing along beside. Jessica watched them reach the door. She saw Georgia stop and flash another anxious look over her shoulder.

"See you at home time!" Jessica called out, only too aware of the trembling in her voice.

Then Georgia was gone, swallowed up by the school building. Jessica stood there for a minute longer, eyes fixed on the closed door, fighting the urge to race inside and pull her daughter back out.

"It's going to be fine," she told herself. "Everything is going to be just fine."

26

As EMILY WALKED SINGLE FILE, hugging the building as they left the visitor centre and crossed a cold concrete yard, she stole little glances at the adults and children among the group, all walking in subdued silence with prison officers to the front and back. There were mothers and fathers, wives and girlfriends, brothers and sisters, sons and daughters, all here to visit a loved one who had committed a crime.

Upon arrival, Emily had been stripped of her belongings except for her ID, subjected to a body search, then made to wait for what seemed like an unnecessary length of time. Although she knew it was standard protocol, she'd found the experience uncomfortable and invasive, yet these families had to endure it every time they visited. It was a necessary evil, she supposed, rewarded by seeing someone you loved.

Now they were being filed through another door and along a stark white corridor towards the visitor's room. The children bristled with anticipation of seeing their fathers. Some of the adults looked less enthused, anxious even, and Emily could understand why. The atmosphere was oppressive, the harshness of the overhead lighting exposing every nerve and worry. And being here, surrounded by high walls and locked doors and security cameras, being herded along by uniformed guards, Emily almost felt like a prisoner herself.

They'd reached the end of the corridor. One of the officers pushed open a door and welcomed the visitors in. They stepped into a large, brightly coloured room that looked more like an office floor than the dank, concrete space that Emily had imagined in her head. The prisoners sat at individual tables, bright red tabards over jeans and sweatshirts, their faces lighting up with smiles as their loved ones joined them. The officers present stood back against the walls, giving families space and a little privacy.

As the air came alive with chatter, Emily moved further into the room, until she spied Wesley Harris, who was sitting alone, fingers drumming on the table as he slowly met her gaze. Until now, the idea of meeting the man had filled her with intimidation, but as she approached, she could see that the short time he'd spent on remand had already drained the life from him. Photographs of Wesley Harris had presented a tall, toned man with a strong posture, tanned skin, and a smile that bordered on arrogance. But the man before her was hunched and thin, with a pale, drawn complexion and eyes that darted about like bees trapped in a jar.

"Wesley Harris? I'm Emily Swanson. Thank you for agreeing to see me."

Sitting down, she held out a hand, which he stared at but made no move to shake. Instead his eyes shifted from her face, to her chest, and back up again.

"I must say," he said, a smile cracking his dry lips, "I was expecting Columbo, but I'll take Charlie's Angels any day."

Emily shifted in her seat and cleared her throat. "If only private investigation were that glamorous. I wanted to talk to you about the letters your wife has been receiving, written by someone calling themselves The Witness. I wanted to ask if you know anything that could help me identify who's behind them."

Wesley Harris leaned back on the chair and gazed at her for a long while. "What makes you so sure I'd know anything at all?"

"I don't. That's why I'm asking." Emily held his gaze until she felt his eyes penetrate her skull. She turned away for a second, fixing her attention on a woman in her mid-twenties and a little boy who were visiting a young man barely out of his teens. Wesley's gravelly voice pulled her back.

"Who do you work for?"

"Braithwaite Investigations."

"I mean who hired you? Because I know it wasn't my wife. She doesn't have the money."

"Who hired me isn't important," Emily said. "What's happening to your family is."

"All the same, someone's paying you to ask questions. So if you're here to cause trouble for my family, you won't be getting any answers from me."

Glaring at her, Wesley pushed his seat back an inch and tried to attract the attention of a guard.

"I'm not here to cause trouble, Mr Harris. If anything, I'm trying to help," Emily said quickly. "The people who hired me believe your wife is responsible for the letters, that it's a scam to make as much money as she can before the government takes your house. But I don't believe that. I believe someone is trying to scare Jessica and the children. Maybe even do them harm."

Wesley was quiet for a moment, watching her through scrutinising eyes.

"That doesn't make sense to me," he said. "You don't know my family. They mean nothing to you. So why would you want to help them when someone else is paying you to drag them through the dirt?"

Emily leaned forward. "Because believe it or not, people's lives are worth more than money; stolen or otherwise. Your wife is in trouble, Mr Harris. Your children, too. And they have no one else to turn to."

A sly smile spread across the man's face. "Is that a dig at me?"

"Not a dig, an observation. You're not the only one living inside a prison, Mr Harris. Jessica and the children have been living in fear for weeks now, too afraid to open the blinds because of who they might see peering in. They can't go on like that. They'll lose their minds. Poor Georgia is—"

Emily cut herself off and stared at the table. She was saying too much, letting her emotions get the better of her.

"Poor Georgia is what?" Wesley said, all traces of amusement gone from his face. Now he looked like a concerned father worrying about his daughter.

Emily glanced up. "Your family needs your help, Mr Harris."

"Break me out of here and I'll see what I can do."

"You can still help. Why don't you tell me who you think could be behind the letters and the other incidents? One of the clients you stole from, perhaps?"

"Incidents? I thought it was just a few letters."

Of course, Emily thought. Jessica hadn't contacted her husband in weeks, which meant he only knew half of what had been happening to his family. Sucking in a breath, she told him about the other strange occurrences, including the hideous gift box of spiders. She knew it wasn't her place, that if Jessica found out she'd be furious, but if Harris knew something, prodding at his emotions might make him talk.

The man was quiet, his fingers gripping the table edge. Emily sat back, watching him.

"Most of the people I stole from were rich, middle-aged men with paunches, who played golf on Sundays and cheated on their wives during the week," he said. "I doubt any one of them would have the spine or the creativity to go after my family." He paused to glance at the fathers and children around the room, and Emily saw him wince. She found herself pitying the man, but only for a moment.

"So you're saying you don't think it's any of them?"

Wesley stared at her, his smug smile slowly returning to rub against her nerves. "What I stole from them was a pittance in comparison to what they've amassed. Oh, I'm sure it caused them a minor annoyance, but no more than a bee sting. Eventually bee stings fade."

"I see. Anyone else? Perhaps a criminal connection you've inadvertently upset?"

"Who do you think I am? The Godfather?" Now, Wesley was staring at her, sizing her up. "How does someone like you become a private investigator? You seem, I don't know . . . a little wet behind the ears. Have you been doing this long?"

Emily glared at him. "Long enough."

He smiled, exposing his teeth, but his eyes remained pained and haunted. "You know, instead of asking me about clients and imaginary criminals, maybe you should ask me about my wife."

Across the room, one of the visitors—a woman in her fifties—had started to cry. On the opposite side of the table, the young prisoner flinched as if he'd been slapped. Then he stiffened, his expression hardening; an expression he'd no doubt come to learn in prison.

"What do you mean by that?" Emily asked.

"Just that maybe Jessica isn't the helpless, innocent victim you want her to be." Wesley leaned forward, conspiratorially. "You honestly think she had no idea where the money came from? Oh, I wasn't poor, don't get me wrong, but my salary didn't make me Saint-Tropez rich and Jessica knew it. Yet she didn't bat an eyelid when I brought her fancy clothes and expensive jewellery, or when we did eventually make it to Saint-Tropez."

Wesley flashed another full-toothed smile.

"I haven't seen my kids in over a month. That bitch won't bring them to visit. What kind of a mother stops her children from seeing their father?"

Anger boiled Emily's insides as she flattened her palms against her sides. "The kind who wants to protect them from criminals."

His smile vanished as he tipped his head towards a guard, signalling that the conversation was over.

"Nice to meet you, Miss Private Investigator," he said, barely glancing at her now. "Tell Jessica I want to see my kids. They're mine. They belong to me."

Then he was gone, escorted away by one of the guards, while Emily sat, red-faced and fuming.

27

FROM HER POSITION behind the steering wheel, Jessica watched the gathering crowd of parents at the school gates with growing unease. She'd been sitting here for two hours now, after spending most of the day obsessively watching the camera feeds in between manic bursts of housework. It had been a long time since she'd spent time alone in the house and she had found herself feeling desperately isolated, the walls closing in on her as she grew increasingly worried about Georgia. By the time the afternoon had come around, she'd called the school three times and had only succeeded in irritating the office staff. Now here she was, waiting for the end of the school day and trying not to lose her mind.

The other parents were all gathered around, some of them chatting and laughing together, while others waited quietly alone. None seemed aware that they were being watched. Jessica was an outsider to them, she knew that. After moving here, she'd barely had time to introduce herself or get to know some of the other families before her husband's arrest had been splashed all over the newspapers. Then it was too late. She was married to a criminal and therefore not to be trusted. It still shocked her how many of the other parents had judged her so harshly. Only a handful continued to talk to her, most of whom were deemed outsiders themselves. But even those budding relationships had eventually fallen by the wayside. Friendships needed at least two people to keep them alive, but Jessica had withdrawn from the world long before the letters. And this—a hive of parents on one side of the road and Jessica on the other—was the price.

Yet it was a price she would willingly pay over and over again if it meant keeping her children safe.

From somewhere inside the school building an electronic bell rang. The tall, imposing gate unlocked and slowly swung open. The parents swarmed, buzzing through the gates and into the playground. Jessica reached for the door, her fingers hovering over the handle. She waited until most of the crowd had thinned, then left the confines of the car and crossed the road, eyes swinging left to right.

More parents were hurrying up the street, some of them noticing her as they approached. Heart racing, eyes fixed on the ground, Jessica stepped through the gate.

It had already begun. The whispering and the pointing, her name being passed along the crowd like a hushed Mexican wave. She risked a glance upwards and saw a multitude of faces staring back. Then doors were opening and the children were flooding out of the building, and suddenly Jessica was no longer of interest. Parents surged forwards, seeking out their sons and daughters. She should have felt relief, but all she felt was rising panic as she searched the crowds for her daughter.

Where was she?

Her eyes found Georgia's teacher, Mrs Wernick, who looked too young to be in charge of a class of thirty vulnerable children.

She was leading Georgia's cohort of classmates to their usual collection point next to the basketball court. Now she was assembling them into a neat line and doing a headcount. Jessica worked her way towards them, scanning the children's faces as she moved, her breaths growing thin and fast.

She wasn't there. *Georgia wasn't there.*

Jessica rushed forward, eyes bulging, mouth agape. Mrs Wernick turned and spotted her almost immediately, her smile faltering for a second.

"Where is she?" Jessica said, a little too forcefully. "Where's Georgia?"

Before Mrs Wernick could reply, a cry rang out above the din. "Mummy!"

Jessica spun around to see Georgia running from the school building with Ms Craven, the teaching assistant, struggling to catch her up.

"She forgot her coat," Mrs Wernick said softly. "Ms Craven took her to get it."

Jessica was dizzy with relief. She opened her arms and Georgia ran into them, her smile a beam of sunlight, her complexion full of colour. Jessica pulled her daughter into her embrace, at once thankful and wracked with guilt.

"Did you have a good day?" she asked.

Georgia nodded enthusiastically. "We did painting and maths, and I won the spelling quiz!"

"Ten out of ten," Mrs Wernick smiled. "We're glad to have Georgia back. But I think Georgia and her friends are happier still." She leaned in closer and placed a hand on Jessica's shoulder. "We took good care of her. She was perfectly safe."

Jessica smiled but couldn't meet her gaze. "Thank you."

"You're welcome. We'll see you tomorrow?"

She watched her daughter chat excitedly with her friend, Adora. It had been weeks since she'd seen her so alive.

"We'll see you tomorrow," she said, meeting the teacher's gaze.

Mrs Wernick smiled and gave her another affectionate squeeze, then turned around to talk to another parent.

People were still staring, still whispering, but Jessica barely acknowledged them. She watched the way her daughter's face lit up as she and Adora giggled and chatted, and it was suddenly all that she needed.

"Jessica? Is that you?"

An olive skinned woman with dark wavy hair was smiling at her. Adora's mother, Delfina.

Jessica opened her mouth to speak but the words wouldn't come out.

"It's nice to see you," Delfina said, in her warm, Spanish accent. "Adora's been missing Georgia like crazy. How are you doing?"

Delfina had been one of the few parents who hadn't branded her a criminal's wife, yet Jessica had still abandoned their friendship out of fear. Now her face flushed red.

"I'm fine," she managed to say. "We've had a rough couple of months, but we're getting there."

Delfina shot her another warm smile. "It can't be easy going through the shit you have, especially with these piranhas on your back." She nodded at a group of mothers who were huddled together as they stared and stage-whispered. "But screw them. You give me a call whenever you feel like it, even if it's just to scream and shout."

Jessica smiled, simultaneously embarrassed and grateful for

the woman's words. A tug on her sleeve pulled her gaze downward and she saw Georgia beaming up at her.

"Adora said I can have a sleepover if I want. Can I, Mum?"

"I'm not sure that—"

"Please, Mum! Pleeease!"

Jessica stared at her daughter, already seeing the sparkle in her eyes starting to dull.

"Well, Adora should check with her mother before inviting people over," Delfina said, winking at Jessica. Adora, who until now had been all smiles and giggles, shot out her lower lip. "Soon, okay, honey? Maybe Georgia's mum can come along too and us mums will have a pyjama party of our own."

Jessica smiled, then returned her gaze to her daughter. "Come on, we'd better get home."

28

As EMILY HEADED towards the M25, with the intention of returning to Raven Road, she found herself increasingly troubled by her visit to Stollingbrook Prison. With just a few deliberately chosen words, Wesley Harris had managed to plant a seed in her mind that was already sprouting tendrils of doubt, making her question Jessica's innocence. But were they the bitter words of an imprisoned man who had not seen his children in weeks? Or was he speaking the truth? Harris had seemed genuinely wounded when he'd talked about his children, but then he'd gone on to describe them as if they were mere possessions. Emily didn't know what to believe, but one thing was clear. Harris had been steering the wheel of the marital ship, but now the balance of power had shifted in Jessica's favour—and she was using it to hurt him, denying him the right to see his own flesh and blood.

Was it because she was angry for having her comfortable lifestyle torn away? Or was Jessica simply trying to protect her children from further harm?

"Facts," Emily muttered unhappily. It was becoming painfully clear that she didn't have many.

She wished she could shake off the bad mood that was clinging to her, but the oppressive hour she had spent trapped within the confines of the prison had somehow seeped into her bones. Perhaps seeing Jessica right now was a bad idea; her emotions were running high and likely to cloud her judgement if she decided to confront her. And yet, she felt she'd told so many white lies now that time was fast becoming her enemy. If she didn't uncover the identity of The Witness soon, Erica Braithwaite and the Fishers would find out they'd been deceived.

Screw it. It was the weekend. Even private investigators were entitled to a day off. Perhaps if she spent some time with the letters, she'd find something hidden between their words; a thread that she could pull on to unravel the truth.

Turning off at the next junction, she pressed her foot down on the accelerator, dreaming of a hot bath and an early night as she headed home.

29

A WEEK PASSED WITHOUT EVENT. The temperature grew colder, the sky turning cotton-white, the air thin and biting. At 57 Raven Road, some equilibrium had returned. For the first time in months, Georgia smiled and laughed about the house like a normal eight-year-old child, her complexion restored to a healthier colour. Jessica had taken the dramatic leap of returning to work three days ago. She'd been deeply reluctant at first, but a call from her boss had given her little choice—she'd taken all the compassionate leave they could allow, and unless she returned to work, they'd have to make some difficult decisions about her future at the company.

Her first day back had been filled with nerves. After dropping Georgia off at school, she'd found herself feeling disoriented and worrying about her daughter's welfare and what might be happening at the house. Emily had provided her with a phone app from which to view the camera feeds, but although she still checked them several times a day, her focus was slowly shifting to the rhythms and routines of her job. Perhaps all the trouble they'd experienced had finally come to an end, the cameras and Emily's presence a successful deterrent.

Only Ethan hadn't changed. He remained sullen and mono-syllabic, coming home late from college and spending unhealthy amounts of time alone in his room. Twice, Jessica had knocked on his door in the evenings to discover he'd slipped out of the house. When she'd seen his grainy image returning on the camera feeds later, she'd resisted confronting him. Ethan had been through enough lately, and she had to take some responsibility for that. Besides, he was seventeen years old—what seventeen-year-old didn't sneak out sometimes?

Today was Wednesday. Jessica had taken Georgia to school, where a handful of the other parents had started to acknowledge her presence, even going as far to smile and nod, then she'd walked the ten minute journey to the office. Now she sat in front of the computer at the reception desk, trawling through emails. Occasionally, her eyes drifted up to stare through the glass front of the office at the busy street beyond, then down to her mobile phone, the temptation to check the camera feeds calling to her like a Siren. But she found herself resisting the lure. Emily was right—the more she gave into temptation, the more she fed her fears. And Jessica was tired of being afraid.

One day soon, she hoped that life would return to normal. Whatever that meant now. But with Wesley's impending court case and her own civil lawsuit against the Fishers, normality still seemed like a distant dream. More than once this week, she'd been tempted to drop the lawsuit; the legal fees were already eating through what money she had left. But with her family's financial security swinging in the wind like a hangman's noose, what else could she do to protect her children?

She glanced around the office. Working as a receptionist for a recruitment agency was not exactly her dream job. It paid the bills—just—but she found little satisfaction in answering phone calls and replying to emails. Not that she had any idea of what else she might do. She'd met Wesley when they were still at school, had given birth to Ethan at the age of eighteen. She'd loved being a stay-at-home mother, caring for Ethan's every need, being there for his first words, his first step, his first smile. When he'd reached school age, she'd wanted to return to work, but by then Wesley was making waves on the financial scene and he'd showered her in gifts and clothes and fancy holidays.

When she'd eventually grown tired of trying to fill her days, she'd looked into returning to work once more. But Wesley had decided they should have another child, so along came Georgia. It wasn't until years later that Jessica had realised it had all been by design; one that she'd been completely seduced by. Wesley wanted her to be kept a woman. She was his possession. A trophy. Something to show off at dinner parties and functions. Just like one of his cars. What a sham, she thought. Just like everything else connected to her husband.

So no, this job wasn't her dream job, but it was hers by choice.

"Jessica?"

The voice, rich and melodic, startled her. She looked up to see it belonged to a handsome, bearded man in his mid-thirties with soft, smiling eyes. Zach from Accounts.

"I heard you were back," he said, his face crumpling with concern as he spoke. Genuine concern, she noted. "It's good to see you. How have you been?"

Jessica smiled. "We're getting back to normal. Or at least, trying to."

"Good to hear it. Sounds like you've been through a tough

time."

Her mind flashed with newspaper headlines and snapshots of her husband's arrest. Face flushing, she nodded and glanced away at the computer screen. She could feel Zach's eyes still on her skin.

"Well, I for one am glad to see you back," he said, his voice soft and reassuring. "And if there's anything I can do to make your return easier, I'm on extension 213."

Grinning, he made a phone signal with his hand.

Jessica's face was burning. "Were you just stopping by to say hello or is there something you need?" She winced, not meaning for the words to sound so sharp, but it had been a long time since someone had shown her genuine concern without then passing judgement. Except for Emily Swanson, she supposed. She forced a smile to her lips, meeting Zach's confused gaze.

"Just saying hi." His smile crumbled a little and they stared at each other, both suddenly awkward, yet both seemingly unable to look away.

The ensuing quiet was broken by another voice.

"I hope I'm not interrupting something?"

Alison Middleton, senior manager, was leaning out through a half-open door on the left, staring at the two of them with sharp, observant eyes. Zach took a step back, straightened his tie. Jessica's gaze flicked back to the screen.

"Just a reminder about the team meeting at three-thirty. Jess, you good to take the minutes?"

Jessica's breath caught in her throat. Her eyes shifted from her boss to her phone. "Three-thirty? I thought that—"

"We've swapped things around while you've been away," Alison said, following her gaze. It's not a problem, is it?"

Zach cleared his throat. "I should probably get back to work.

See you later, Jess."

Flashing her a smile, he drifted off to the right and vanished through one of several doors. Jessica turned back to Alison, who was still leaning half in, half out of the doorway, as if she simply didn't have time to make a full entrance.

"My daughter. I usually finish at three to pick her up from school."

"Which is fine every other day of the week. Sorry, I should have mentioned it before you came back. Is there someone else who could pick her up? Your son, perhaps? Or does the school have some sort of afterhours club?"

Jessica was still staring at her phone, heart racing in her chest. "Well I—It's just that . . ."

She glanced up at her boss, whose sharp eyes were piercing right through her. Now Alison moved fully into the room, the door swinging shut behind her as she moved up to the desk and dropped her voice to a hush. "It would be really good if you could stick around this afternoon. You know, with it being your first week back. I do appreciate you've been through a lot recently, but things have changed here and we're trying to run a tighter ship, which means we need *everyone* on board."

Panic and irritation were churning Jessica's stomach. Alison was talking as if she'd been away for months, not a few weeks, and she didn't like the accusatory tone of her voice—it was all too familiar: guilty by association. She pressed her fingers against the surface of the table. Her mind raced. Right now, this job was all that stood between her family and the breadline. Georgia had been going to school for a week without incident. And Ethan finished at two on Wednesday afternoons . . .

Alison was staring at her, growing impatient.

"I'll give Ethan a call," Jessica said, aware that her voice was trembling slightly.

Alison smiled. "Great. We'll be done by five so he won't have to watch her for too long."

When she was gone, Jessica picked up the phone and dialled Ethan's number. To her surprise, he answered right away.

"Why aren't you in class?"

"It's break time," he said, and she could almost hear his eye-roll. "What do you want?"

"I need you to pick up your sister from school this afternoon. I have a meeting."

"No way. I have plans."

"What kind of plans?"

"Nothing. Just meeting the guys."

"Well if it's nothing, you won't mind putting it off for another day. Come on Ethan, I never ask you to pick up your sister. But I need you today, just this one time."

She waited as he huffed and puffed and swore under his breath. "Please, Ethan. I'll be home just after five."

"Fine, I'll be there," he said at last.

"Thank you. She gets out at three-twenty so you need to be there at least five—"

"I said, I'll be there."

"Okay. Thanks. I owe you one."

"Whatever."

Ethan hung up. She should have felt relieved, but the anxiety in Jessica's stomach was turning in on itself, twisting and knotting. She glanced over the reception desk, watching people walk by. She swiped the screen of her phone, brought up the camera feeds, and reviewed the morning's footage. Nothing. Just passing cars and the occasional flitting bird. She hoped it stayed that way.

30

WHILE THE HARRIS family was cautiously testing out a semblance of normality, Emily had been busy fending off Erica Braithwaite's over-inquisitiveness and dodging Meredith Fisher's mounting frustrations. It had taken almost a week to investigate the fifty investors Wesley Harris had stolen from, running background checks and searching for criminal convictions or connections, only to learn that all fifty were wealthy enough that the embezzled money had barely made a dent in their bank accounts. Which meant that Harris had been right—it was unlikely any of them would be bothered enough to devise something as elaborate as The Witness just to exact a little revenge. Add to the fact that the letters had also incriminated the Fishers, it was not an unreasonable move to strike the investors from the suspect list. Which is exactly what Emily did.

Next, she moved onto the residents of Raven Road. Accessing the electoral roll, she'd gone house to house, scrutinising each resident, searching criminal records, social media accounts, and a whole host of other resources that had all returned the same result: except for Reginald Collins of number fourteen, who had several points on his driver's licence caused by speeding, Meredith Fisher had been right—the street was filled with outwardly good people, made up of families and the elderly, who might not be happy about the presence of the Harris family, but were unlikely to cause them harm.

While she didn't remove them from the suspect list entirely —outwardly good people could also harbour cruel intentions— Emily moved the residents of Raven Road down a few notches.

There were other people still to run checks on—co-workers, extended family members—but the Harrises still remained in pole position; Wesley in first place, closely followed by Jessica. It troubled Emily that she had been unable to move Jessica down the list, not even by a single notch. Was there a chance she was wrong about the woman? Or was the doubt Wesley had instilled in her mind now clouding her judgement?

"Facts," she reminded herself.

If only she had some. With the suspect list dwindling and with little else to go on—DC Ryan had let her know that the gift box had come back clean—Emily was fast running out of options.

31

THE REST of the day had passed sluggishly. Jessica had found herself distracted, her attention torn between her work and her mobile phone, her anxiety growing with each passing minute. It was three o'clock. Ethan would have finished for the day, and now he would be leaving college on his way to pick up Georgia from school.

What if he's forgotten?

Anxiety somersaulted in her stomach. Picking up her phone, she swiped away from the camera feeds, which had revealed nothing out of the ordinary, and dialled Ethan's number. The line connected and started to ring. Only this time, it continued to do so.

Jessica shut her eyes and waited for his voicemail message to kick in. *It's fine,* she told herself. *He's on his way. He's probably sick of you calling.*

The sound of her son's recorded voice played in her ear: "It's Ethan. Leave a message or whatever."

"It's me," she said, trying to keep her voice steady. "I hope you're on the way to your sister. You have remembered to pick her up, haven't you? You need to be there at three-twenty, five minutes before if you can. Call me to let me know you haven't forgotten."

She hung up, realised she was breathing fast and shallow. *You're overreacting. If Ethan's late, the school will keep hold of her. They know he's coming to pick her up.*

Jessica glanced over the desk at the glass front of the office, where passers-by sauntered along the high street. She watched as a man on a motorbike pulled up outside, noting the storage box on the back of the bike. It was the courier company they used. She recognised the logo. Now the man was climbing off the bike and opening the box. Jessica glanced down at her phone screen. Ethan hadn't called her back. With trembling fingers she quickly tapped out a text message—*Please let me know you're on your way to your sister*—and pressed 'send'.

The courier was pushing open the main door, letting in the din of car engines and voices, and the choke of traffic fumes. He pulled off his helmet as he made his way towards the front desk, a smile on his face.

"Special delivery," he said, as he reached the counter. "How are you doing? Haven't seen you here for a while."

Jessica smiled, but struggled to hold it there. She recognised the man. He'd delivered packages here countless times, but panic was clouding her memory, making her forget his name.

"I'm fine," she said. "You need a signature?"

The courier nodded, passing her a handheld device. Jessica wrote her signature and handed back the device, just as her mobile phone vibrated with a text message alert. Ignoring the courier, she swiped a finger across the screen and read Ethan's message:

I'm almost at the school. Stop being a freak.

Relief flooded through her body like a sedative, leaving her limbs soft and spongy.

"Everything okay?" The courier was watching her, eyebrows raised.

Jessica smiled again and this time, managed to hold it. "Fine."

"Well, see you around. Nice to see you back."

The man handed her a letter and turned to leave. She watched him slip his helmet back on as he exited through the door, before picking up the letter to see who it was for.

Blood rushed from Jessica's face. The world fell away as she stared at the familiar handwriting: *To The Harris Family.*

She tried to breathe, but it was as if her throat had closed up and now her heart was hammering against the blockage, trying to smash through it. Somewhere to her left, she saw a door open and Alison Middleton appear in the gap.

"We're just about to get started." The manager's voice sounded far away, as if she were speaking through a hundred walls.

Slowly, robotically, Jessica nodded her head. "I'll—I'll be right there."

Alison disappeared again and Jessica was left alone. She stared at the letter, at the handwriting that seemed to leap off the paper to burn her retinas. Her body was trembling now, nausea threatening to spill from her guts. She glanced up at the glass front, saw the courier pulling away on his motorbike. With shaking fingers, she carefully peeled open the envelope and removed the letter. The paper was the same as always—A5, blue lines, folded neatly in half.

It took her a moment to force herself to look at the words, and even longer to read them. But when she did, her eyes grew round and wide, and her mouth fell open in a silent scream. Before she knew what she was doing, she'd grabbed the letter and shoved it inside her bag. Then she was dashing across the reception floor and rushing out to the street.

As she pushed through the crowds, hands shoving at backs and shoulders, breaths rushing in and out of her lungs, the words replayed in her mind, over and over, taunting her until she could see nothing else.

Heading in the direction of Georgia's school, Jessica pulled out her phone and dialled Emily Swanson's number.

32

THE SCHOOL BELL had rung five minutes ago and now the playground was a roar of chatter. Crowds of parents and children filled the tarmac. Georgia stood in line, trying to peer through the shifting bodies, eyes flicking back towards her dwindling classmates as parents came to take them home. Ethan was supposed to be picking her up; Mrs Wernick had said so at lunchtime. But Ethan wasn't here.

Another of her classmates, Abdul, was being taken away by his mother and father. Now there were only six of them left. Georgia's heart thrummed in her chest. She glanced over her shoulder. Ms Craven was nowhere to be seen. Meanwhile, Mrs Wernick was in the middle of what looked like a heated exchange with Jimmy Rodrick's mother, who was always having a heated exchange with someone. Poor Mrs Wernick, Georgia thought. She was nice and kind, and she had nice stickers to wear on your chest if you did all your homework. She didn't deserve to be shouted at.

Where was Ethan?

A tight feeling was gripping her chest and the top of her

head had started to itch. Through the crowds, she saw Adora and her mother collecting Adora's older brother, Victor. She wished she could go with them instead of waiting here for Ethan. He was always in a bad mood lately, and he almost never wanted to spend time with her, or even talk to her. Once, when they'd lived in the old place, Ethan had drawn comics with her, starring Caesar the Ninja Cat, but now he told her to draw comics by her *fucking-self.*

It was all her dad's fault. If he hadn't broken the law, their family would still be together. Her mother would be happy. Ethan, too.

As Georgia waited for her brother, she thought about her life from before. She missed her old friends. She missed sleepovers and dance class, and horse riding on Saturdays. Since her father had gone away, there'd been no classes at all, and no sleepovers or birthday parties to be invited to. There was just Georgia and her mum and stupid Ethan, who was always in a bad mood. And who was late.

Now there was only Georgia left in her class and another boy, Andy. But his mum was always, always late. Andy's dad was in prison, just like hers. She wondered if that meant that soon, her mother would always be late to pick her up, too. But now Andy's mum was pushing through the crowds, red-faced and sweaty.

"Sorry! So sorry!" she cried between breaths, and Georgia noted that she was saying it to Andy, not Mrs Wernick, which was a good thing because it showed that she cared.

Mrs Wernick turned to smile down at Georgia. "Well, looks like it's just you and me."

Georgia liked the idea of it being just the two of them. For a second, she daydreamed about going to live with her teacher.

She bet Mrs Wernick had a nice house which let in lots of light. She bet she had a dog, and that no one ever got into a bad mood or cried at night-time through the walls. She bet that at Mrs Wernick's house, you didn't even have to play tricks to get what you wanted.

Georgia thought about what she wanted. Until recently, the thing she wanted most was to go back to her old house and her old friends and her old school. But lately, well, this week, she'd decided that she liked her new school after all. And now that she was back with Adora and Stacey and Tracy-Ann, she supposed she didn't need her old friends anymore, either. If only things at home were better. If only her mum could be happy and Ethan could be less angry. It was because of all the bad things that happened. That were still happening. Georgia wondered if she could make them stop. She wondered if she could make all the bad things go away.

She stared up at Mrs Wernick, who was still smiling down at her, her kindness as warm as the sun in the wintry sky. Then she turned and saw Ethan pushing his way through the crowds, his angry, dark eyes fixed on her.

The itchiness at the top of Georgia's head grew more intense, the tightening in her chest unbearable. If only she could make the bad things go away.

"Hello Ethan," Mrs Wernick said. It was funny how her voice sounded like a smile. "Nice to see you. How are you doing?"

Ethan glanced at her, then down at the ground. "I'm fine."

"Everything okay at home?"

He narrowed his eyes, peering through his curtain of lank hair. "Why wouldn't it be?"

Mrs Wernick smiled. Ethan glared at Georgia.

"Come on."

As Georgia followed Ethan out of the emptying playground, she turned to glance over her shoulder and Mrs Wernick gave her a little wave. She was still smiling, but there was something else in her eyes, dampening the light.

"Hurry up," Ethan growled, wrapping one of his large hands around Georgia's wrist and almost yanking her off the ground.

Outside the school gates, he released his hold on her and took off down the street. She hurried behind, trying to keep up with his large strides. She wanted to ask why their mum was working late. She wanted to tell him about the science class they'd had today, where they'd made a homemade volcano out of vinegar and baking soda. But Ethan wasn't interested. He was busy talking on his phone to someone, muttering quietly so she couldn't hear what he was saying. Then he shot a glance back at her, staring at her like she was something nasty stuck to his shoe.

They reached the end of the road and turned left. Finished with his call, Ethan stuck his phone in his pocket and started walking faster.

Georgia was half-skipping, half-running now, afraid that she would be left behind.

Then Ethan was grinding to a halt where this street met the next. He stared at her, tapping his foot while he waited for her to catch up. When she finally did, he pointed to his left.

"Home's that way. You know the way, right?"

Georgia followed his gaze, staring down the long street. She knew the way, but she wasn't supposed to be walking home on her own. She cast a worried glance at him.

"I have to be somewhere," Ethan shrugged.

"Can't I come?"

"No. You've got your key and you know the way. You'll be

home in a few minutes. Watch TV or something until I get back."

Georgia continued to stare at him, a frown making her head ache, her face heating up despite the cold. "But I'm not allowed to go home by myself. Mum said. That's why you had to pick me up."

"Mum's full of shit. You're old enough to start taking care of yourself. Just keep going that way, then turn left at the end and you'll be on our road. I'll be back before Mum gets home."

"But when will that be?"

"By five." He sighed, staring down at her, then looking away. "I won't be long."

"But where are you going?"

"None of your damn business. Just go home. And don't tell mum. If you do, you'll be sorry." He leaned closer, until his face was inches from hers. "*Really* sorry."

Just then, a battered black car pulled up to the kerb a few metres ahead of them. Loud music vibrated through its body and a funny smell wafted through a gap at the top of the passenger window, making Georgia's nose wrinkle.

"Get going," Ethan said, nodding towards the street.

Georgia stood where she was, unmoving, eyes flicking between the car and her brother.

"Get!" he yelled, making her jump out of her skin.

Her lips quivered. Her eyes filled with tears. She didn't want to walk home alone. She didn't want to be in the house, where anyone could break in and get her. But then she remembered the cameras that lady, Emily, had put up. They would protect her. Keep her safe from harm. And they'd also let Mum know that Ethan had made her go home all by herself.

Georgia turned away. Even though she felt scared, she smiled to herself. That will teach him, she thought. Stupid Ethan—too dumb to even remember the cameras.

Ethan was glaring at her. Someone yelled out from the car for him to hurry up.

Georgia started walking, slowly at first, then gathering speed, the fear of being alone pushing her along. When she'd walked a few metres, she glanced over her shoulder and saw Ethan climbing into the car and then the car driving away.

Now, she really was on her own. If anything happened to her, anything bad, it would be all Ethan's fault. She got walking again. At least when she got home, she'd be able to watch cartoons in peace without him trying to change the channel.

Making her way down the street, she spied other children from her school walking home with their parents. Some of them chatted excitedly about their day, while others sucked on sweets and lollipops. Georgia wished she had a lollipop. Or someone to talk to about her day. But she didn't. Instead, she put her head down and sped up, walking faster and faster. At last, she reached the end of the street and turned the corner onto Raven Road. In a couple of minutes, she'd be home.

She slammed straight into a pair of legs.

Georgia caught her breath. Her heart began beating like a hummingbird's wings. Slowly, she stared up at the towering figure that was blotting out the sinking sun. The figure stared down at her, a looming shadow against the cold, white sky.

"Hello Georgia," the figure said, and she felt a chill shiver from the tip of her head all the way down to her toes. "What are you doing out here all alone? It's not safe."

Trembling, Georgia took a slow step back and felt a sudden, desperate need to pee.

"What are you doing here?" she said, her voice a trembling whisper.

The figure leaned down, filling her vision. "A girl your age shouldn't be walking home alone. Here, take my hand. Don't be afraid—I'll walk with you."

Georgia began to cry. Mum was going to be so mad.

33

Before Emily could press the buzzer, the door swung open and Jessica's pale, tear-stained face appeared.

"I'm sorry it took me so long. The traffic was a nightmare," Emily said, as she was ushered through the hall and into the living room. "What's going on?"

"It's Georgia," Jessica cried. "She's missing."

Emily stared at her. "What do you mean, missing?"

"I had to work late. Ethan collected her from school. I told him to bring her straight home, but they didn't make it! There's no sign of them on the cameras and Ethan's not answering his phone."

Before Emily could say something, Jessica pulled an envelope from the bag that was still slung over her shoulder and handed it to her. Trying to keep her breaths steady, she carefully removed the letter and began to read.

Harris Family,

I was pleased to see you opened the blinds so that I may do my duty, serving Him. But He is not appeased. You have angered

Him! The woman who brought cameras into your home—Emily Swanson—she must leave. She is dirtying consecrated ground. Remove her, Jessica Harris or He will exercise His wrath. Your youngest lamb will suffer. She will feel the pain that's waiting behind the walls. He will rip her apart and the well will boil with her blood.

Emily Swanson must leave. She must take her cameras with her so I may continue the watch.

Who am I?

I am The Witness. I am watching you all.

Goosebumps crawled over Emily's flesh. He knew her name.

"This was at the house? Have you checked the cameras?"

She turned to head for the kitchen, where Jessica's laptop would be waiting, but Jessica shot out a hand and gripped her by the arm.

"It arrived at the office this afternoon, by special delivery."

Emily stared at her, mouth hanging open. "Then It has to be someone who knows you've returned to work. Who did you tell?"

"I don't know, I can't think straight." Jessica turned away. "I've told my solicitor, Georgia's school, a couple of the other parents. Obviously my colleagues know."

"What about Wesley?"

"I still haven't spoken to him."

"Extended family?"

Now, she hung her head, avoiding Emily's gaze. "There isn't anyone. I haven't spoken to my parents in years—we fell out after I got pregnant with Ethan. And we haven't heard from any of Wesley's family since his arrest."

Emily watched her pace the room, terrified eyes darting

towards the living room window. "What about me? Who've you told about me?"

"No one. I promised I wouldn't and I've kept my word."

Her mind was racing, making it difficult to process her thoughts. She watched Jessica move back and forth in front of the window like the pendulum of a clock. Last week at the prison, had she let it slip to Wesley that she was helping Jessica? No, she was sure that she hadn't, only telling him that she'd been hired by the Fishers to investigate The Witness. Her eyes returned to the letter.

"This is a threat, right here in black and white," she said. "Whoever's behind this wants me gone, which means I'm getting close to the truth."

"Or you're getting in the way of whatever they're planning," Jessica said, her voice breaking.

Emily nodded. "Call the police. Tell them the kids are missing."

Jessica stopped pacing, her complexion souring, waxen and pale. "I can't."

"Why not? What do you mean? Your children are missing!"

"No, I just—"

Emily pulled her phone from her pocket. "Fine, I'll call them."

She shot Jessica an angry look as she unlocked the screen with a swipe of her thumb, then brought up the keypad and dialled 999.

Jessica lunged forward, grabbing her by the wrist.

"Hey, what the hell are you doing?"

"Please, Emily." Tears were spilling down her face. Her eyes were red and raw. "Please don't call the police!"

Emily stared wildly, her thumb hovering over the call button. "What do you know? What aren't you telling me?"

Jessica shook her head, over and over as the tears streamed in an uncontrollable flow. "I don't want to believe it. I don't want it to be true. But I think Ethan may be The Witness."

Emily glanced down at her phone screen. Slowly, she removed her thumb. "Why do you think that?"

Jessica's body slumped, as if someone had punched her in the stomach. "I've been thinking it for a while. He keeps disappearing. Sneaking out at night and coming back home in the early hours. He's secretive. Moody. Always in his room, making calls or chatting online to people I don't know."

"You're not telling me anything that doesn't sound like a regular teenage boy."

"No! It's more than that. He never wanted to come here. He's always struggled to fit in, always been a little different. He's been through three secondary schools and had to leave each one because he was always getting bullied. You know what kids are like. They fear anything different, anything that doesn't fit the norm is a threat."

"Not just kids," Emily said, as Jessica's gaze drifted over to the family portraits hanging on the wall. Where was all this leading?

"When Ethan started college, he finally found a place where he could fit in. He made friends. Kids who dressed the same, liked the same kind of music. He was happy. Probably for the first time since he was little. Then Wesley tore it all away. He wanted to move, to get out of the city. I didn't know it at the time but he was scared he was about to get caught. He quit his job and we pulled the kids out of school and forced them to come here. Ethan hated it. He hated us for taking him away from his friends, from the place he felt he belonged."

Emily thought about it. She'd had her own experiences of being on the outside, of not fitting in, feeling like the only person in the world who didn't. But was it enough to drive Ethan to terrorise his family like this?

Jessica had started pacing the room again, her red eyes flicking back towards the living room window and the street beyond.

"Ethan was never good enough in his dad's eyes. Wesley was always complaining about the way he dressed or wore his hair, about the music he listened to and the films he watched. None of it fitted into Wesley's idea of how a man should be. They fought all the time. Once they even came to blows." She glanced at Emily, her carefully applied makeup now smudged and smeared. "I used to tell Wesley to leave him alone. I used to say to him, 'not everyone is cut from the same cloth.' Then Wesley got arrested, and ever since, every time I look at Ethan, I see his father. It's funny. I never noticed it before, but underneath all the clothes and the hair, underneath all their differences, they look so much alike. Even in the way Ethan stands. In the way he gets mad and loses his temper."

"Ethan's not responsible for his father's crimes," Emily said, staring at her.

Jessica looked up, struggling to lift her head. "But I pushed him away, all the same. Now he's punishing me for it."

"How can you be so sure it's him? Where's your proof?"

"It's in the way he looks at me, like he wants me dead. He wants to go back to where we used to live. Back to his old college and his old friends. He's been writing those letters to scare me. He's been making it difficult to live here, so I'll change my mind and move us back. But he has no idea what's looming over us. How much we stand to lose if the courts have their way. Ethan hates me. He thinks it's all my fault because I never stood up to his father. Because I never said no."

"Even if that's true," Emily said quietly, "do you honestly believe your son would go this far? To terrorise you? Georgia, too? And what about the box of spiders? He was here with you, upstairs when someone knocked on the door and left it on the step."

Jessica was quiet for a minute, staring numbly into space. "I don't know. Maybe he's had help. Maybe he's working with his father."

"His father who he hasn't seen or spoken to in weeks?" Emily's head was throbbing. She pinched the bridge of her nose, trying to rid herself of the ache. "What if you're wrong? What if it's someone else? That means your kids are out there somewhere. We should call the police."

They stared at each other, the air between them thickening like cement. Then they heard the front door open. All the tension flooded from Jessica's face.

"Thank God!" she cried. "Thank God!"

She rushed from the living room with Emily close on her heels. They entered the hall in time to see Ethan shutting the door behind him. He spun around as they approached, a startled look rippling over his face as he stared at his mother.

"I—I can explain," he stammered. "I've only been gone for ten minutes. Maybe fifteen."

All the relief in Jessica's eyes splintered and crumbled away. "Where is your sister?"

Ethan stared at her, open-mouthed, his body pressed up

against the door. Confusion swept across his face like a shadow. "What do you mean? She's here, isn't she?"

"No, she's not. What have you done with her?" Jessica lunged at him, grabbing the collars of his jacket. "Tell me where she is!"

Ethan flinched as he tried to free himself from his mother's grip. "I don't know. Let go of me!"

Emily stepped forward. "Jessica, you need to calm down."

"Don't tell me what I need!" she barked, before turning back to her son, her face inches from his. "It's you, isn't it? You're the one."

"I don't know what you're talking about!" Ethan yelled. Then he shoved Jessica hard, knocking her to one side, and ran for the stairs.

"Don't you walk away from me!"

But Ethan was already halfway up the steps. Jessica raced after him, screaming and shouting. Emily followed behind, her headache thrumming. As she reached the landing, she saw Ethan duck inside his room and Jessica leap forward, wedging herself between the door and the jamb.

"What have you done to Georgia? So help me God if you've hurt her—"

"You're crazy. Get the hell away from me, you fucking psycho!"

"This isn't helping," Emily said, raising her voice. "Everyone needs to calm down."

But now Jessica was inside Ethan's room, yelling and crying at the top of her lungs. Swearing under her breath, Emily followed, finding Ethan with his back to the window, his body recoiling from the fury emanating from his mother.

"I haven't done anything," he wailed.

"You're a liar! You've been sneaking around, coming and going at all hours, making secret phone calls, conspiring. You've been hiding something from me for ages. What is it?"

Ethan was no longer angry, Emily saw. His complexion had paled, and his eyes were large and round, his pupils dilated and oscillating, as he stared at Jessica. He's afraid, she thought.

"I—I . . ." he stammered.

Jessica advanced upon him, hands balled into fists.

"I . . ." But then Ethan screwed his face up into an angry ball. "Go to hell, you stupid bitch!"

Before Emily could move, Jessica lashed out, slapping Ethan hard against his face, the sound like the crack of a whip in her ears. He reeled back, his spine hitting the window as Jessica raised her hand once more.

"Stop it! Stop it!"

The voice was high-pitched and terrified, making all three of them turn.

Georgia stood in the bedroom doorway, large eyes peering from her tear-stained face, fingers pinching at her skin. Jessica turned, the fire burning in her eyes quickly dissipating. Tears came as she rushed forward.

"My darling! My baby girl! Where have you been?" She was on her knees, sobbing hysterically as she wrapped her arms around her daughter, squeezing the life out of her. By the window, Ethan had crumpled like a tissue, leaning against the wall for support, tears spilling down his face, where a large, hand-shaped welt was already reddening his skin.

"You're hurting me," Georgia managed to say, pushing against her mother's shoulders. Releasing her grip, Jessica searched her daughter's face.

"Where have you been? I've been out of my mind with worry! Was it him? Did he hurt you?"

"I . . ." Georgia began, her eyes shooting across the room at Ethan. "I got lost."

"What are you talking about?" Jessica twisted around, glaring at her son. "You were supposed to take her home. You were supposed to be with her."

She turned back to Georgia, who was pale and trembling, eyes brimming with tears. "Did he hurt you?"

She pulled at the girl's clothes, checking her legs, then lifting her school shirt to examine her torso.

Emily watched in horror, memories of her mother flooding her mind.

"Jessica, stop," she whispered.

"He hurt you, didn't he?" Jessica continued as she pulled off Georgia's jacket. Georgia tried to wriggle free, but Jessica held her fast as she pulled back the sleeves of her school shirt.

She froze, staring at the large, finger-shaped bruises on her daughter's forearm. Slowly, she got to her feet and turned on Ethan, holding Georgia's arm up for him to see.

"You're just like him," she spat. "You're just like your fucking father."

Ethan straightened, his face contorting with shock. "It wasn't me. I didn't do that."

Emily stared at the bruises, remembering something that Geraldine Butcher had told her. She had seen Ethan in the garden that day, slapping Georgia so hard he'd knocked her off her feet.

"You're The Witness," Jessica said in a half whisper. "I knew it. I always knew it."

Launching himself from the window, Ethan stormed across

the floor. As he ran for the door, he shouldered Emily out of the way.

Jessica sprang forward, trying to block his path, but Ethan was too fast. A second later, they all heard his feet hammering on the stairs, followed by the deafening slam of the front door.

Emily glanced at Jessica, who stared numbly at the open door, her mouth moving up and down, then at Georgia, who was shell-shocked and shaking.

"Wait here," she said, her voice sharp and angry. "I'll go after him."

As she moved past Georgia, she placed a gentle hand on her shoulder. The girl flinched, staring up at Emily with wide eyes.

"I got lost," she said. "It wasn't his fault."

Then Emily was hurrying through the house and out through the front door, chasing after Ethan.

34

It was already growing dark outside, bruises spreading across the sky, bleeding into each other. The temperature had dropped again, biting at Emily's exposed skin. She hurried down the drive, pushing open the gate and stepping onto the pavement. She looked both ways. There were people moving up and down the street, a few cars driving past. It was home time for the town's workforce. Across the road, the living room window of the Butchers' house was illuminated in soft orange light, Raymond Butcher's crooked silhouette standing at its centre.

Emily headed right, moving along the street, searching for Ethan. She could still hear Jessica's angry shouts in her ears, could still see the children's frightened faces. Jessica was a woman at the end of her tether, terrified and lashing out. Emily wondered if Ethan really was The Witness. It was certainly possible. If he hated his mother that much, especially when she treated him so coldly . . .

But he couldn't be in two places at once, which meant he wasn't working alone. She quickened her pace, eyes darting left to right. Then she saw him, ducking under a pool of streetlight up ahead.

Emily skidded to a halt and pressed up against the hedgerow. He had come to a standstill beneath the light. She couldn't see his face, but even from this distance, she could read his body language. He was furious, his shoulders up to his ears, his fists clenching and releasing then clenching again at his sides. He turned, glancing back down the street, and for a second, Emily thought she'd been seen. Then Ethan was digging into his pocket and pulling out his phone to make a call.

A car drove past, headlights splashing over parked cars. A woman walked by, hand clutching the straps of her shoulder bag, her head down but her eyes pointed forward as she passed.

Emily edged closer, keeping to the shadows, aware that at any minute Ethan could look up and spot her. She could hear his voice now but wasn't close enough to decipher his words. He sounded angry, hurt, not caring who was listening in. The call ended. He jammed the phone back inside his pocket then walked on, until he reached the end of the road, where he slid to a halt again.

Emily watched him from the shadows. She saw him bring a cigarette to his lips and light it, the tiny flame flickering in the dark. Smoke billowed into the icy air. Emily wondered if Jessica knew her son was a smoker—and judging by the pungent smell drifting from where he stood, not just a smoker of cigarettes.

Why was he just standing there, waiting around in the cold?

He's waiting for a lift. Whoever he called is coming to get him.

Which meant she needed to get to her car, fast.

Heading back along Raven Road, she quickened her pace and cast occasional glances over her shoulder, keeping Ethan in her sights. Another car drove by, making Emily break into a jog and hope it wasn't the one that was picking him up.

By the time she reached her car and switched on the engine, her body was aching from the cold. She pulled away from the kerb, driving slowly along the street. Another car appeared behind her, forcing her to speed up then drive past Ethan, who was still standing there, cloaked in shadows. Reaching the end of the road, Emily headed left, driving away from her quarry. As soon as she could, she turned the car around, heading straight back—just in time to see a battered old Corsa pull up in front of Ethan, its colour difficult to discern in the darkness.

Emily slowed down, watching him climb into the passenger seat and close the door. The Corsa drove away from Raven Road and Emily followed it, keeping her distance, thankful that the roads weren't jammed with traffic, as she followed them through the suburban maze until they were on the outskirts of town.

Twice, she almost lost sight of the car, other vehicles getting in the way, or because she was dropping too far behind. She wondered where they were going, Ethan and the mystery driver. She wondered what was happening back at the house, if she'd been right to leave Georgia alone with her hysterical mother.

Up ahead, the Corsa was turning off at a junction. Emily reached it moments later, heading onto an old dirt road that led away from the town and into more rural surroundings. Hedgerows grew up. The road twisted and coiled, slowing her down, until she was afraid that she had lost Ethan altogether. But then the road was straightening out again and she saw the rear of the Corsa dangerously close up ahead, taillights glinting like cats eyes as it disappeared down an even narrower track.

Emily flicked off the headlights. Anxiety shivered beneath

her skin as she slowed down, then took the turning. Trees grew up on both sides of the track. Without the safety of the headlights, she reduced her speed to a crawl, tyres running in and out of potholes, shaking her body from side to side. The track twisted and she caught sight of the Corsa in the near distance. The vehicle had come to a halt, its headlights illuminating a grassy space surrounded by woodland, where the track had come to an end.

Emily quickly pulled over, parking the car on the roadside and switching off the engine. She sat in darkness, eyes fixed on the lights in the distance. She saw the passenger door open and Ethan step out. Then the lights were snuffed out, plunging the lane into absolute darkness.

Slowly, quietly, Emily exited the vehicle and stepped onto the stony ground. The night was freezing cold, making her teeth chatter. She had no idea where she was, and the lack of manmade light and the cover of the trees was making it hard to see anything at all.

She walked on, keeping her tread light and her feet steady. Then stopped still. She could hear them talking up ahead, Ethan and his companion. She listened, holding her breath, tracking their direction. They were on the move, heading away from her. But where were they going?

Emily moved to step forward, but her body held her back. She had no idea who Ethan was with, or what they were doing out here in the middle of nowhere. For all she knew, they were aware that she was following, and were leading her somewhere isolated, far from people, where no one would hear her scream.

He's just a boy, she thought. A seventeen-year-old, angst-ridden boy who's angry at the world. But if Jessica and Geraldine

Butcher were to be believed, Ethan was more than that. He was a hateful boy, a bitter and twisted young man, who lashed out at little girls and terrorised his family out of spite. And he was not alone.

Had Emily lost her mind to be following him and his companion into unknown territory? She wavered, listening to their voices moving further away. Turning around, she hurried back to the car, opened the door, and rifled through the contents of her bag on the backseat, until she found what she was looking for. Pepper spray was illegal in Britain, but she'd managed to acquire it from another private investigator. She had never used it, and never hoped to, but it gave her an extra layer of safety during the several hours she spent alone on surveillance.

Sliding the can inside her coat pocket, she locked the car door, then headed in the direction Ethan had taken.

She could still hear their voices, somewhere up ahead in the distance, fading fast. She quickened her pace, reaching the end of the lane and the parked Corsa. It was hard to see anything in the darkness, but a torch or her phone light was out of the question. Cocking her head, she honed in on the voices, which were now somewhere ahead to the left. There had to be a path. She found it moments later, her eyes finally adjusting to the shadows. She followed the muddy track through the trees, pulse beating in time with her steps. The voices were growing louder, clearer. She couldn't hear words exactly, but she recognised Ethan's angry tone.

A beam of light cut through the darkness, painting the tree trunks. Emily ducked down, holding her breath. She was much closer to them than she'd realised and saw two figures splashed in phone lights, disappear around a bend. Then she was on the move once more, following them, all too aware of foliage crunching beneath her feet.

Soon, the path was turning again. Beams of light bounced off concrete walls up ahead.

"Through here," she heard Ethan say, followed by the screech of rusty hinges as a door was pulled open.

Emily stole forward, her heart beating erratically. This was reckless, she told herself. Dangerous. She was breaking every safety rule Erica Braithwaite had attempted to instil in her. Yet Emily ploughed forward, unable to stop, almost losing her balance as she stumbled over a broken branch. The trees parted. Above her, the clouds shifted, exposing the moon. Emily saw a cluster of abandoned warehouses, weeds growing up from the cracked, concrete ground. Monochrome rays bounced off shards of broken glass. A light was flickering through an unbroken window. Pressing herself up against a wall, Emily slid along until she reached an open door.

Ethan's voice came in loud and clear. "She's a fucking bitch! A stupid whore! She deserves to suffer for what she said to me!"

His companion spoke, his voice calm and deliberate. "Everyone gets what they deserve in the end. It's only a matter of time."

Blood pounding in her ears, Emily stepped through the doorway, her hand subconsciously reaching for the can of pepper spray.

"She thinks I'm just like my father, but she has no idea who she's fucking dealing with!"

"You're nothing like him. You're stronger."

"That asshole got caught. That's how strong and clever he is!" Ethan laughed, a high-pitched, desperate and angry sound that bounced off the walls. "I should teach that bitch a lesson. If she's scared of a few letters, she should wait and see what I could do!"

Emily moved closer, keeping to the shadows as she edged further inside. The warehouse was L-shaped and she was reaching the corner where it turned. One more step and she would be exposed.

"I'm not my father. I'm not anything like him. Why can't she see that?" Ethan's voice had dropped down low, fractured by sadness.

And then he was quiet. They both were.

Emily twisted her neck to the right and peeked around the corner.

At the far end of the warehouse, Ethan stood bathed in torchlight, his back turned to her and a beer bottle swinging loosely in his hand. Standing in front of him, his face pointed in Emily's direction, was a young man, tall and lithe, shadows flickering across his handsome face.

"I never wanted to come to this place!" Ethan was crying now, his face pressed against the boy's shoulder.

She watched the boy lean forward, wrap his arms around Ethan's neck. "I know. But I'm glad you did."

Emily's eyebrows shot up to her hairline and her mouth fell open as she watched them kiss.

They'd got it all wrong. Ethan wasn't The Witness. This was something else entirely. She watched them embrace, feeling like a voyeur, her face burning despite the cold. Then something scurried over her feet and made her shriek.

The two young men spun around, shocked expressions staring in her direction.

Slowly, Emily moved into the light.

Ethan stared at her, horror creeping over his face as he backed away from his companion.

"You can't tell her," he said, eyes round, voice shaking. "You can't let her know."

Emily shrugged her shoulders. "Honestly, I think your mum has bigger worries right now. But you and I, we need to talk."

35

THE HOUSE WAS QUIET, the only sound the soft hiss of the radiators. Jessica had closed every blind and curtain, and now she sat in the living room, swirling whiskey around a glass. She hated the stuff—it was Wesley's drink of choice, not hers—but she needed to feel numb and alcohol was the quickest solution. Except it wasn't working.

What had become of her family?

Wesley's arrest had been like lighting a trail of gunpowder, and she had watched helplessly as it crackled and sparked, getting closer and closer to the explosives. But she had been the one to explode.

She remembered lashing out at Ethan, the brutal crack of her open hand against his face. The look of utter horror and betrayal in his eyes. She hadn't meant to do it. She'd never hit her children, not once. But she'd been consumed by panic and rage, convinced that he was responsible for all the stress and fear she'd endured these last few weeks.

Was Ethan The Witness?

She desperately wanted to be wrong. But what if she was

right? Did it mean her son truly hated her? Did it mean he wanted to cause her harm? Earlier, she had tried to get Georgia to speak, to admit that Ethan was behind it all. But Georgia had been dazed, disoriented, unwilling or unable to talk. Now she was in bed, the traumas of the day having taken their toll.

Jessica emptied her glass, wincing at the burn, then refilled it. She glanced at her phone screen, wishing that Emily would call or text.

If Ethan was The Witness, she had serious decisions to make, starting with what she should do about it. She'd already decided that she wouldn't involve the police. If Ethan was The Witness, it wasn't his fault—his actions were a reaction, a by-product of his father's own crimes, indirect or otherwise.

If Ethan was The Witness, it meant she had wasted time and money bringing a lawsuit against the Fishers, and that the lawsuit would be brought to a swift end. Where would that leave her family?

Penniless and on the streets, that's where.

Jessica looked around the room, its emptiness pressing down on her. She thought about her parents. If only she still had some sort of relationship with them, she could pick up the phone right now and ask for their help. Maybe send Ethan to stay for a while, which would give them both time and space to work things out. But the truth of the matter was that she hadn't spoken to her parents in years and didn't even know if they still lived in the same house.

For a long time, she'd blamed them for not accepting her relationship with Wesley, or her pregnancy at seventeen. But she'd done nothing to repair that relationship. Even years later, when her mother had reached out, asking for forgiveness and begging to meet her grandchildren, Jessica had ignored her.

People never changed. No matter how much they said they were sorry.

She had thought Wesley the perfect man, sweeping her off her feet. But he'd lied to her. He'd cheated. Once, he had even hit her. Yet she'd stayed with him, dazed and deluded, while he'd chipped away at her self-confidence and her ego, until she could barely stand to look at herself in the mirror.

No. People never changed.

She still had her parents' old phone number in a notebook, tucked away in a kitchen drawer. She'd never called it. Never tried to put things right. But now she needed to talk to someone. To anyone that would listen. She imagined calling her parents. Imagined hearing their voices for the first time in years. Imagined them shaking their heads and saying, "We told you so. Didn't we tell you he was no good?"

There was Adora's mother, Delfina. She was kind and a good listener, and she'd said just the other day that she was there if Jessica needed to talk. Putting down the whiskey, Jessica picked up her phone from the coffee table and swiped through her contacts until she found Delfina's number.

A noise made her look in the direction of the open living room door. Georgia was standing there in her pyjamas, hair springing out like a tangle of weeds.

"What are you doing out of bed?" Jessica asked. "Is everything all right?"

Georgia nodded, blank eyes shifting towards the kitchen. "Getting a drink of water."

Jessica stared at her, her heart breaking at the pale, exhausted form of her daughter. She wanted to ask her again about what had happened earlier that day. She wanted her to confess that it had been Ethan all along.

Georgia was staring at her, swaying tiredly on her feet.

"Okay, well get your water, then straight back to bed. We can see how you're feeling in the morning and decide if you should go to school."

A crease appeared between Georgia's eyebrows. She turned wordlessly, shuffling off in the direction of the kitchen.

Jessica's phone vibrated in her hand, startling her. It was a message from Emily. Her thumb hovered over the screen. Her throat dried up. Was Emily about to tell her the horrible truth about her son?

"You're his mother," she whispered. "No matter what, you're his mother."

She swiped the screen and read the message: *I'm with Ethan. Heading back now. We need to talk.*

Jessica stared at the words, frustrated and relieved. She looked up to see Georgia passing by the living room door once more, then heard the soft tread of her feet on the staircase.

She found herself almost wanting Ethan to be The Witness, because even if it meant he hated her, at least the horrors of the last month would be at an end. Jessica picked up the whiskey glass and swallowed its contents. The gunpowder trail crackled and sparked, setting alight to her heart. Outside the window, a shadow moved.

———

The man stood at the centre of the driveway, his tall, powerful frame staring up at the house. The blinds were all closed. But there was a light on in the living room. He stood there, perfectly still, his breaths heaving in and out, growing faster with excitement. He watched the window, saw movement behind the blinds. Inside his jeans, he felt himself grow hard.

Stepping quietly, he made his way up the drive, then followed the narrow path that led along the side of the house. He passed windows, blinds shut, the rooms beyond hidden in darkness, until he emerged in the back garden. A security light snapped on, illuminating the patio and the children's toys scattered across it. He stared at the light, unafraid, his excitement growing.

Running a tongue over his lips, he stepped forward, bathing himself in the security light, until he was standing outside the back door. Now his heart was hammering. Saliva was filling his mouth.

He thought about what he was going to do to her. About how scared she would look when she discovered him inside. He grinned, felt the throb against his jeans.

With a large, powerful hand, he gripped the door handle. He pressed down. The door was unlocked.

36

THEY HAD LEFT the cold and gloom of the warehouse. Emily sat in the driver's seat of her car, rubbing her hands together, feeling grateful for the warm air blasting out from the heaters. Ethan sat in the front passenger seat, his head bowed and his eyes fixed straight ahead, the yellow glow of the overhead light painting his skin in a sickly hue. They'd been sitting in silence for over two minutes now, Emily waiting patiently for him to speak. She glanced through the windscreen at the Corsa, which was now parked in front of the Audi. The boy Ethan had been with—Adam—sat behind the wheel, a similar, shocked expression on his face.

Emily heaved her shoulders. Teenagers, she thought, feeling a surge of pity. Puberty was hell; all those bodily changes and uncontrolled hormones and terrible mood swings. She'd rather die than be forced to relive her formative years.

Her passenger was still unmoving, still staring miserably into space.

"You know," she said softly, "sometimes it helps to talk to people who don't know you."

Nothing. Not even a blink of an eye.

"I'm not here to judge your private life. As far as I'm concerned, who you choose to spend time with is your own business and nobody else's."

Ethan sucked in a breath, then slowly let it out. His silence continued.

"But we should probably talk about what happened earlier today," Emily said.

Shrugging a shoulder, Ethan turned to stare at the darkness on the other side of the passenger window. "Nothing to talk about," he muttered. "My mum is a bitch. End of story."

Emily clenched her jaw. "First of all, if you use that word again, I'll leave you here to freeze to death in the cold. Second of all, your mother has been through hell these last few months. She's a human being, which means she makes mistakes. We all do sometimes."

"I knew you'd take her side," he grunted, shaking his head.

"I'm not taking anyone's side. I'm just trying to encourage you to be mature and look at the bigger picture. I didn't say she was the only one who's been through hell. It's not been easy for you and your sister, either. You've had to live with the consequences of your father's bad choices. You'll have to live with them for the rest of your life, and that's not fair. But so will your mother." Emily paused, staring at the young man in her passenger seat, who was looking more and more like a child by the second. "She shouldn't have hit you like that. She shouldn't have said all those terrible things. But she did, and that's on her. It's down to you to decide how to deal with it; whether you choose to forgive her, or don't."

Ethan turned his head, eyes flicking towards her, before focusing on the windscreen.

"My mum wasn't perfect," Emily said, brushing hair from her face. "Far from it, in fact. She was paranoid, agoraphobic, beaten down by life. When I was your age, I could barely leave the house without her blowing up into a full scale panic. She made it difficult for me to have friends. Impossible for me to have a social life. I felt guilty if I left her alone, and alone when I was with her." She paused, surprised at the words that were flooding from her mouth. She never talked about the past. Especially not about her relationship with her mother.

"Why was she like that?" Ethan was staring at her again.

"I have no idea. I used to think it was mental illness. Or maybe something terrible happened to her before I came along. She'd never talk about it, so eventually I gave up asking."

"What about your dad?"

"Never knew him. I don't even know his name." Emily leaned forward, scratching a mark on the dashboard. "The thing is, whatever my mum's problems were, they weren't my fault. The same way that whatever your mum is going through isn't your fault. But getting angry with her, deliberately doing things to hurt her—or lashing out at your sister and knocking her to the ground—that's not going to help anyone." Ethan's face turned scarlet as he hung his head in shame. Emily sighed. "Where did you go earlier? Was it to meet Adam?"

"I wasn't even supposed to be picking Georgia up. And I—I didn't want to let Adam down."

"But it was okay to let your sister down? To leave her wandering the street alone with everything that's been going on?"

He was quiet, his eyes pointing to the floor.

"We all make bad choices. God knows I have," Emily said. "Sometimes we even deliberately hurt the people that we love.

But you shouldn't have left Georgia alone. You know that, right? And you certainly shouldn't be hitting her."

Ethan nodded, refusing to look at her, his mortified expression telling her all she needed to know.

"She's your sister," Emily said. "You need to take care of her, especially now."

"Because I'm the man of the house."

"Actually, you're not. You're a boy. Your mother is in charge and you should do well to remember that. What I mean is that your sister's vulnerable. She's not old enough or strong enough to defend herself. She needs you right now, and she should be your priority. Not some boy you've only just met, no matter how cute he is. Which is quite a lot, by the way."

Ethan's face burned redder. "Are you going to tell her? Will you tell Mum about . . . about Adam?"

"It's not for me to tell. In a perfect world, this shouldn't even be a big deal. As my good friend Jerome would say, 'Some people are gay. Get over it.' Don't you think your mum would say the same? Don't you think she'd love you anyway?"

Now Ethan did meet her gaze, and she saw how sad he looked. How young and alone. "It's not my mum I'm worried about."

"Well, you don't have to tell your dad anything. Besides, whatever your dad thinks—whatever anyone else thinks—it doesn't matter. What matters is that you're happy in yourself. That you accept who you are." Emily reached out and touched his shoulder. "Look at me."

Ethan glanced up through his hair.

"I need to ask you something and I need you to answer honestly. Are you The Witness?"

His gaze wavered, his eyes shifting towards the car in front, then back at Emily. He was quiet, chewing on his lip.

"No," he said. "I'm not."

"Do you know who is?"

"I wish I did. But I don't. That's the honest truth."

Emily slowly nodded. "I believe you. But I'm not sure your mum does, which is why we need to go home and talk to her right now."

Tears sprang up in Ethan's eyes as he shrank further into the seat.

"You don't have to tell her anything you don't want to," Emily said, offering him a reassuring smile. "But you do need to tell Georgia you're sorry for leaving her alone. You can let me take care of the rest."

She smiled again, watching the relief flood through his body. "Now go and say goodbye to lover boy over there before he thinks you've forgotten about him."

Eyes widening, Ethan ran fingers through his hair, then cleared his throat. "Fine. Whatever."

Emily watched him push open the door and climb out. She watched Adam look up, eyes bright and hopeful. For a moment, she found herself thinking about Carter, and about how badly she was handling their relationship. You should take some of your own advice, she told herself, then reached for her phone. She tapped out a text message to Jessica, telling her they were coming home. Then, to give the boys some privacy, she reached inside her bag and pulled out her tablet.

As she activated the camera feeds, she caught her breath. A tall, shadowy figure was standing on the driveway of 57 Raven Road. He was completely still, watching the house. Her blood froze as she watched him step forward and disappear from view.

Fingers shaking, Emily flicked to the camera feed coming from the rear garden. The man appeared a second later, stepping from the shadows as the security light flicked on.

Emily moved to grab her phone from the dashboard, knocked it with her hand and watched it slide off to drop beside her feet. Panicking, she reached down, scrabbling with fingers. Now the man was beside the back door. Now he was turning the handle and the door was opening. Why wasn't it locked?

Her blood rushing in her ears, Emily found the phone and scooped it up. As she unlocked it with one hand, she tapped the tablet screen with the other, bringing up the feeds of the hidden cameras.

She watched in horror as the man entered the kitchen through the back door, his tall, powerful frame moving stealthily across the floor. Locating Jessica's phone number, she hit the call button. On the camera feed coming from the living room, she saw Jessica sitting on the sofa, a glass in hand as she stared into space. The line connected, and she saw Jessica pick up her phone from the coffee table.

"Emily?"

"Listen to me very carefully," Emily breathed. "Don't speak. As fast as you can, get out of the living room and go upstairs, get Georgia and lock yourself in somewhere."

"What's going—"

"Not another word. Someone is inside your house. Do as I say right now."

She watched Jessica's grainy image turn to face the door. "But I—"

"I'm calling the police," Emily said. "Go. Now!"

She hung up. Watched Jessica leap to her feet and dash towards the hall.

Emily dialled 999 and threw open the driver door.

"Ethan! Get here now!"

The calm voice of an operator spoke in her ear, asking which emergency service was needed.

"Police," Emily said, trying to remain calm. "Please hurry."

37

JESSICA RACED across the living room floor and through the open door. Her heart was pounding. Nausea churned her stomach. Her vision swam and spun. *Someone was inside her house.* That was what Emily had said. But she'd locked every window and door. Sliding to a halt in the centre of the hall, she spun around on her feet and stared at the smoked, patterned glass of the kitchen door. Just in time to see a shadow move behind it.

Strangling a scream, Jessica tried to keep her feet quiet as she hurried towards the stairs. Reaching the bottom step, she shot out a hand and clutched the rail, then twisted herself around. Behind her, the kitchen door began to open.

She took the steps two at a time, terrified tears stinging her eyes, until she reached the landing and raced towards Georgia's room. She threw the door open, watching it crash against the wall. Georgia sprang up from her bed, eyes wide, mouth open, a crease in the centre of her forehead. She was about to speak when Jessica lunged forward and clamped a hand over her mouth.

She shook her head violently, then carefully removed her hand.

"We have to go," she whispered. She pulled back the covers and took hold of Georgia's wrist, forgetting the bruises on her daughter's skin. Together they crossed the room, heading back out to the landing. Footsteps, heavy and solid, were coming up the stairs.

Georgia craned her neck to see, but Jessica pulled on her arm, dragging her along, lifting her feet from the floor, leading her into the master bedroom. Releasing her grip on her daughter, she swung the door, catching it before it could slam shut, then closed it gently and spun around, pressing her back up against the wood.

Whoever had broken into her home had reached the landing.

Georgia stared at her mother, eyes bulging from her sockets, confusion and fear making her unsteady on her feet.

Jessica's gaze darted around the room. There was no lock on the bedroom door. She could move the dresser, use it as a barricade. But could she move it before the intruder got inside? Even if she could, it wouldn't stop them from breaking in.

"Mum?" Georgia whispered.

Jessica shook her head, eyes darting with panic.

The bathroom.

Moving quickly, she scooped up Georgia's hand and pulled her through the bedroom, towards the en suite. She spun around, in time to see the bedroom door handle slowly turning. And her phone lying on the carpet.

"No!"

Now the bedroom door was opening.

With a cry, Jessica pulled Georgia inside the bathroom and

slammed the door. Her fingers fumbled with the lock, a flimsy bolt that a couple of swift kicks could easily demolish. It was all that stood between them and the intruder.

She slammed the bolt across and backed away from the door, bumping into Georgia.

"I'm scared, Mum. I didn't—"

"Quiet!" Jessica hissed. She backed further away from the door, taking Georgia with her. "You have to be quiet."

She felt the sink pressing against her back. She'd run out of space. She turned, eyes finding the bathroom window. She tried the handle, but the window wouldn't open. It was jammed. Had been on the to-do list for weeks. And even if she could get it open, they were two floors up with a sheer drop down to the garden below. She would probably survive with a few broken bones, but Georgia . . .

She shook the bloody image from her head.

The bathroom door handle was turning. Jessica clamped her hand over her mouth and pushed Georgia behind her. Whoever was standing on the other side knocked three times then rattled the handle.

"Let me in, you dirty slut," a deep, lust-filled voice said. "You've got me hard, chasing after you like this. If only you could touch it right now. You'd like that, wouldn't you? Why don't you let me in and give you what you asked for?"

Jessica's body was trembling uncontrollably. Her eyes swept the bathroom, searching for a weapon.

"Is this how you like it? You sick and twisted bitch. Is this what turns you on? I'll give it to you hard while you scream. Does that turn you on? Does it make you wet?"

She wrenched open the medicine cabinet and pulled out a

pair of scissors. They were small and blunt, but shoved into an eye socket or soft tissue . . .

The man on the other side of the door knocked again.

Jessica screamed. "Leave us alone!"

Behind her, Georgia was hyperventilating, with tears splashing down her face. Wrapping an arm around her daughter, she pulled her close. She pointed the scissors at the door.

"Shall I break it down?" the man said. "Or is that going too far? I can break it down, then split you apart, just like you told me you wanted!"

He shook the door so hard, it sounded like the whole room was coming down around Jessica's ears.

"Stop it!" she screamed. "Please, stop it!"

But the man wouldn't stop. He laughed and hammered on the door. "Come on, bitch. You've got me here and you've got me hard. What more do you want? Come out so I can give it to you. Come out and let me fu—"

An explosion of sound interrupted him, quickly followed by a flurry of shouts and crashes. Then the man was screaming in pain at the top of his lungs. Jessica held her breath and her daughter tight. She heard another crash, running footsteps, and more shouting.

Silence fell, as if the world outside had suddenly vanished. Then someone knocked gently on the bathroom door.

"Jessica?"

Relief washed over her in a flood. A sob escaping her lips, Jessica released her grip on Georgia and slid back the door bolt. The door swung open and she saw Emily, who stood with her shoulders heaving up and down, her face red with exertion.

"Thank God," she said. "We got here just in time. Are you both okay?"

Jessica fell into her arms, weeping uncontrollably, one arm opening up to let Georgia in.

"It's all right," Emily said. "You're safe. You're both safe."

A second later, Ethan burst into the room, terrified eyes fixed on his mother.

"They caught him!" he cried. "The police are outside and they caught him!"

Pulling away from Emily, Jessica reached out for Ethan. He came forward, gingerly at first, then rushed into his mother's arm. She hugged her children tightly, their sobs mingling with each other as Emily stood to the side, watching over them.

38

THEY WERE SITTING in a medium size room, plain blue carpet on the floor, a grid of ceiling tiles hanging above their heads, strips of fluorescent lighting hurting their eyes. Emily sat on a plastic chair. Two seats down from her, Jessica stared blankly into space, the after-shock of the attack still haunting her. A female police officer sat close to the door, watching over them. She looked tired as well, Emily thought, probably pulled out of bed as an extra pair of hands.

The children were both asleep; Ethan lying across a row of seats with a blanket thrown over him, and Georgia curled up in an armchair, cradling a doll that the police officer had given her. Emily sighed. The family had been through so much lately, long before The Witness had entered their lives to make everything worse. She couldn't help but feel sorry for them. And now they were here, in the early hours of the morning, at the police station. Both she and Jessica had given separate statements then been sent back to this room, where they'd been waiting for almost two hours. Hopefully, there would be some news soon, and Jessica would be allowed to take the children home. If she could face taking them back there.

Emily watched as Jessica stretched her arms and glanced at her children.

"How are you doing?" she asked her.

"I think I'm still in shock. I'm not sure I'll ever get over it."

"You will, in time. I'm just glad we got there when we did."

Jessica visibly shuddered. "I don't even want to think about that. I can't."

"You don't need to. The police have him in custody and they'll have answers for you soon."

Jessica stared at her, slowly blinking. "Thank you. Again."

Emily smiled, glanced at the police officer by the door. "I wonder what's taking so long."

"I can't believe I thought that Ethan was The Witness. What kind of mother am I?"

"A good one," Emily said. "But you've been under a lot of pressure, both you and the kids. Besides, you told me that Ethan's behaviour has been erratic lately, that he's been sneaking around, keeping secrets from you. It's easy to jump to conclusions in situations like this."

Jessica glanced at her son, sadness creeping into her eyes. "Where did you find him?"

Shifting on the hard chair, Emily stuck her hands inside her jacket pockets and pictured Ethan's shocked expression when she'd walked in on him and Adam.

"Around. Just walking the streets."

"He didn't tell you anything?"

"Like what?"

"I don't know. I just feel like something's there. Something he wants to say to me. Or maybe I'm just imagining things. Maybe I'm just losing my mind."

"Give yourself a break. Especially tonight."

Jessica stared up at the ceiling. Then her brow crumpled and she turned to face Emily.

"How did you know?" she asked.

"Know what?"

"That I was in the living room. When you called, you said, 'Get out of the living room and go upstairs.' How did you know where I was?"

"I—" Emily's gaze shifted back to the police officer, who was still staring into space, but who was also clearly listening in. "I just—"

Jessica's eyes narrowed. "You just what?"

"I may have put a camera in the living room."

Slowly, Jessica's mouth swung open. She leaned back a little, moving away from Emily.

"And maybe one in the kitchen."

"You were *spying* on me?" Jessica said in a loud whisper.

Across the room, the police officer's eyes shifted towards them. Emily was squirming now, pressing her knees together as she pushed herself up in the seat.

"Not spying, exactly," she said. "More like keeping an extra eye on you."

"Except that you didn't tell me about the cameras, which meant you didn't want me to know they were there. You were trying to catch me out."

It was pointless to lie now, especially after everything Jessica had been through tonight. "Okay, fine. Yes, I was spying on you. It was the only way I could find out if you were telling the truth."

Jessica was glaring, her cheeks flushing red. "Or you could have just asked me."

"I didn't know you so well then. You could have told me anything you wanted. At least now I know you're telling the truth."

Jessica stared at Emily, her upper lip pulling into a sneer. "And all it took was a psychopath breaking into my house."

She turned away, shaking her head in disgust.

Emily dropped her gaze to the floor. Fair enough, she thought, but she still didn't regret doing it.

The door swung open and DC Ryan entered, followed by another detective in her fifties, who had furtive eyes and a stern expression that said she wasn't happy about being dragged out of bed in the middle of the night. As they approached, Emily and Jessica got to their feet.

"Sorry to keep you waiting," DC Ryan said. "This is Detective Inspector Trent."

The woman nodded then turned to observe the children. "Perhaps we should talk outside. PC Walker here will watch the kids."

The detectives turned, heading for the door, with Jessica and Emily following behind.

Out in the corridor, DI Trent ran a hand through her hair. "As DC Ryan said, apologies for the delay, but we had to wait for the suspect to receive medical treatment before questioning him."

She stared at Emily, who immediately glanced away.

"Who is he?" Jessica asked.

The detectives eyed each other, something passing between them.

"You don't know him?" DI Trent said.

"How the hell would I? Why are you even asking me that?"

The detective inspector raised an eyebrow. "The suspect's name is Tom Crank. He claims to know you."

Jessica shook her head, face crinkled with confusion. "Well, he's lying. I don't know any Tom Crank!"

Emily watched the detectives. There it was again—the shared look that suggested they knew something.

"Crank claims he's been engaged in online conversation with you on an adult website called . . ." DI Trent paused to glance at the clipboard in her hand. She looked up again and cleared her throat. "RolePlayingSluts.net. That doesn't ring a bell?"

The colour drained from Jessica's face. She was silent, her mouth hanging open, eyes darting between the detectives.

"He claims he's been chatting with you for a couple of weeks now," DC Ryan continued. "Says you've been engaged in various conversations of a sexually explicit nature."

"He's lying!" Jessica hissed. "I don't know him! And I would never—I would never go on a website like that."

DI Trent arched an eyebrow as she removed several printouts from the clipboard. "So the username 'Jessica236' means nothing to you? How about 'BigManXXX'? What about these conversations?"

Taking the printouts, Jessica slowly sifted through them, her eyes growing wide as she pored over the words. Emily peered over her shoulder, trying to get a glimpse. As she read, she felt her face heating up.

"As you can see," DI Trent said, her expression indifferent, "the conversation between the two of you suggests that tonight was nothing more than an elaborate sexual fantasy; a role play acted out in real life. The burglar and the hapless victim, submit-

ting to her intruders demands, which was unfortunately miscon-
strued as an actual crime."

Emily continued to scan the words, nausea churning her
stomach.

– *I love to be scared by big, nasty men breaking into my home.*

– *It turns me on thinking about those huge hands pushing me
down onto the bed. Putting a knife to my throat.*

"It's all there," DI Trent said. "The time and date, even you
agreeing to leave the back door unlocked for him to gain entry."

Jessica was shaking her head, over and over, tears spilling
down her face. But they weren't tears of sadness, Emily realised.
They were tears of pure rage.

"This is bullshit!" Jessica cried. "My daughter was in the
fucking house!"

She shoved the printouts back at DI Trent, who reattached
them to the clipboard.

The detectives stared at each other, then back at Jessica.

"You think I'm lying, don't you?" she yelled, tears flying
from her eyes. "What, because I made the mistake of marrying a
criminal, I'm a sick-minded pervert, too? What is it going to
take for you people to believe someone is trying to hurt me and
my children? Do I have to die first for you to take me seriously?"

Her shoulders were heaving up and down, her face a
worrying shade of purple. She turned and stared at Emily with
pleading eyes, who placed a hand between her shoulder blades,
offering her reassurance.

"You know, there's a simple way to find out who's behind all
this," she said. "And you have the means in your hands right
there."

DI Trent looked her up and down. "And you are?"

"Emily Swanson. Private investigator. Would you care to see my licence?"

DC Ryan stepped forward. "I met with Miss Swanson a few days ago. She brought us evidence concerning the harassment complaint."

"I see." DI Trent was still staring at Emily, still trying to figure her out. "Well, Miss Swanson, is it? Let me tell you something. As a senior detective, I also happen to have a few tricks up my sleeve." She turned to Jessica, her expression softening. "We'll get the tech team onto it, see if they can trace the sender of these messages. With a bit of luck, they'll not only be able to find out where they were sent from, but the exact identity of who sent them. Which means there's a very good chance the culprit will be apprehended very soon."

"Please," Jessica said, the fight leaving her now. "Please just make it stop. My child was in the house tonight."

"We'll get onto it" DI Trent placed a calming hand on her shoulder. "We'll contact the tech team first thing in the morning, then it's just a waiting game. Whoever's behind this, their days are numbered." The detective inspector smiled sympathetically, then raised an eyebrow at Emily. "DC Ryan, I'll leave you to see these women out."

She turned and walked away, disappearing through a door at the end of the corridor.

"I'll have PC Walker drive you and your children home," Ryan told Jessica. He turned to Emily. "If I could have a quick word in private?"

Wiping tears from her eyes, Jessica returned to the room where her children still slept, curled up on chairs. Now that they were alone, DC Ryan cleared his throat.

"I just wanted to say you acted quickly tonight. If you hadn't, things could have been much worse."

Too tired to smile, Emily nodded.

"But I have to ask about the pepper spray. It's illegal to carry in this country. You do know that, right? I'm assuming you just happened upon it?"

Emily froze. "I guess the suspect must have dropped it?"

DC Ryan arched an eyebrow and flashed her a wry look.

"What's going to happen to him?" she asked.

"We're still trying to decide, but it's not for you to worry about. You should go home and get some sleep." He paused, glancing towards the room where Jessica waited with her family. "You believe her, right?"

"You still don't? You honestly think she'd put her daughter in danger like that?"

The detective shook his head. "This will all be over soon."

Stifling a yawn, Emily said, "I hope you're right. I really do."

39

Friday morning came around in what seemed like minutes. The little sleep that Emily had managed had been fitful and restless, sullied by dark dreams. Now she was awake, feeling sluggish and irritable, cold winter light seeping in through the curtains as she lay on her back, wondering if she should have taken a different career path; one that was safe and boring and allowed her the joy of peaceful slumber. But then what? She would quickly find herself bored and yearning for something more. Even though she was currently undecided if Braithwaite Investigations was the right place for her, she felt certain she was heading along the right path. It wasn't private investigation that was wrong for her, it was how she was going about it.

She had some serious thinking to do about the future. But not before her morning coffee.

On the bedside table, her phone started to buzz. Scooping it up, she pressed it to her ear.

"Are you awake?" It was Jerome. His voice was laced with worry.

"What's wrong?"

"You need to come into the office," he said. "Erica is pissed off and she wants to see you."

Emily's breath caught in her throat. She didn't know why she felt so shocked that Erica could have found out about her misdeeds. After all, the woman owned a private investigation company. Sucking in a shallow breath, she struggled to let it out.

"Fine," Emily said. "I'll be there soon as I can."

She hung up and lay there for a minute, staring up at the ceiling. Perhaps Erica Braithwaite was about to make up Emily's mind for her.

———

Grosvenor Square was cold and frosty, the first snow of the year starting to fall in a light drift over the park. Travel mug of coffee in one hand, Emily exited the lift and started down the corridor, towards the smoked glass doors of Braithwaite Investigations. Jerome was at his usual position behind the reception desk. He glanced up as she entered, his face taut and lined.

"She's in her office," he said in a hushed whisper. "She says to go and see her as soon as you come in."

Emily swallowed, eyes moving across the room towards the solid wood of Erica's office door.

"Do you think she's found out about the cameras?" Jerome asked. "Because seriously, if I lose this job right now, I'm screwed."

"Don't worry about it. If she asks, I'll tell her it was all me." Emily heaved her shoulders. Her heart was palpitating, making it hard to breathe. Flashing Jerome one last look, she handed him her mug of coffee.

"Wish me luck?"

"It's not luck you need," he said. "More like full body armour."

Steeling herself, Emily crossed the room until she was standing outside Erica's door. She breathed in for a count of five, held it for a count of eight, then exhaled for a count of seven.

She knocked on the door.

A sharp, commanding voice told her to enter.

Here goes nothing, she thought.

Erica was standing by the window, her back turned to the immaculately kept office.

"You wanted to see me?" Emily said, trying to sound calm and failing miserably.

Erica nodded stiffly. "Sit down."

She did as she was told, feeling like a naughty schoolgirl in the headteacher's office as she waited for Erica to join her at the desk, but the woman remained at the window, her gaze fixed on the snow that was gently falling outside. For a long while, they were both silent, the mood in the room growing heavy like the air before a storm. Then Erica turned around and Emily immediately wished that she had stayed at home.

"I trusted you," Erica hissed "You told me you were up to the job and I believed you, in spite of my doubts." She crossed the room, planting herself in her chair, spine upright, gaze rendering Emily paralysed. "You've broken every code of practice in the book. You lied to me. You lied to your client and went directly against her wishes. If that wasn't bad enough, you endangered the lives of the very people you were supposed to be investigating."

Emily opened her mouth, ready to argue that she'd not been

the one who'd broken into Jessica's house and attacked her. She shut it again.

"You broke a contractual agreement, for God's sake!" Erica continued, refusing to release Emily from her glare. "You're lucky that Meredith Fisher is a good friend of mine, because if the client had been anyone else, I would be facing a lawsuit right now!" She glanced away, giving Emily temporary release. "Of course, that doesn't mean that Meredith is happy with your actions. Far from it! By hiring us, she'd been hoping to put the whole sorry mess behind her, allowing John to recover. But instead, you've made everything so much worse."

Emily lowered her head, eyes searching out wear marks on the desk. She had no idea what to say, so she said nothing at all.

Erica puffed out her cheeks and leaned back in her chair, slowly shaking her head. "It's my fault. I should have listened to my doubts. You weren't ready for something like this. You're too naive, too led by your emotions. I picked you, out of everyone in that class, because I thought you had what it takes to be a commendable, dedicated investigator—someone I would be proud to have working on my team. Instead, you do something like this. What the hell were you thinking?"

Cheeks burning, Emily risked a glance upwards. "Jessica caught me watching the house," she began. "It was either give up then or try a different tactic. I thought that if I could talk to her, if I could win her trust, then I could find out the truth." She leaned forward, staring earnestly at Erica. "And I did, because Jessica Harris is innocent. The attack last night proves it."

"Does it?" Erica said, narrowing her eyes. "Or does it prove you've become too involved? You've sided with that family, given them your sympathy and your understanding. Meanwhile, you've let facts and reasoning fall to the side.

Where's your proof? Where's the evidence you can hold in your hand and prove to the Fishers that Jessica Harris isn't lying?" The anger faded from Erica's eyes, swallowed up by disappointment. "This is why you aren't ready, Emily. This is why I should have given this case to someone more experienced."

Emily leaned back and threw her hands in the air. "The police are just one piece of evidence away from finding out who The Witness really is. And once they do, Jessica will realise that the Fishers are innocent and she'll drop the case. The Fishers will get the outcome they're looking for, the police will apprehend The Witness, and the Harris family will be safe at last. Everyone wins."

"Except for Braithwaite Investigations," Erica said. "Because all we will have proved is that we don't honour our clients' requests. That we can't stay within boundaries legally imposed upon us by contracts. Or did you forget that it wasn't just *your* reputation on the line?" She shot Emily another glare and slowly shook her head. "I'm sorry, but you leave me with no choice. You're off the case. In fact, right now, I think you should go home. Because if you say one more word to try to justify your behaviour, it will be your last as an employee of Braithwaite Investigations."

Stunned, Emily stared at Erica, who picked up a pen and pulled some papers from a drawer.

"Go home," she said. "Don't return to the office until you hear from me."

Emily couldn't move. Couldn't find the will to push herself onto her feet; not until Erica looked up, eyes burning into her skin.

Slowly, Emily stood, thought about apologising, then

remembered Erica's warning. She walked to the door, her head weighing down her shoulders.

"And I want those cameras back. Today, if possible," Erica called out behind her. "You can give them to your co-conspirator out there while he still has a job."

40

SHE DIDN'T WANT to go home to her empty apartment, where all she would have for company were her feelings of guilt and failure. She'd let Erica down. She hadn't stopped for a second to think about the woman's reputation, or the fact that Erica had gone out on a limb to help her further her career. It wasn't that she had acted selfishly; all Emily had been trying to do was help Jessica and her family and to bring the Fishers some peace. Maybe prove to herself that she was worthy of being a private investigator in the process. But now she wasn't anything. Temporarily, at least. If she couldn't even follow a few rules, how was she going to carve out a career that depended on discretion and trust?

No, she didn't want to go home with these feelings and thoughts. Instead, Emily drove across the city in the lightly falling snow, until she reached West Hampstead. Carter wasn't at home. She hadn't bothered to call before making the journey, but she had a good idea where to find him.

His workshop was at the far end of a cobbled stone court-yard, where vines of ivy spread across the walls, impervious to the winter chill. Stopping outside a battered and chipped door, Emily listened to the rhythmic buzzing of an electric lathe and inhaled the pleasant aroma of sawn wood. Pushing open the door, she stepped inside, where Carter was bent over a workbench, busy working on an indiscernible lump of timber. Sensing her presence, he glanced over his shoulder.

A smile spread across his face. Brushing sawdust from his overalls, he went to greet her. "This is a nice surprise. Don't you have a case to solve?"

Emily avoided his gaze, glancing around the workshop at the various tools and benches, stacks of wood and pieces of finished furniture.

"*Had*," she muttered. "As in past tense."

"What happened?"

Heaving her shoulders, she told him about her meeting with Erica and the incidents of the last two days, brushing over her involvement in preventing last night's attack on Jessica. By the time she'd finished talking, she felt utterly miserable, the room pressing in on her to squeeze the air from her lungs.

Concern creased Carter's face, bringing out the laughter lines she liked so much. Only he wasn't laughing now.

"So you've been suspended?" he asked. "How are you feeling?"

Emily arched an eyebrow, then pulled away from him to examine the rows of tools hanging on the wall. "Oh, I feel great. Never better."

She was aware of the sarcasm in her voice, but for now, she was too distracted to care.

"What can I do?"

Emily just shook her head.

"It's my own fault," she said at last. "Jerome's right. I'm a bull in a china shop, always stamping my way to the truth, never mind who gets hurt along the way."

"Jerome said that?"

"Don't you think it's true?"

"Well, I—"

"Oh. So, you do."

"I didn't say that. What I meant to say was—"

"What? Go on, spit it out."

She could hear the venom in her voice and yet she couldn't seem to stop it. This was what she did, wasn't it? Trampled on everyone's feelings, so she could prove to herself that all those negative thoughts about herself were true.

Carter fell silent, shrugging his shoulders. "You want to get out of here? We could go do something. Catch a film, or we could go back to my place and I could make you lunch."

"Maybe. No. I don't know."

Why had she even come here? She should have gone home to wallow. Because Carter was too nice, trying to make her feel better when she didn't deserve it. Picking up a chisel, she flipped it over in her hand. If only she could chip away at all her self-doubt. If only she could scrape away the voice that crawled inside her skull and always whispered that she was no good. She put the chisel down and glanced over at Carter, who was staring at the ground and scratching the top of his head.

"Erica said I wasn't ready," she told him. "She said I can't see the facts because I'm blinded by my emotions. Do you think I'm like that? That I can't see the truth because I've already made up my mind about how things are?"

"I honestly don't know."

"Why not?"

He stared at her nervously.

"Go on," Emily said, softly this time. "You can say."

"Because half the time it's hard to know what you're thinking at all," Carter said. "We've been together a year and I hardly know anything about you."

"Yes, you do," she said defensively. "You know lots of things."

"I know that you're no good in the mornings until you've had coffee. I know that you need time alone to re-energise. I know you secretly love reality TV even though you swear you hate it." He smiled, but only for a second. "But I don't know anything about your family, except that your mother died. I don't know anything about where you came from or your life before moving to London."

Emily's shoulders tensed. "I told you. It's all online. All you have to do is type in my name and read it for yourself."

"But I shouldn't have to find out about you that way. It's not normal." Carter stepped forward, a pained look on his face. "You should feel like you're able to tell me."

She glared at him. Then she remembered sitting in the car with Ethan last night and talking about her mother. She'd told Ethan, a boy she'd barely known for a week, more about her past than she'd ever told Carter. But it was easy, wasn't it? To tell strangers your deepest, darkest secrets. Because it didn't matter to them. Because they had no reason to judge you.

She watched Carter for a second, noting the confusion and frustration in his eyes.

I could tell him right now. Just spit it out and be done with it. Then I could walk away and never have to see him again.

She got angry. "What about you? We've been through this before—I'm not the only one with secrets!"

Irritation lit up Carter's eyes. Crossing the room, he pulled up two chairs. He sat down on one of them and nodded to the other. Emily stayed where she was.

"You want to hear about my sister? Fine, I'll tell you," he snapped. "Her name was Jamie. She was eleven years old when she disappeared. I was fifteen and supposed to be babysitting her, but instead I chose to smoke weed and hang out with my friends. When I finally decided to go home that evening, she was gone. She'd run away. Left a note saying she was too scared to stay at home anymore because our father was abusing her. No one believed it. Certainly not me. I thought she was acting up, doing it for the attention. She was *always* doing something for attention. Now it's obvious why. But by the time I started believing, it was too late. She was gone. No one ever saw her again. And it's all my fault."

Emily shuddered, staring at Carter open-mouthed, feeling all his hurt and pain rushing out of him to flood the room. He was shaking, angry-looking. He nodded at the empty chair.

"Your turn."

Emily stared at it, imagined a spotlight shining over her like a scene from a spy film, where the hero is about to be interrogated by the enemy.

"I . . ." She began. She thought about Phillip Gerard. About that day, when he'd gone sailing past her classroom window, clothes fluttering in the breeze. She thought about the sickening crunch of his body hitting the playground. It was all imagined, of course. She hadn't really seen him go past the window or heard him hit the ground. But she had heard the screams of horror that followed.

She stared at Carter, mouth opening and shutting, as he got up and crossed the room, then stopped just in front of her.

"You don't trust me," he said quietly. "At some point, when

you're ready, you need to trust someone. Even if that someone isn't me."

Emily stood, completely still and silent, avoiding Carter's gaze, until he gave up.

"I should get back to work."

She watched him turn away and walk back to the lathe. She hurried from the building and through the courtyard, where the snow was starting to stick, back to her car, where she sat behind the steering wheel, motionless, not knowing where to go. Not home. Not to the office. Not to see Harriet, even though she'd promised to visit but had let her down again.

There was only one place left to go.

Erica wanted the cameras back. Today, if possible.

Starting the engine, Emily pulled the car away from the kerb.

Yes, she would go get the cameras. And even though she'd been removed from the case, even though she'd been warned to stay away, perhaps while she was there, she'd be able to find out if the police had come any closer to unmasking The Witness.

41

THE DOOR OPENED and Jessica stared out, tired eyes growing as icy as the falling snow. "Oh, it's you. Come to spy on me some more, have you?"

Emily glanced away, shook her head.

"I'm sorry. But it was the only way I could be sure of your innocence. I was hired to investigate you, so that's what I did, but in the small amount of time I've spent with you and your children, I can see that, well, you've been through enough."

Jessica continued to stare. Emily sighed, shivering as a bitter wind bit into her exposed skin.

"I've come to collect the cameras. I've been taken off the case."

Jessica's expression remained the same. "Well, maybe that's for the best. You have everything you need to take them down?"

Emily nodded. She didn't know why she'd been hoping for any other reaction.

"Good. I'll be in the kitchen," Jessica replied then closed the door.

Grabbing a toolbox and stepladder from the boot of her car,

Emily got started, first detaching the camera from the porch, before climbing up to retrieve the second camera from the Rowan tree. The snow continued to fall, whipped about by the wind, making it dance in swirls around Emily as she perched on top of the ladder. As she pulled the camera free, her gaze wandered across the street. Raymond Butcher's tall silhouette stood at his living room window, watching her.

By the time she'd reached the rear garden, her fingers were red and stinging, her cheeks completely numb. A thin layer of snow had already settled on the lawn and borders of shrubs, and she had to brush snow away from the camera to get to it. Placing it inside the silver case, she stood and straightened her spine, aware that she was now shivering beneath her coat. Glancing up, she saw Ethan watching from his bedroom window. She raised a hand, but he only stared at her.

Trudging towards the back door, Emily stamped the snow from her shoes and reached for the handle. She hesitated, then knocked.

Jessica let her in. She had expected to see the same steely expression melded to the woman's face, but she only looked sad now. Sad and disappointed.

"That's all done," Emily said, shutting the door behind her and glancing around the kitchen. "I just need to—"

Jessica uncurled a hand and held it out, revealing the two mini cameras. "Here. They were easy enough to find once I knew where to look."

Silently, Emily plucked them from her palm, one at a time, returning them to the case. The two women stood, staring at each other, the air around them growing awkward and tense.

This is it, Emily thought. Time to say goodbye. Yet she wasn't ready to leave. Despite having been suspended from the case, despite Jessica's clear disappointment in having been deceived, Emily still felt the desire to help. Even if her help wasn't wanted.

Her chest heaving up and down, she glanced over her shoulder at the back door.

"Was it unlocked?" she asked. It had been puzzling her ever since last night. "Was that how he got in so easily?"

Eyes darting towards the door, Jessica's expression suddenly collapsed. "I've gone over and over it in my head. I'm *positive* that I locked it. I always do after dinner, it's part of my evening routine. And with all that's been happening lately, there's no way I would have forgotten to do it."

She stared at Emily, eyes desperate for answers.

"Well," Emily said, glancing down at the silver case in her hand. "There's one way we can find out."

———

Two minutes later, the women were at the kitchen table, a tablet in front of them and the camera feed dashboard filling the screen. Selecting last night's recorded footage from the hidden kitchen camera, Emily pressed play. They watched in silence, Jessica shifting uncomfortably and muttering under her breath as she watched a black and white version of herself lean against the kitchen counter and wipe tears from her eyes, before pulling out a whiskey bottle from under the sink. Emily felt her face burn, not daring to look at Jessica for fear of meeting her gaze. She was about to apologise for so wilfully invading her privacy, when they saw Jessica's grainy image move over to the back door and turn the key in the lock.

"I knew it! I knew I wasn't going crazy! But then how did he get in without forcing the door?"

Emily tapped the fast forward icon and they watched the footage speed up, Jessica's grainy figure racing around the kitchen at high speed before switching out the lights and leaving the room. Emily doubled the speed, watching the time counter in the corner of the screen go faster and faster, until the kitchen lights flickered on again and they saw a figure enter the room. It was Georgia, dressed in pyjamas, shuffling over to the kitchen sink.

"She came down to get a glass of water," Jessica explained. "I told her to go straight back to bed."

But as they watched, they saw that Georgia didn't go straight to bed. She drank the water, placed the glass in the sink, and crossed over to the back door. She hovered there for a minute, head swivelling over her shoulder to check the kitchen and the hall beyond.

"No," Jessica gasped.

They watched in shock as the child reached out and turned the key to the right, unlocking the door. Then they saw her hurry from the room, turning out the light as she went.

No one spoke. Emily's mind raced. What was going on? She glanced at Jessica, who had grown deathly pale, her eyes darting back and forth as she continued to stare at the now dark kitchen on the tablet screen.

"We need to go and talk to her," she said at last. "Right now."

————

They found her in her bedroom, sitting on the bed, propped up by pillows and surrounded by soft toys. She was reading a book, although Emily could see that she wasn't really reading. She looked exhausted, shadows lurking under her eyes, the colour that had returned to her complexion a week ago now drained.

"Sweetheart?" Jessica said softly. "We need to talk to you."

Emily hung back by the door while Jessica sat down on the edge of the bed and reached a hand towards her daughter.

"I need to ask you a question," Jessica said, keeping her voice calm and steady. "And I need you to tell me the truth. You're not in trouble and no one is going to get angry. We just need to hear what you have to say."

Georgia heaved her shoulders, avoiding her mother's gaze.

"Why did you unlock the back door?"

Instantly, the girl's body grew rigid, and even from her position by the door, Emily heard her catch her breath.

"It's okay," Jessica said. "We're just trying to understand what happened. Did someone tell you to unlock it?"

"I—I didn't do anything!" Georgia suddenly yelled. Tears sprang from her eyes. "It wasn't me!"

Jessica turned to Emily, slowly nodding, who handed her the tablet. She stood back again, watching Georgia as the footage was played, noting how all the tiny muscles in her face were twisting into knots.

"You can tell us," Jessica said, her voice still quiet and soothing. "Who told you to do this?"

Georgia turned away, shaking her head violently. She raised a hand to rub tears from her eyes and her sleeve fell down to expose the finger-shaped bruises that her mother had discovered only yesterday.

"Who hurt you?" Jessica's calm demeanour was breaking

now. She reached out to touch her daughter, but Georgia shrank away. "Was it the same person who told you to unlock the door?"

"I didn't want you to get hurt!" the girl wailed. "She didn't tell me that would happen!"

Emily and Jessica exchanged worried looks.

"Who didn't tell you?" Emily asked.

Georgia shook her head, over and over, as braying sobs caught in her throat. Jessica tried to reach out again, but she pushed her away, then sprang from the bed and into a corner, pressing her back against the wall like a trapped animal.

"I can't tell you!" she shrieked. "If I do, she'll hurt me!"

She slid down the wall until she hit the floor, then she pulled her knees up to her chest and buried her face in them, long, drawn-out sobs making her body tremble.

Jessica stared helplessly. Emily nodded towards the door and the two women went outside, leaving Georgia to weep in the corner.

"Who is she talking about?" Jessica's voice was choked with horror. "Who's making her do this?"

Up ahead, a door swung open and Ethan leaned out. "What's going on? What's wrong with Georgia?"

Emily and Jessica stared at him, then at each other.

"What other women has she had contact with?" Emily asked. "Besides you."

Jessica narrowed her eyes. "I hope you're not suggesting—"

"Think, Jessica. Who else has Georgia had contact with in the last few weeks?"

Jessica shook her head. "There is no one else! And the only other place she's been is . . ."

Her voice trailed away, the realisation hitting her. She glanced up, confusion and shock in her eyes.

"Hello?" Ethan said, waving a hand. "Am I invisible?"

A chill wrapped itself around Emily's spine as she finished Jessica's sentence for her. "Her school."

42

Emily parked outside the police station and climbed out of the car, almost skidding on a patch of ice. Out in the street a salt truck was rumbling by, spitting out chunks of rock salt onto the tarmac, a little too late in the day. Pushing open the double doors, she hurried to the reception area, where the same paunchy and belligerent duty officer she'd encountered on her first visit was manning the desk.

"I need to speak to DC Ryan," she said, aware that her tone was unnecessarily sharp. But she couldn't help it; her heart was pounding so hard in her chest that she was finding it impossible to stay calm. She had always believed that school was meant to be a haven—a home from home where children could feel safe and protected. Yet Georgia's safety had been violated, leaving her in danger from the very people who were meant to keep her from harm. She had seen it happen once before with tragic consequences. She wasn't about to let it happen again, especially to Georgia.

The officer stared at her, an amused look on his face.

"Today would be nice!" Emily snapped.

"DC Ryan isn't here," he said, his smile fading.

"Where is he?"

"I'm afraid I can't tell you that, Miss. If you'd like to leave your name and number, I'll—"

"What about DI Trent?"

"What about me?"

Emily spun around to see Detective Inspector Trent leaning out through a half open door.

"I need to talk to you," Emily said.

"Is that so?" DI Trent stared at her doubtfully. "Because if you're after information about the Harris case I'm afraid that won't be possible. Since the break in last night, this has become a serious criminal investigation and we don't have time for Nancy Drew types."

"Actually, I have information for you," Emily said, ignoring the sting of her ego. "Whoever's behind The Witness has been manipulating Georgia. Getting her to do things."

"What kind of things?"

"Unlocking the back door so that psychopath could get in last night, for one."

DI Trent's mouth dropped open an inch. "And you know this how, exactly."

"Because I have it on camera."

"You're telling me you have incriminating evidence that you haven't submitted for investigation? Do you know that with-holding evidence is a—"

"Here," Emily said, pulling her tablet from her bag and shoving it into the detective inspector's hand. "Consider it submitted. And here's something else for you while you're waiting on your tech team—whoever's manipulating Georgia and terrorising her family is connected to her school."

DI Trent stared at Emily, then at the tablet in her hands. Slowly, she smiled.

"I like you," she said. "Come with me."

43

THE SNOW HAD FALLEN throughout the weekend, but now on Monday morning it was already turning to slush. Which meant no snow day for Georgia. She arrived at school at the usual time, hordes of children already gathered in the playground and making an unearthly din. She held her mother's hand, which in any other circumstances would have been humiliating. But now she was afraid.

As they passed through the school gate, she stared up at her mother, who returned her gaze with a reassuring smile.

"It's okay," she said. "You're completely safe."

Georgia saw her mother's smile waver, as if she didn't believe her own words, and fear grew inside her like a snake uncoiling in her stomach. She slowed down, dragging her heels, not even smiling when Adora came running over, calling her name.

The fear continued to grow, reaching out to her fingers and toes, making them tremble as her mother kissed her goodbye then left her alone to line up with the rest of her class. She watched her mother walk through the gates, waited for her to look back, to change her mind and come get her. But she didn't.

She continued to walk, her step more hurried than usual, until she disappeared from sight.

Georgia looked around at the sea of bodies. She watched her classmates forming a tidy line, with Mrs Wernick standing up front. Then a shadow fell across Georgia and she looked up. Ms Craven was looming over her.

"Time to get in line," she said, and Georgia felt a shiver move all the way from the tip of her head down to the base of her heels.

———

Ten minutes later, their coats hanging on hooks and their packed lunches handed to the lunch monitor, the children sat at their desks while Mrs Wernick took the morning register. When she was done, she told them to get out their reading books for ten minutes of silent reading.

Removing a copy of *Hansel and Gretel* from her book bag, Georgia opened it up and turned to the first page. She knew she was probably too old for such a childish fairy tale, but it was one of her favourites and she'd read it several times. The best part was when Gretel pushed the evil old witch into the fire and stood there, listening to her screams of pain and watching her burn alive.

She glanced up at Mrs Wernick, who was standing by her desk, rifling through some worksheets. Most of the other children were sitting quietly, eyes on pages, faces lined with concentration, while a few were whispering to each other, hiding their mouths behind their hands. Ms Craven was sitting across the room, next to Alison Keith, who always needed extra help with reading. But Ms Craven wasn't helping Alison. She was staring straight at Georgia, her eyes unblinking. And she was smiling.

Soon, silent reading was over and it was time for maths. As the children put away their reading books, Mrs Wernick cleared her throat.

"Would you mind collecting a tray of set squares from the Maths cupboard, Ms Craven?"

"Of course." Ms Craven smiled and turned to the class. "Now who did all their reading and would like to be my assistant?"

"I think it'll be hard for you to choose today," Mrs Wernick said.

Every child in the room raised their hand, except Georgia, who kept her eyes fixed on an ink stain that she'd found on her desk.

"Let me see," Ms Craven said, looking around the room. "I think . . . Georgia! Yes, she was doing very well with her reading. She didn't make a peep."

A bubble of nausea popped in Georgia's throat.

"I think that's a good choice," Mrs Wernick said. "Well done. Off you go with Ms Craven."

Georgia sat still, her heart tap dancing on her spine.

"Come on, slow coach," Ms Craven said.

Slowly, Georgia got to her feet. She moved around the side of her desk on shaking legs.

Ms Craven held out a hand and waggled her fingers. Georgia stared at them, thinking they looked like a nest of snakes.

"Come on," Ms Craven said again, and she saw a flash of something dangerous in her eyes. She offered up her tiny hand and Ms Craven closed her fingers over it, squeezing a little too tightly.

Together, they left the classroom, shutting the door behind them and walking down the corridor. It was quiet now, all the children inside their rooms, lessons in full flow. They walked in silence, Georgia's heart pounding so hard that she was worried it would burst right out of her chest. She didn't dare look up at Ms Craven. Instead she kept her eyes fixed firmly in front of her as she counted her steps.

The maths storage cupboard was halfway along the corridor, on the right, in between the boys and girls toilets. They stopped outside and she felt Ms Craven squeeze her hand even tighter.

"The cat got your tongue today?" she said, but there was no humour in her voice. Taking out a large bunch of keys, she slid one into the lock of the maths cupboard door and turned it.

The door swung open, revealing a tiny room with barely enough room to fit two people, and with shelves running from ceiling to floor filled with trays of equipment. Ms Craven waited for Georgia to step inside. When she didn't move, the woman gave her a hard shove, making her trip over her feet and land in a heap on the storage cupboard floor. Ms Craven shut the door behind them, snapped the lock into place, and switched on the light.

Georgia's whole body started to tremble. Tears, hot and stinging, filled her eyes. For a long time, Ms Craven didn't speak, just stood there, her large, powerful frame looming like a giant.

Then she smiled.

"I heard the police came to your house. Did your mummy enjoy her surprise?"

She grinned wickedly, exposing her teeth. One was missing, Georgia noted, from the upper jaw on the left side.

"Well, did she?"

Georgia shook her head. She tried to speak, but it was as if her throat had sealed up.

"Good. She wasn't supposed to." Ms Craven bent down and grabbed Georgia's hand again, squeezing it so hard that tears came spilling down her face. "What did she say? Did she tell you that you have to move out?"

Again, Georgia shook her head, tears flying through the air to splash on the wall. Ms Craven squeezed her hand even tighter, making her squeal. Slowly, the woman released her hold.

"What's it going to take?" she hissed. "If your mummy doesn't move out very soon, I'm going to get very cross. And when I get very cross, I don't know what I might do."

Georgia pulled at her clothes as she stared up at the woman's towering shape. Her hand throbbed with pain.

"We're going to try again." The woman leaned down, her shadow spreading across the wall as she reached into her cardigan pocket and pulled out a small brown bottle.

"Take it."

Georgia stared at it, wondering what it was.

"You're going to go home this evening," Ms Craven said. "And you're going to empty this into the milk carton. You mustn't drink it, not if you don't want to get sick. But you must make sure your mummy takes a drink. Maybe that brother of yours, too."

Ms Craven smiled as Georgia stared at the bottle.

"I—I don't want to," she stammered, shaking her head.

Ms Craven leaned in, her face growing dangerously close. "You will do it. Your mummy needs to be punished for being a stubborn criminal's whore. Now take it, or you'll be very, very sorry."

She thrust the brown bottle at Georgia.

"Take it," Ms Craven hissed. "You know what will happen if you don't."

Georgia stared at the bottle. She didn't want her mummy to get sick. But she didn't want to get hurt either. Not again. But then Ms Craven was snatching up her arm and pinching her skin, as hard as she could. She winced, hissing through her teeth. More tears ran down her cheeks. She took the bottle, trying to hold in the sobs as she slipped it inside her skirt pocket.

Ms Craven stood up, a triumphant smile on her face.

"Good girl," she said. "Your mummy deserves a taste of her own medicine, don't you think?"

She glanced over her shoulder, towards the locked door. Someone was walking past; a child, singing to themselves. Georgia thought about calling out, but she knew what would happen if she did.

When it was quiet again, Ms Craven turned back to her. "Now, tell me—what are you going to do tonight as soon as you get home?"

"I . . . I'm going to put it in the milk," she said.

"That's right," Ms Craven's eyes were glinting as she reached for something inside her pocket. "Because if you don't, you'll wish that you'd never, ever been born."

In a flash, she grabbed Georgia's face with one hand, squeezing her cheeks, and with the other thrust a large darning needle towards her eye.

Georgia squealed, watching its sharp point glint in the light. Ms Craven leaned in. She smiled, baring her teeth, but her eyes were cold and dead. Like sharks' eyes.

"It would pop so easily," she whispered, the point of the needle getting closer and closer. "Like a burst little grape!"

Georgia tried to turn away but Ms Craven held her face in a

cast iron grip. Squirming, she squeezed her eyes shut and thought about nice things, like her toys and her books, and that time before her dad got taken away and they all went on holiday to a place called Florida.

She felt Ms Craven retreat, the light shifting behind her closed eyes. When she opened them again, Ms Craven was unlocking the door. Then she was reaching for a large tray of set squares, the shiny triangular rulers all the colours of the rainbow.

"Let's get back to class," she said, a pleasant smile on her face. "Today we're learning about right angles!"

They walked the length of the corridor. Georgia was deathly pale. Her hand throbbed and her eyes stung, and she felt that somewhere deep inside her, part of her was broken. Ms Craven walked ahead, a strange smile on her lips. Georgia wiped her eyes with the back of a sleeve, trying to stay focused on the nice things.

They reached the classroom door. Ms Craven glanced down at her, shooting her a vicious, warning look.

"Rosemary? Ms Craven!"

The voice was cold and stern, making Georgia turn around. Principal Owen was standing behind them, dressed in a black trouser suit, her usual kind face pulled into an angry scowl. And she wasn't alone. Two uniformed police officers stood on either side of her.

Georgia's heart jumped into her throat. She glanced up and saw Ms Craven's mouth had dropped open into a perfect circle.

There were more people coming down the corridor. Among them was the policeman in the suit, who had told her a funny joke earlier that morning.

"You need to come with us," Principal Owen said, angry flames burning in her eyes. Georgia didn't think she'd ever seen her so mad. "These police officers would like to have a word with you."

Ms Craven let out a strangled noise, somewhere between a squeal and a laugh. Her eyes flicked down to Georgia, who scratched at the funny wire that a policewoman had taped to her skin beneath her shirt, wishing she could take it off now. Ms Craven dropped the plastic tray and the set squares rained down on the carpet, one of them landing on Georgia's feet. Then she began to wail and pull at her hair. It was a strange noise, Georgia thought; like when you accidentally stood on a cat's tail. And she looked frightened. More frightened than her dad had looked when the police came to arrest *him*.

Good, Georgia thought. She was glad Ms Craven was scared. She hoped that she'd cry until she wet herself. Just like she'd made Georgia do before.

44

Emily sat in the back of a patrol car, eyes fixed on the school gates, her mouth running dry. Just being here, staring up at the building, was bringing back all kinds of unpleasant memories that she'd worked so hard to block out. But now wasn't the time to immerse herself in guilt and imagined scenarios in which she saved Phillip Gerard from death. Now was the time to be here for Jessica.

It had been a near-impossible task to convince her to agree to the plan. And rightly so.

The person responsible for terrorising Jessica's family was lurking somewhere inside Georgia's school. DI Trent wanted to send Georgia inside to lure the suspect out into the open. It didn't matter that the detective thought it was no longer safe to wait for the tech team, who were still tied up in bigger cases, or that her daughter would be wearing a wire, or that the police would be right outside, listening in and ready to strike; to Jessica, they were sending a mouse into a lion's den. *Her* mouse. *Her* little girl. And there was no way on this green earth that she was going to let that happen.

It was Emily who had finally convinced Jessica, telling her that this was the only way, promising her that Georgia would be safe and that it would bring the horrors of the last month to a swift end.

Now, her stomach churning and twisting in knots, Emily hoped that she was right. She glanced at Jessica, who was sitting next to her, eyes fixed on the school building. She looked so tired, Emily thought. Beaten down by all the terrible events life had thrown at her these past months.

"What's taking them so long?" Jessica pressed her face against the window of the passenger door.

Emily glanced at the young police officer sitting up front, his fingers nervously drumming on the steering wheel. It was like they were all waiting for a gun to go off.

The crackle of the police officer's radio made Emily jump out of her skin. A tinny voice spoke. The officer responded. Then twisted around in his seat.

"They're coming out," he said.

Jessica and Emily glanced at each other, then peered through the window and saw two uniformed police officers crossing the playground and heading for the gate, quickly followed by DC Ryan and another plainclothes detective, who were escorting a large middle-aged woman, her arms handcuffed behind her back. The woman was shrieking hysterically, her face twisted into a grotesque mask. Above her, rows of curious faces filled the windows of the school building, all staring and whispering.

Jessica gasped, her eyes growing wide. "Ms Craven?"

Emily watched as the woman was led through the school gates, the envoy of police officers surrounding her. She saw Jessica reach for the door, felt anger pulsing from her in waves. She put a hand on her shoulder.

"Let them do their job," Emily soothed. "She can't hurt you anymore."

They watched as Ms Craven was pushed into the back of a police car and driven away. Then they returned their attention to the playground.

"Where is she?" Jessica hissed, her voice trembling now.

And there she was, holding DI Trent's hand as they walked out of the building.

Jessica threw open the car door. Emily climbed out after her and crossed the road, sliding to a halt at the gate. She hadn't stepped onto school premises in over two years. She thought it best to keep it that way. Besides, this wasn't about her. She watched mother and daughter run towards each other; Georgia wrapping arms around her mother's waist, Jessica sobbing and pressing her close.

Emily watched them, relief flowing through her body like nectar, glad that it was all over.

45

THE SNOW STARTED UP AGAIN, covering the city in a soft, white blanket. This time, Emily thought it might stay for a little while. She met up briefly with Jerome at a cafe two streets away from Braithwaite Investigations and handed him the case of surveillance cameras. Erica had hauled him over the coals, he told her, and was still deciding whether he could keep his job.

"I'm sorry," Emily said, prompting Jerome to roll his eyes.

"You need to get over this guilt complex. I've told you a thousand times, I'm a grown adult and I make my own choices." He paused, shaking his head. "By the way, Erica wants the car back."

Emily's heart sank into her stomach. "Guess that's me looking for a new job, then. I'll return it tomorrow. Right now, I want to go home and sink into a hot bath."

Driving back to The Holmeswood, she about to let herself into her apartment when Harriet Golding's voice rasped behind her, "Hello stranger. Haven't seen you in ages."

Emily turned and forced a smile to her lips. "Tomorrow, I promise."

She spent the rest of the evening, soaking in the bathtub, her mind processing the events of the day. Carter called but she didn't pick up. He sent a text message, but she didn't read it. Instead, she sank into her bed and slept for eight hours.

The next morning, she woke to a call from Jessica Harris, inviting her back to Raven Road, and now she found herself sitting in the living room, along with Jessica and DC Ryan, who looked like he hadn't slept last night and was nursing a much-needed mug of coffee. Ethan was busy watching over Georgia upstairs.

"Why did she do it?" Jessica asked.

It was the one question that Emily had been unable to answer.

DC Ryan shook his head; not because he didn't have the answer, but because he couldn't quite believe it.

"She wanted the house," he said.

Jessica stared at him, open-mouthed and incredulous. "She put my family through hell. She terrorised us. All because she wanted this house?"

DC Ryan looked as perplexed as Emily felt. "Apparently, she'd had her eye on your home for a long time. She says it was her dream house, something she wanted to have for herself. Rosemary Craven has never had much of a life from the sounds of it. She's spent much of it caring for her elderly parents, who'd had her later in life. They both died within a month of each other, right around the time Rosemary started working at your daughter's school. She walked along Raven Road, every morning on the way to work, daydreaming of living on a nice street like this, in a nice big house instead of the cramped two bedroom flat she shared with her parents. When number fifty-seven was put up for sale, she made an offer. And the Fishers were going to accept it, until your husband swooped in with a better offer—one that Rosemary Craven couldn't compete with."

Jessica was quiet, trying to make sense of it all.

"She was angry," DC Ryan continued. "Bitter and outraged, especially when she'd read about Wesley's arrest. She didn't think a bunch of criminals deserve such a nice house." He raised his hands defensively. "Her words, not mine. Anyway, Craven thought that with your husband on remand, you'd be feeling vulnerable, so if she could scare you badly enough, you'd put the house back on the market and want to leave. Then she'd make you an offer—a familiar face from your daughter's school—and she'd have the house of her dreams at last. She's completely fixated by it, like this house has become a symbol for her. An escape from a desperately unhappy life."

The three sat in silence for a moment, contemplating Rosemary Craven.

"What about Georgia?" Emily asked.

"She'd once confessed to Craven that she'd never wanted to move to Amberwell. That she was desperately unhappy and wanted nothing more than to go back to her old home and be with her old friends. Craven manipulated her; told her she could help make that happen. She used Georgia, just for information at first. Then things turned nasty." He stared at Jessica, his eyes sad and sympathetic. "She hurt your daughter. Threatened to do worse if she didn't comply. Craven made her unlock the door that night, and yesterday, she'd given her a vial of rat poison and told her to put it in the milk to make you sick."

Jessica grew pale, her eyes filling with tears. Then her face turned crimson with anger. "I hope she fucking rots in prison."

DC Ryan cleared his throat and adjusted his tie. "Craven has admitted responsibility for all the harassment—pretending to be you online and goading that man to break into your home, sending the spiders, the adult magazines, and the obscene note to your neighbours—but she completely denies writing the letters. She says the first she heard of The Witness was when she read about it in the local newspaper. She says that's what gave her the idea to jump aboard and help out, thinking she could force you to sell the house."

"Bullshit." Jessica leaned back on the sofa. "You don't believe that, do you?"

"Not really. I think Rosemary Craven has realised how much trouble she's in and is now doing her best to reduce the charges." The detective put down his coffee mug and got to his feet. "I should probably go. We'll need to take a full statement from Georgia, sooner rather than later, but I'll have the family liaison officer arrange that with you." He smiled then, a warm, reassuring smile. "It's over. Your family is safe. Maybe now you can get back to some semblance of normality."

Jessica scoffed. "I think normality might have to wait. I just found out this morning a date's been set for Wesley's trial."

"Well, good luck." Detective Constable Ryan said his goodbyes and left, nodding at Emily as he went.

When they were alone, Emily stared at the floor. "I suppose I should get going myself. Will you be okay?"

Jessica nodded. "My kids are depending on me." She paused, her eyes softening. "I wanted to thank you. You were supposed to be investigating me but instead you helped to protect my family. Now you'll probably lose your job because of it, and I'm sorry. But I want you to know how grateful I am. How grateful we all are."

Shrugging a shoulder, Emily smiled.

"What will you do now?"

She thought about it. Jessica was right—her role at Braithwaite Investigations was almost certainly at an end, which now left a blank space where her future was meant to be. She should probably try to fill it somehow.

But with what?

She smiled again. "I'll think of something. How about you? I assume you'll be dropping the lawsuit against the Fishers?"

"I already spoke to my solicitor this morning. I feel terrible."

"If it makes you feel better you're not the only one to have got on their bad side." She squeezed Jessica's arm. "Now I really should go."

She turned to leave, but Jessica lunged forward and hugged her tightly. Emily resisted at first, then slowly forced herself to relax.

"Thank you," Jessica said again.

"You take care of yourself and the kids. Go easy on Ethan—he's angry but he's not all bad. One day he might even surprise you."

Leaving Jessica in the living room, Emily made her way outside, where a thin blanket of snow had settled over the street. The salt trucks had visited again last night, leaving the road a black streak slicing through the white.

As Emily approached the car, she turned to see Ethan and Georgia watching her from an upstairs window. They waved at her and she waved back. Then she stared across the street and saw Raymond Butcher's silhouette. She raised a hand, but he stood unmoving, statue-like at the living room window.

Climbing into the driver's seat, Emily strapped herself in and started the engine. An uneasy feeling fluttered in her chest, like a butterfly trapped in a jar. She wasn't sure if it was because of something DC Ryan had said, or if it was because she was about to head to the Fishers, hoping to rebuild some burned bridges.

46

As EMILY KNOCKED on the front door of the Fishers' home, the uneasy feeling in her stomach continued to unfurl. A moment later, the door opened and Meredith peered out, her curious expression suddenly hardening like ice.

"You shouldn't be here," she said. "Erica's taken you off the case."

Emily stared down at her boots, which were caked in melting snow. "She has. But I wanted you to know the police have arrested a suspect they believe to be The Witness. And Jessica Harris is dropping the lawsuit."

Emily waited, hoping that her news was enough to grant her a reprieve. Slowly, Meredith's lips parted, but no words came. Her narrowed eyes grew soft and watery, filling with tears.

"Oh, thank God!" she cried, clutching at her chest and leaning against the door jamb, as if she didn't have the strength to stand.

Emily arched an eyebrow. She had expected Meredith to be relieved, but this was something much bigger than that.

She cleared her throat, eyes finding the ground once more. "I also wanted to apologise. You put your trust in me and I betrayed you, ignoring your request to stay away from the Harrises. And even though it got the results you wanted, it wasn't my place to make that call. I'm sorry, Mrs Fisher. Sorry for any distress I caused you and your husband."

She glanced at Meredith again, who was still pressed against the door, hand to her chest, and who clearly hadn't heard a word.

"Is everything okay?" Emily asked. Because now Meredith was silently crying, tears running down her face.

Removing a tissue from her sleeve, she carefully dabbed her eyes. "I'm sorry. It's just that—" She hesitated, glancing over Emily's shoulder into the snowy drive. "Well, the truth is . . ."

Her voice trailed off again.

"Mrs Fisher? What's wrong?"

Meredith ushered her in from the cold and shut the door. They stood in the hallway, shadows dancing over the walls, the ticking of a clock the only sound.

"I'm just so relieved, that's all," she said, pressing her hand to her chest once more. "But I feel so guilty."

"About what?"

Now, Meredith glanced over her shoulder, back into the house. When she turned to Emily again, she looked awkward. Embarrassed, even.

"I lied to you. To everyone," she said, dropping her voice to a hush. "My husband didn't have a stroke."

Emily's jaw dropped open an inch. "He didn't?"

"John isn't well, and I don't mean physically." She nodded as she gazed at Emily, testing to see if she had understood. "He had a nervous breakdown. A bad one. John had always been . . . sensitive, shall we say? Ever since I've known him, he's been prone to bouts of depression and anxiety, sometimes wishing to be left alone for days, other times clinging on to me like a child. Some people struggle in this world. Some people have terrible things happen to them that leave them broken."

She continued to stare at Emily, her strange gaze penetrating her skin. The butterfly trapped in Emily's stomach broke free and fluttered up to her chest, wings flapping out of control.

"We'd only lived there for a year," Meredith continued, "but in that time I saw John grow progressively worse. He'd been so keen on that house. To me, it wasn't anything special, but when he saw it was for sale, he became obsessed with it, insisting that we put in an offer. So I agreed; anything to keep him happy. But the longer we stayed in the house, the worse he became. He grew depressed and withdrawn. He would have terrible nightmares and he would sleepwalk.

"Then one night, I found him in the basement, naked and screaming, pressed into a corner like a terrified child. Whatever it was about that house, it was making him sick. So the next morning, I insisted we put it on the market."

Meredith paused, momentarily lost in dark memories. "When I first heard about the letters, I became afraid."

"Afraid of what?"

She looked up, staring Emily straight in the eye. "Afraid that John was writing them."

Emily's mind was racing, making tiny connections, trying to make sense of it all. "Why would you think that?"

"It was the handwriting. It was different from John's but similar enough to make me wonder. When I saw that the first letter mentioned the basement, I felt this terrible feeling in my gut, like something was eating away at me." Her face was haunted, her eyes lost and searching. "That's why I reached out to Erica in the first place. I needed to know that it was the Harrises who were behind the letters. More than that, I needed to know that it wasn't my husband."

Panic was hijacking Emily's mind, making it hard to think straight. Through the chaos came DC Ryan's voice, clear as a warm, spring sky. Yet his words were like icicles.

"Where's John right now?" she asked.

But Meredith wasn't listening. "The truth is, I've been fussing over him so much lately that I probably haven't helped his recovery at all. It was because I was terrified, you see. Terrified of what you might find out." She wiped a tear away and laughed. "But now I know that the only thing my husband is guilty of is being unwell."

"Meredith!" Emily said sharply. "Where is your husband?"

The woman blinked. "He's out on one of his walks. Which is a good sign because John always used to love going for walks. Sometimes he'd be gone for hours. He says walking brings him peace. And this week, he's been out walking almost every day."

She smiled, beaming with pride.

But Emily could only stare as a paralysing chill clawed at her bones.

47

THE DOUBLE DOORS of the library flew open and Emily came hurtling in, heading straight for the counter, where two shocked librarians stood, gaping at her. Before either could speak, she held up her private investigator licence.

"Sorry for the entrance," she said. "I need to access newspaper archives. How do I do that?"

The librarians, two women of indeterminate age, stared curiously at her. One of them, an olive skinned woman named Flora, according to the badge pinned on her chest, cleared her throat. "All the newspapers are stored on microfilm, right at the back on the left."

"Lead the way."

Emily followed her past shelves of books, where a handful of patrons turned to stare, until they reached the far end of the library and a table of bulky, dated-looking projectors, which stood next to several wide filing cabinets containing hundreds of small trays.

"This is it," Flora said. "These filing cabinets contain the micro-films. You use these projectors to examine them. Which newspaper are you looking for?"

Emily stared at the rows and rows of filing drawers, overwhelmed by the sheer mass. "I don't know. Something local and old enough to go back fifty years."

Flora stared at the drawers, rubbing a thumb against her chin. "Well, the Amberwell Herald has been going since the turn of the century. That should do." She spent a minute locating the section of drawers dedicated to the Herald, then ran a finger down them. "The drawers are labelled by year. You know how to use one of these things?"

Emily shook her head.

Pulling open a drawer labelled '1969', the librarian removed a small plastic box and brought it over to one of the projectors.

"It's old film that the newspapers have been scanned onto," she explained, showing Emily how to attach the reel to a spool on the left side of the projector, then feed it beneath a microscope to attach to a spool on the right. "Use this button to scan through each page, this one to speed forward, and this one to go back. Don't press the red button, or you'll have Heather over there breathing down your neck."

With the first film fitted, Flora pressed a button and the projector screen lit up, displaying a row of condensed newspaper pages. She showed Emily which buttons to use to zoom in and out, then she stood back, allowing her to sit.

Emily stared at the pages on the screen and fiddled with the zoom button. Flora was still standing there, watching.

"Looking for anything interesting?" she asked.

"Murder, mostly."

The librarian raised her eyebrows then made her way back towards the front desk.

Emily got to work, scanning through each page until she

came to the end of the first newspaper. She moved on to the next issue. Her eyes shifted back and forth as she zoomed in and out, turning the dials to advance the film.

Minutes ticked by, her frustration growing as she skimmed page after page, finding nothing but stories about local flower shows, housing issues, and petty crime. Soon, she had reached the end of the reel and 1969. Carefully removing the film as shown, she returned it to the drawer and loaded up '1970'. She started searching again, trawling through numerous stories, but not one about murder on Raven Road. She had no idea if the murders Raymond Butcher had told her about were even true, but the tightness in her chest was growing more urgent, like she was running out of air.

She decided to stop scanning each newspaper in its entirety and concentrate on the front pages. If there was one thing about local newspapers, murder always got top billing. 1971 raced by, quickly followed by 1972 and 1973. She loaded up the film roll for 1974.

And there it was, in the third week of July, in bold, black letters: *Family Slain In House Of Horror. Only One Survivor.*

Emily read through the columns of the story, her breaths growing thinner by the second. By the time she'd finished, the hairs on the back of her neck were standing to attention. Leaving the film roll still attached to the projector, she jumped up from the table and ran through the library, mobile phone pressed to her ear. As she dashed past the front desk, Flora and the other librarian glanced up, mouths hanging open.

"Hey, wait a minute!" Flora called. But Emily was already through the door and hurrying to her car.

Jessica wasn't answering her phone. Emily climbed in and started the engine, driving away from the library, one hand on the wheel, the other dialling the police station's number. The line connected and a familiar voice spoke in her ear.

"I need to speak to DC Ryan now. It's an emergency," she gasped, her voice taut and thin.

"I'm afraid DC Ryan is unavailable," the duty officer said.

"Then you need to make him available because Jessica Harris and her children are still in danger."

"Is this some sort of prank? Because the suspect has already been charged."

The car skidded on a patch of ice. Emily threw the phone onto the passenger seat and spun the wheel between both hands, gaining control of the vehicle.

"Shit!" she yelled.

She was just two minutes away from Raven Road. She would get there before she could make another call. She just hoped that she wasn't too late.

48

PARKING the car with one wheel on the kerb, Emily grabbed her phone from the seat and dialled another number. This time the caller answered and she barked commands at them, not caring how angry or terrified she sounded.

Hurrying across the road towards number fifty-seven, she slipped on more ice and twisted her ankle, sending bolts of pain shooting up her leg. Swearing, she wrenched open the gate and limped her way up the drive, where she hammered on the front door.

Five seconds ticked by. Ten.

Emily hammered again, then dialled Jessica's number. As she waited for her to answer, her eyes scanned the street, landing on the Butchers' house. Perhaps they had seen something.

Hobbling back down the drive, she returned to the street and crossed the road, Jessica's automated voicemail playing in her ear. Emily hung up and entered the Butcher's front yard. She pressed the buzzer and stepped back. When no one answered, she hammered on the door then hobbled across the drive to the living room window, where she cupped her hands to the sides of her face and peered in.

Raymond Butcher was sitting in an armchair that faced away from the street. His head was tipped to the side, his arm hanging down, knuckles touching the carpet.

Emily hammered on the window. "Mr Butcher? Raymond!"

The man remained unmoving. Colour drained from Emily's face as she hurried back to the front door and flipped open the letterbox. She was about to call through when the stench hit her, rotten and putrid like days old meat. Her stomach somersaulted as she peered through the slot.

She saw the foot of the stairs. She saw coats hanging from hooks. She saw Geraldine Butcher's lifeless eyes staring back at her from down the hall, where her body sat propped up against the wall.

With a strangled cry, Emily staggered backwards. Images of Raymond Butcher standing at the living room window assaulted her mind. She'd seen him just this morning, watching her as she climbed into her car.

Except it hadn't been Raymond Butcher, not today or on the previous days.

Because Raymond and Geraldine Butcher had clearly been dead for at least a week.

Emily panicked. Her vision stretched out before her like chewing gum, then snapped back like elastic. She stood, frozen to the drive, her mind jamming like trapped microfilm.

"Move!" she hissed.

Pulling out her phone she dialled 999, then set off again, stepping off the kerb and onto the road. The emergency operator asked her which service she needed.

"Police," she said, her voice thin and high-pitched. She was halfway across the road now. The police operator spoke in her ear.

"They're dead," Emily heard herself say. "He killed them and the Harris family are next."

She gave the operator the address then hung up. There was no time to wait for the police. If she did, Jessica and the children would die.

Emily hurried up the family's drive, her twisted ankle throbbing painfully. She tried the front door, which was locked, then she circled the house, making her way to the rear garden.

The back door was locked, too. She spun around, searching the shrubbery, until she found a fist-sized rock. Without hesitating, she smashed through one of the back door windowpanes. Slipping a hand through the hole, she turned the key and let herself in.

The house was quiet and deathly still.

"Jessica?" Silence answered her. "Ethan? Georgia?"

The kitchen was a mess. Chairs were turned over. Shards of broken crockery lay scattered on the floor.

Hurrying over to the counter, Emily wrenched open a drawer and removed a large steak knife. She turned, fighting for air and trying to control the dizziness that threatened to overwhelm her.

She already knew where he'd taken them. There was only ever one destination.

The basement door was already open. The light already on. Emily froze, a terrible pressure building in her temples. She waited, listening as she peered into the depths.

From below came a terrified, strangled cry.

Forcing one foot in front of the other, Emily made her way down to the basement.

49

THE SOBS and cries grew louder. Her senses screamed at her to turn around, but Emily forced her feet onward, descending the steps to reach the cold concrete floor.

Again, she was struck by how ordinary the basement appeared. Until she saw the horror show that was playing out.

Georgia had been shoved into a corner, wrists and ankles tightly bound and tape over her mouth. Ethan and Jessica were at the centre of the room. Like Georgia, they were tied and gagged, only they were on their feet, tip-toeing precariously on top of footstools, nooses of rope dropping down from the central support beam to loop around their necks. Like Georgia, their desperate, frightened eyes swung towards Emily.

She stared back, horrified and sick to her stomach. Then she saw John Fisher. *The Witness.*

He stood at the edge of the room, half in shadows, mouth pulled into a sneer, a hammer swinging loosely in his hand.

"You're not supposed to be here," he said, his voice low and trembling, the claw of the hammer pointed at Emily. All three members of the Harris family began to struggle against their bindings, cries muffled by their gags. Emily barely noticed. She kept her gaze fixed on John Fisher and her grip tight on the knife, as the thick, terror-laden air of the basement invaded her lungs.

"John," she said, failing to keep her voice steady. "You don't have to do this."

He smiled. "I do and I'm sorry. As He is my Witness, I shall be theirs."

Emily took a step closer, the blade trembling in her hand. John hissed, baring his teeth, the naked, overhead light reflected in his black eyes.

"Please, John," she said. "I know what happened to you. I know what your father did to your family."

In the corner, Georgia began to wail hysterically, choking on the gag. Jessica twisted her head, the noose tightening around her neck, her eyes begging, imploring.

Emily stepped forward, but John was closer, blocking her path. "Your father was ill. Very ill. He abused you and your brothers. Your mother, too. He did terrible things to you all. And then he led you down to the basement one night. He tied you up, just like you've done to Georgia, and then he made you watch as he murdered them all, one by one, right in front of you. Until only you were left."

Jessica's eyes grew impossibly wide. Two metres away, Ethan shook his head and choked on the gag, the toes of his left foot balancing dangerously on the edge of the stool.

John was crying now, his terrible gaze paralysing Emily as she watched the horror of that night return to haunt him.

She tried again. "Your father slaughtered your family and

then he killed himself, leaving you to witness it all. You must have spent your entire life wondering why. *Why* did he make you watch? *Why* did he let you live? But I don't think there's an answer, apart from madness."

Saliva dripped from John's mouth and he made no effort to wipe it away. "Because it was my turn," he whispered. "Because I was a rotten apple. Because it was time to pass on the torch."

"You were a child. Innocent. What your father did to you wasn't your fault."

"No! He gave me a job. He handed the duty to me, from father to son. I am The Witness and I watch you all!"

Her legs quaking beneath her, threatening to collapse, Emily stepped forward.

"Put the hammer down, John. Let's talk."

"No!" He swung the hammer through the air, threatening her. "This is your fault! You were supposed to leave, so I could watch in peace. I told you all what would happen if you didn't go."

"It's not their fault. The only mistake these people made was to move into this house. Please, John. Let them go."

Emily watched as he backed away, circling like a shark, until he stood behind Jessica, one foot resting on the leg of the stool. Her eyes darted up to Jessica's face, which was contorted in blind terror, her skin white as bone, the gag sucking in and out of her mouth as she tried to scream.

"John, please! Let them go."

Slowly, sadly, he shook his head. "No. I'm tired. It's time to pass on the torch."

His gaze travelled to the corner of the room, where Georgia had grown deathly still, transfixed and terrified.

"As I was his witness, she will be mine," John Fisher said. He kicked away the stool, sending it clattering across the floor.

Jessica dropped. The rope grew taut, squeezing the life from her lungs. Her body bucked as her face turned red and her eyes bulged, legs kicking furiously in the air.

Emily dashed forward, dropping the knife and grabbing Jessica's legs. She held on tight, taking her weight and loosening the pull of the rope.

John was on the move, stalking towards Ethan, eyes wild and rolling.

"Don't!" Emily screamed.

But John was already reaching for the stool.

With a smothered cry, Ethan lashed out, kicking backwards and knocking the man to the ground, where he struck his head on the concrete.

Emily stretched out a leg, reaching for Jessica's stool with her foot and falling short by an inch. She screamed in frustration.

John was sitting up now. Climbing onto his hands and knees.

Jessica squirmed and thrashed in Emily's grasp. She shook her head wildly, screaming through the gag, pointing at Ethan with her eyes.

"Let me go," Emily thought she heard her say through the gag. "Save my son!"

John was on his feet, his face twisted with rage and grief. Jessica stared at Emily, her eyes suddenly calm and pleading.

"Let me go."

Horrified, confused, Emily loosened her grip.

John lunged at Ethan.

And then a voice, shrill and broken, pierced the air. "John, no! What are you doing?"

John Fisher froze on the spot.

Clamping her arms around Jessica once more, Emily twisted around to see Meredith standing at the foot of the stairs, a look of pure disbelief on her face.

"What are you *doing*?" she repeated, as if scolding a child.

John stared back at her. And then it was as if all the anger, all the fury and despair drained from his body and seeped into the floor. He folded in on himself, hammer swinging loosely in his hand, chin dropping onto his chest. He wept.

"John," Meredith said, her voice soft and soothing now as she stepped forward, moving closer until she was right in front of him. Gently, she reached out and placed a hand over his. "Listen to me, put the hammer down."

Emily heard sirens, somewhere in the distance but getting closer. Her arms trembled under Jessica's weight, her muscles threatening to snap. But she tightened her grip, refusing to let go.

"Come on, put it down," Meredith said, stroking the side of his face. "Let's go home. We'll put you to bed and you can have a nice, long sleep. Tomorrow you'll feel better. Tomorrow you'll feel as right as rain."

Tyres screeched out in the street and the sirens cut out. There was a dull thud and a crack, then feet were thundering across the floor above. The basement door flew open and voices filled the air, along with the crackle of police radios.

John Fisher looked at his wife, all the sadness in the world pressing down on him.

"I'm tired," he said. "Very tired."

As the first police officers reached the basement, Emily screamed: "Georgia, close your eyes!"

In one lightning movement, John raised the hammer and

smashed it into the side of his head. His body crumpled. Meredith screamed.

Everyone witnessed him die, except for Georgia, who kept her eyes squeezed shut, thinking of all the nice things she could think of, until her mother told her she could look again.

TWO DAYS PASSED. Emily hadn't slept much, lying awake at night, replaying those awful images from the basement, hearing the Harris family's terrified screams and Meredith Fisher's heartbroken cry as her husband took his own life. Jessica, Ethan and Georgia were safe, mostly unharmed, but Emily couldn't help but wonder what lasting effects their ordeal in the basement might have. She'd let them be for now, with a promise that she was a phone call away if they needed her help.

She still hadn't seen Carter, only sharing a handful of text message exchanges since their last, strained encounter, and turning down his request to come over after he'd heard the news about John Fisher.

Now, she found herself in Erica Braithwaite's office, tiredness still tugging at the edges, feeling strangely calm and collected for someone who was about to be fired. Erica sat on the other side of the desk, a grave expression on her face as Emily recounted the frightening events that took place at 57 Raven Road. Outside, the snow continued to fall, overstaying its welcome.

"According to the news archives and John Fisher's police

statement at the time, his father, Terrence Fisher, was convinced that an evil presence lived within the walls of Raven Road. Of course, he was completely unstable, but he nonetheless believed this entity commanded him to watch over the house. And that it also required sacrifice. John's father slaughtered his entire family in front of him, hanging them, one by one, in the same way John tried to murder the Harrises.

"Before taking his own life, Terrence told John that he was leaving him alive with the sole purpose of carrying on his duty as watcher of the house. Unsurprisingly, the ordeal left eight-year-old John completely traumatised and deeply disturbed. He spent much of his adolescent life in and out of institutions before eventually getting lost in the foster care system, but at some point, he re-emerged as an adult, apparently able to stand on his own two feet, holding down a successful career, then meeting and marrying Meredith. Only, that traumatised little boy was still trapped inside, slowly coming undone." Emily paused as Erica let out a long, faltering sigh. "I'm sorry. This must be difficult to hear."

"I remember when Meredith met John," Erica said with a sad smile. "It was at an engagement party of a mutual friend. He seemed so pleasant. So down to earth. I would never have guessed in a million years the horrors he'd endured, or what was festering beneath the surface. Oh, Meredith would mention his bouts of depression and anxiety over the years, but she was a proud woman, battling with her own conflicting feelings and the stigma of mental illness. But she loved him dearly."

Emily had her own conflicting feelings about Meredith. She may have loved her husband, but she'd clearly had her suspicions about him and had chosen denial over action.

"I can only guess," she said, "but I imagine that over the

years, John had taken the duty of watching over the house on Raven Road seriously. From afar at first, then from inside its walls when he'd bought the place with Meredith. God only knows what possessed him to move back there, but clearly the impact on his mental health was catastrophic.

"Once they had sold the house to the Harris family, the knowledge that children were living at number fifty-seven again, especially Georgia, who was the same age John had been at the time of the murders, must have triggered something in him. Something irreparable that he couldn't come back from."

Emily paused, staring out the window as terrifying images from the Harris' basement haunted her mind. "The coroner believes Geraldine and Raymond Butcher had been killed at least a week before I found them. The police think that, faced with the surveillance cameras, John had needed somewhere to watch the house from without getting caught. I reviewed the footage from the street. You can see him coming and going from the house. I thought it was Raymond . . ."

Emily clenched her jaw, feeling the sting of tears as she tried to force them away.

"Something still puzzles me," Erica said. "That first letter. Why incriminate himself and Meredith like that?"

"Perhaps that wasn't his intention. Perhaps it was a reference to his father. Or a cry for help. I guess we'll never know."

Erica shook her head, her expression morose. "It's a tragedy. From start to finish, a terrible tragedy."

"How is Meredith?"

"As to be expected. I've called but she needs time. As her friend, I'll be there as and when she needs me. I'm just sorry that all of this has happened." Erica looked up. "Which brings me to you."

Emily stared down at the table. "Oh."

"This is hard for me to say, so I'll be as succinct as I can. You went against everything I taught you. You broke every rule, every protocol I tried to instil in you as a good private investigator. You compromised my business and my friendship with Meredith. You became personally involved with the Harris family, which I supposed turned out to be a blessing for them, but you also put your life at risk for people you hardly know. Which, depending how you look at it, was either commendable or incredibly stupid."

Erica paused, her shoulders heaving as she let out a heavy breath. "You've broken a bond of trust, Emily. Right now, I'm not certain that it can be fully repaired."

Emily was silent, eyes fixed on the desk, bracing herself for the inevitable.

"But, I suppose," Erica said, leaning forward, "with the lives you saved and the truth you exposed, you've actually proved yourself to be a highly skilled investigator. Unorthodox, yes. Bloody-minded, without question. But you have passion and commitment; two fine qualities that I cannot deny. Which is why, if you're prepared to play by the rules, I think I'd very much like you to stay."

Emily looked up, mouth agape.

"Don't get your hopes up just yet," Erica continued. "You need to regain my trust. Which is why I'm putting you back into insurance investigation for a probationary period of three months. During that time, if you can prove to me that you're capable of following the rules down to the last letter, then I'll consider—*consider*—giving you something more substantial."

Erica shot a familiar, authoritative glare at Emily, who flinched but held her gaze.

Nicely played, she thought. And no less than she deserved.

———

Jerome was at the reception desk, deep in conversation with Lee Woodruff, a fellow private investigator that Emily had spoken to a handful of times and had yet to decide whether she liked him. As she closed Erica's door and crossed the floor, she noted the way Jerome was leaning in, his smile bright and charming.

"I hope I'm not intruding on anything . . ."

Lee glanced up, nodded at Emily, then turned back to Jerome. "I'd best get on my way. Cases to solve and all that."

"Go Sherlock." Jerome flashed a blinding smile.

Reaching the desk, Emily watched the investigator disappear through the smoked glass doors. "I didn't think he was your type."

"Oh, please! I never mix business with pleasure. Anyway, how are you still alive?"

"I'm not sure. Erica wants me to stay. I mean, she's putting me on probation, but still . . ."

"It's a post-Christmas miracle." Jerome glanced nervously at Erica's office door. "Did she say anything about me?"

"Not really. Only that she wants to see you in her office."

"What? Oh shit."

"I'm just kidding. She's letting you stay. For now. I guess Erica Braithwaite isn't the monster we thought she was."

Jerome shot another worried glance across the room. "So it's back to small time fraud for you?"

"Looks that way." Emily shrugged, searching Jerome's desk for coffee but only finding an empty mug. "Who knows, maybe it'll be good for me. Maybe I'll even learn to enjoy it."

"What kind of sick-minded masochist are you?"

Smiling, Emily punched him playfully on the arm then made her way towards the smoked glass doors. "One that's not done eating humble pie for the day."

"Huh?"

"See you tomorrow, Jerome."

———

Carter had finished work for the day and was fresh out of the shower and dressed in more comfortable clothes, when Emily came barging in through the front door. Without a word, she grabbed him by the hand and pulled him into the living room, where she pushed him down on the sofa.

Carter stared at her, open-mouthed. "Emily, what's—"

"No," she said, raising a silencing hand. "Let me talk."

He closed his mouth and waited, staring up at her with his curiously-coloured eyes.

Emily sucked in a breath, held it, then let it out. "Before I came to London, I lived in a small village in Cornwall—the same village I grew up in. I lived with my mother, whose mind was broken and who was afraid of the world. She would never let me have friends, or out of her sight. On bad days, she would obsessively scrub her hands clean with steel wool, until they bled. Then she would do the same to mine." Emily paused, holding out trembling hands, showing him the thin white scars on top. "As soon as I could, I moved away, trained to be a teacher in Somerset. My mother couldn't cope. I was going to travel the world, but she emotionally blackmailed me into coming home and taking a job at the school I went to as a kid. The school I hated.

"But I loved being a teacher, and I found happiness helping children learn all they needed to know. There was a boy from my village. A boy named Phillip Gerard. His father was a drunk who beat him and his brother on a daily basis. Everyone knew it was happening, but no one did anything to stop it. Not even me. Oh, I'd let Phillip stay with me at lunchtimes and we would talk and hang out, and I thought I was helping him, but I saw the bruises just like everyone else.

"Then my mother got sick. I took compassionate leave to nurse her. But she died and my world fell apart. I returned to work too soon. I thought I was ready, but I wasn't. The day I came back, Phillip was angry with me. He didn't understand why I had to be away all that time. He thought I'd abandoned him while his father got drunker and the beatings got worse. The day I came back, Phillip started acting up, taunting me, saying terrible things about my mother.

"I lost my mind. I screamed at him, slammed his desk, humiliated him in front of the whole class. He ran out of the room, crying. Somehow, he managed to get on to the school roof. And he jumped. Phillip died in the playground; in the one place he should have felt safe."

Emily paused, her voice breaking as tears wet her face. "I used to believe that it was my fault. I used to believe he jumped because I shouted at him. But he jumped because his father was an abusive monster. He jumped because no one did anything to stop him. But I was made a scapegoat, by everyone I knew and by the newspapers. And that's what you'll find when you search for my name online: 'Police question crazed teacher after boy dies.' That's why I couldn't tell you. Because part of me still thinks it's true. Because I care about you, and I'm terrified that you'll believe it, too."

She slumped down on the sofa, exhausted and spent, unable to find any more words. But she felt lighter. Even if Carter walked away now, he would do so knowing her secrets.

But Carter didn't walk away. He sat there, staring, with an unreadable expression on his face.

"Say something," Emily said, unable to bear the silence any longer. "Please."

Slowly, gingerly, Carter reached out and took her hand. "I'm sorry for Phillip. I'm sorry you went through everything you did."

He kissed the back of her hand and the thin, faded scars.

Emily stared at him. "That's it?"

"That's it," Carter said. "Now we know each other a little better and a little worse. Tomorrow morning, if you want, we can talk some more. Or not. Whatever the mood brings."

After he had left her to start on dinner, she continued to sit, perfectly still and silent. As Carter hummed badly to himself in the kitchen, as tantalising food smells wafted through the air, Emily glanced down at her bag.

Before leaving her office, Erica had given her a new insurance fraud case to investigate. Two weeks ago, she would have rolled her eyes, but now people were dead and Erica had predicted it would happen because Emily couldn't follow the rules. But Erica had also given her a second chance. This time, Emily was determined not to let her down.

She stared at her bag again, her fingers itching to remove the case file, her eyes eager to see what lay inside. Then Carter was calling her name. Emily stood up and went to him, deciding that today had been filled with enough surprises, and that any more, no matter how small, could wait until tomorrow.

THE TRUE CRIME BEHIND 'WATCH YOU SLEEP'

When I'm looking for ideas for my next novel, I often turn to the Internet and true crime stories for inspiration (I dread to think what Google makes of my search history). While trawling through the sites one day, I came across a recent news story that made the hairs on the back of my neck stand up.

In 2014, Maria and Derek Broaddus purchased a house in Westfield, New Jersey. Before moving into the property with their children, they decided to renovate the place. A few days into it, they discovered a blood-chilling letter among the mail. The writer referred to themselves as The Watcher and claimed that his family had been watching the house for generations. ('*Do you know the history of the house? Do you know what lies within the walls of 657 Boulevard? Why are you here? I will find out.*'). It went on to describe the family's children and the renovations they were making.

A couple of weeks later, a second letter arrived, this time correctly naming the children and asking if they'd been down to play in the basement yet ('*It is far away from the rest of the house. If you were upstairs you would never hear them scream.*'). When a third letter arrived, the Broaddus family was done. They refused to move into the house, then decided to sue its previous owners after one of The Watcher's letters claimed they knew all about him and had even sold the house at his command.

The identity of The Watcher has yet to be discovered and the case is ongoing. In fact, after failing to sell the house, the Broadduses decided to rent it out. Shortly after their tenant moved in, another letter arrived . . .

While *Watch You Sleep* is a complete work of fiction, it does take its inspiration from The Watcher. I wanted to explore what might happen if a family had already moved in and were at the mercy of such a deranged individual. What would happen if the letters became more than just words on a page?

I encourage you to go online and read the full story about what happened at 657 Boulevard, and to read The Watcher's original letters. They are truly the stuff of nightmares.

THE EMILY SWANSON SERIES

Emily Swanson features in five nail-biting mystery-suspense novels. Although each story can be read on its own, it's best to read the series in order so that you can fully enjoy Emily's efforts to overcome her demons and become a master private investigator.

Next to Disappear - Book 1

When troubled nurse Alina vanishes one night, it's assumed she ran away from her violent husband. Until disgraced ex-teacher Emily Swanson moves into the couple's former home.

Emily's life is in ruins and she's meant to be making a fresh start. But when she learns about the missing nurse, she sees a chance for redemption. Because finding Alina could help right the wrongs of Emily's past. All she needs to do is follow the clues. But what Emily doesn't know is that Alina had a horrifying secret. One about the care foundation where she worked.

And the closer Emily gets to uncovering the truth, the closer she gets to terrible danger.

Mind for Murder - Book 2

Emily Swanson came face to face with a psychopath and survived. But the ordeal has left its scars. Determined to move on with her life, she visits a weekend retreat called Meadow Pines. With its forest setting and strict ban on technology, it's the perfect escape.

Until one of the guests is found hanging from a tree.

The evidence points to suicide. But when help fails to arrive and the guests start turning on each other, it's clear that Meadow Pines is not the haven it claims to be. Miles from the nearest town and with darkness falling fast, Emily must race to uncover the horrifying truth–because there is a killer at the retreat who is about to strike again.

Trail of Poison - Book 3

When environmentalist Max Edwards is found dead on the bank of the River Thames, his widow turns to rookie private detective Emily Swanson for help. But as Emily investigates, a case of accidental death quickly takes a dangerous turn. Max isn't the only one to die in strange circumstances. One of his colleagues has vanished with her sick child. And all of the evidence points to the mysterious Valence Industries.

Out of her depth and with the body count rising, Emily must seek the help of an unlikely ally. Because if she doesn't uncover the truth about Max Edwards soon, more innocent people will die.

Watch You Sleep - Book 4

When Jessica's husband is arrested for fraud, her family's future is thrown into jeopardy. Then the letter arrives. Someone called The Witness claims to be watching Jessica and her children through the windows of their home.

At first it seems like a sick joke. But as more unhinged letters and disturbing events follow, it's clear that The Witness is real and means to do them harm. Yet is everything as it seems?

Private detective Emily Swanson is hired to debunk Jessica's claims. It's the kind of case that could boost her career, but as Emily draws closer to the vulnerable family and the identity of The Witness, she soon finds her loyalty questioned – and her life in grave danger.

Kill for Love - Book 5

When shy student Wendy is found bludgeoned to death, her classmate Bridget is the chief suspect. But what turns a caring teenager into a cold-blooded killer?

Private eye Emily Swanson is desperate to find out. Bridget is the little sister of Emily's oldest friend, and with no motive or history of violence, her role in the crime doesn't add up. Until

Emily's investigation leads to a horrifying discovery. A psychopath is stalking online dating sites, searching for young women to play his sick and twisted games. Games that turn innocent victims into killers.

To clear Bridget's name, Emily must enter the dark world of online catfishing. But can she catch a maniac who doesn't appear to exist—before she becomes his next fatal obsession?

ACKNOWLEDGEMENTS

Never try relocating to a different part of the country while halfway through writing a novel. Just don't do it. Thank you to the following people who helped me over the finish line: Natasha Orme, for your wonderful editorial work that always helps to shape a tighter, more rounded story; my family and friends, who keep me sane with their encouragement and support; my awesome Read & Review team, who make excellent cheerleaders and never fail to lift me up during unavoidable moments of self-doubt; and to Xander, without whom none of this would be possible.